Brightwell Birthright

By the same author

The Glass Unicorn
This Rabbit is Constipated
It's Around Here Somewhere!

Brightwell Birthright

Trish Mills

Quicksilver Publications

Published by Quicksilver Publications
in the United Kingdom in 2016

Copyright © Patricia Jean Mills 2016
This edition published 2016
Reprinted February 2017

ISBN 978-0-9932872-6-8

All rights reserved. No part of this publication may be reproduced, stored in a retrieval system, or transmitted, in any form, or by any means, electronic, mechanical, photocopying, recording or otherwise, without the prior permission of the copyright holder.

Patricia Jean Mills has asserted the moral right to be identified as the author of this work. E-mail: quicksilver7@icloud.com

Typeset in Garamond 12/16 point.
Design by Trish Mills
Printed by www.bookprintinguk.com

Dedication

To Adrian Burns, who inspired this book
with stories of his father, Frederick,
and his own extraordinary childhood.

Chapter 1 – 1882

'There's nothing like a good gallop on a bright spring morning!' called Tristram to Charles, catching his breath. 'God, it's good to be back in England.'

'Yes indeed,' panted Charles, reining in his horse beside him. 'And it's good to have you back too. You've been away too long.'

'I agree!' laughed Tristram. 'But where to settle now I am back, that is the question.'

'Right here in Berkshire might be worth considering?' suggested Charles. 'Yorkshire couldn't hold you, and now your Aunt in America has passed away, I'm the best reason you have for settling anywhere.'

Mr Tristram Sinclair grimaced at his friend in agreement, with the familiarity born of having known each other since their schooldays. As soon as Tristram had written to his longest-standing friend to let him know he had now returned from his travels, and was staying with his brother Hugh in Halifax, Viscount Charles Worth could not rest until he had persuaded his friend to visit him at his home, Tower Court, near Newbury, in Berkshire.

'You have been away so long,' Charles had written, 'I have had time to find myself a beautiful wife and spawn two of the most delightful brats ever born. You must come and visit, I want to show them off to you, my friend.'

Kicking his heels at his older brother's Mill in Halifax, and feeling the onset of boredom, Tristram had needed little persuading. He travelled down by train, a journey that necessitated several changes and even more stops at stations along the way, and the need to be collected from Reading station on arrival.

Intending only the briefest of visits, he had brought so little luggage that Charles was obliged to lend him suitable clothing, and breeches in which to go riding, as well as a mount to ride. His lovely wife, Isabella, was completely unfazed by the arrival of their guest, and set about making him as welcome as possible. With due ceremony he was introduced to James aged five, and to Amelia aged two, and was agreeably surprised by his friend's achievement.

'No wonder you wanted to show them off to me!' said Tristram. 'All three of them are a delight.'

And so it was that they spent pleasant days riding two of Charles' finest horses, relaxing at home if they felt lazy, and dining in style at Charles's table. A week had passed already, and Tristram was anxious not to wear out his welcome.

As they paused after the morning's gallop, and surveyed the beautiful countryside spread before them, Tristram said, 'You will be wishing me miles away if I don't make some sort of arrangement soon. Maybe I should find a property for lease if I can't find anything to buy? And I need to visit Reading to buy some clothes. I can't live in yours for ever, Charles. I need a horse of my own too. I'm growing very attached to Sylvester here, he is a magnificent steed.'

Charles smiled. 'He is indeed. I'm afraid he's not for sale though, Tristram.' As he spoke he gave a light kick to his own mount, Beaumont, and they resumed their ride at a walking pace. 'It seems a lot to have to provide all at once, Tristram. Are you sufficiently in funds . . . ?'

Tristram knew he was being offered financial help if it was needed, but he chuckled at the thought. Finance was the least of his problems. 'God, yes,' he replied. 'Thanks to my late Aunt, I am taken care of until kingdom come.'

'Really?' said Charles. 'That is good news. I was concerned – seeing how little luggage you had.'

'Oh, that's because I like to travel lightly upon the earth. You must blame my military training for that.'

'So you are looking to settle down at last, are you?' said Charles. 'I can certainly recommend it. Does Yorkshire really not hold you? What does your brother do up there?'

'Wool,' replied Tristram, laconically. 'Our father inherited a thriving woollen mill in Halifax, and made it even better. He was one of the first to improve conditions for his workers, and pay them a fair wage. His first wife was from Yorkshire – they both were – and their first born son, Hugh, took to the life and learned the business from the bottom up.

'His mother died in childbirth a couple of years later, along with their second baby, so it was assumed he would be the only child. Our father's sister Harriet came to live with them, and looked after Hugh for some years.

'By the time our father was looking about him for a second wife, he had gone up in the world, become quite wealthy, and was mixing with the local aristocracy. His second wife had a title, Lady Anne, she was, and I was the result of that marriage. Aunt Harriett stayed on to help with both of us for some years. She was always there really, very fond of us both, and I suppose being unmarried, she had nowhere else to go.

'When I was about seven, the Mill was doing incredibly well, and an investor came over from America to take a look, and to see if my father would be interested in joint investment in a cotton mill. I don't know why, nothing came of it, but in the meantime, the American took a shine to my aunt, and she to him. They corresponded after he returned home, and the following year he came again, and asked her to marry him.

'She was well beyond marriageable age, and the American was getting on a bit himself, so it was a match made in heaven. They wed in Halifax and then he took her back to America. Having married that much later in life, they had no children, of course. We kept in touch, she had helped to look after me since birth, and we had been close.

'I missed her hugely after she left, and it was decided that, because of my mother being a minor aristocrat, and my being the second son, I should have a military career. So I was sent to the boarding school where we met, and they educated away all trace of my Yorkshire accent. As you know, I went on to University after that – my father could afford it by then, and my mother wanted it. But I was no academic, and the so-called glamorous years of Wellington's wars were over, and fortunately the Crimean war too, so the military held little appeal either.

'My father – his name was Hugh, and my brother was named after him – continued to work the Mill and my brother continued to help him, learning as he went. When our father died, it was inevitable he would inherit the Mill, and rightly so. My mother had pre-deceased my father, so life for Hugh went on pretty much as it always had done.

'After University, I did a sort of Grand Tour, but not around Europe, but to America. I visited my Aunt, she was quite elderly by then. America was amazing, beginning to boom too. Her husband was big in cotton, as they say over there! I could have gone into that, he did invite me, but I returned to my roots after a lengthy visit.

'Later my Aunt's husband died and she lived alone for many years. We kept in touch but I didn't return. Recently she died, and it was a genuine shock to discover she had left everything to me! She knew of course that my brother had inherited the Mill, and was well provided for. But she knew too that I had not relished the idea of the military career planned for me.

'The least I could do was go over there and sort things out. The cotton mill was long sold, but there were other assets to dispose of, and her husband's relatives to trace. America is booming, literally the land of opportunity, but as I said, it's good to be back in England.'

Charles had listened without interruption, and they had allowed their horses to continue without check. 'My God,' said Charles. 'It sounds as if you are now more wealthy than your brother?'

'Well, yes,' said Tristram, anxious not to appear too pleased. 'I suppose I am. Once I'm settled, I shall make various settlements upon his children, and yours too, if I may, Charles?'

'You are very kind,' said Charles, delighted and touched by his friend's generosity. 'They will of course inherit the house and all that's in it, but being a Viscount doesn't necessarily bring wealth with it any more. I try to make the estate pay its way as best I can, it is doing well at the moment, but that was not always the case . . .'

Their horses now approached a narrowing of the ways and they were forced to go in single file. Suddenly Tristram reined in his mount and stopped, his eyes fixed on the view below. He turned in the saddle. 'Look! Just look.' His outspread arm indicated a house below them, surrounded by outbuildings, unkempt gardens, grounds beyond and a stream running through it.

'I could live there,' he said, his eyes fixed. 'That is lovely, and just the right size for me. I could live there for ever.'

'Probably not,' said Charles, following his gaze. 'Brightwell Manor. The Earl died last year, and it was inherited by his youngest son, Sir Geoffrey Turnbull, he's a Baronet. His two older brother's died, one in a foreign field, one of some illness or other. He lives there now with his mother, and she'll never leave it.'

'Oh well,' conceded Tristram lightly. 'I can dream,' and heeled Sylvester into a walk again.

'Anyway, it is falling into rack and ruin,' added Charles, falling in beside him. 'Years of neglect. It would take all your fortune to put it right again, not to mention the work. Organising a project of that magnitude would take years and leave you time for little else.'

'Well, I'd get an estate manager and leave it all to him!' grinned Tristram, and turning his horse for home, he forgot all about Brightwell Manor. 'We need to get back,' he told Charles, who really did not need telling.

'Isabella, Amelia and James will be wondering where you are.'

'No they won't,' smiled Charles fondly, 'Isabella has gone for a dress fitting. She is so excited about the Fortescue's Ball next week. It's been arranged for months and she has had a new dress made for the occasion. You'll have to come with us, Tristram. We can't leave you at home on your own.'

Tristram raised a doubtful eyebrow but Charles was determined. 'The ladies will love it. Someone new to whom they can cast out their lures for a husband. Handsome, single and wealthy, an irresistible combination!'

Tristram laughed. 'I can't possibly come, Charles,' he protested. 'I have nothing remotely suitable to wear. And the tailors of Reading cannot be expected to make a coat for me in time.'

'I'm sure I can find you something. We're of similar size and I am spoilt for choice.'

'No one's going to consider me as even a possibility if I'm wearing your hand-me-downs. And there really isn't time to have anything made before next week. Apart from which,' he added with some foreboding, 'I am 30 years old! Far too old to be of interest to anyone looking for a husband.'

It was Charles turn to raise an eyebrow at that, but he held his peace.

Chapter 2

Sir Geoffrey Turnbull was not having a good day. Indeed, since his father died over a year ago, and he had inherited Brightwell Manor, there had been very few good days at all, if any.

Taking after his mother, he was inclined to corpulence, which struck him as monumentally unfair since his father had been as slender as a reed. A permanent scowl marred his countenance, and a general air of being extremely hard done by effectively obliterated any attractiveness he might once have possessed.

His mother continually wore him down, telling him he should either be doing something he wasn't doing, or not doing whatever he was. When he complained or ignored her, she told him it was his place to act now that he had inherited the family home. She would go on for ever about how fortunate he was that it was one of the finest homes in Berkshire.

The first time she had said this, her son had stared at her in genuine amazement.

'Finest, Mama?' he repeated incredulously. 'Fortunate?

How can that possibly be? It has been neglected for years, much of it is falling into disrepair, the roof leaks, and the place is bleeding me dry. What is so fortunate about that, pray?'

His Mama sighed. 'Your poor Papa's health did not permit his carrying out his duties as one would have wished,' agreed her Ladyship, fanning herself pathetically. 'But you have no such excuse!' she exclaimed, eyeing her last remaining son distastefully. 'If only Ernest, my first born, had not been taken from us so precipitously . . . And poor Albert too, with that dreadful illness . . .'

Sir Geoffrey raised his eyes to heaven in silent supplication. 'God give me strength,' he muttered, and his Mama turned reproachful eyes upon him. 'I wish you would not blaspheme, Geoffrey. Your Papa never did, and I won't permit it in my hearing.'

Barely pausing to draw breath, she continued, 'And just when, might I ask, are you going to begin to take your duties seriously? There are repairs needed everywhere we look. I have asked you a dozen times.'

'I will begin just as soon as we discover sufficient funds from somewhere to pay for it!' replied her undutiful son. 'I told you, the place is bleeding me dry. I keep discovering nonsensical wasting of so much money, it is simply incomprehensible. I've had a bill from the family solicitor in London, an extortionate amount just for storing the Title Deeds of this house. And that is for just one year!'

His mother felt a sense of foreboding in her bosom. 'Henderson's have kept the Title Deeds safe for us ever since I can remember, and beyond,' defended her Ladyship. 'They are safe there.'

'Well I'm sure we could find a safe corner for them somewhere in this rambling great barn,' replied Sir Geoffrey. 'I shall go and fetch them and relieve them of their duty.'

'Are you sure that is wise, dearest?' His mother decided with so much at stake, the conciliatory approach might be safer.

'Why do we have to use those parasites in London, Mama?' His indignation rendered him incapable of hearing, let alone seeing, any other point of view. 'Surely a solicitor in Reading could do the job and be just as expensive, without my having to travel all the way up to London to fetch them?'

'Henderson's are not parasites, Geoffrey. If you took a little more interest in your heritage, you would know they have served this family well for over 100 years. And you don't have to take the stagecoach! You know there is a perfectly good carriage in the stables . . .'

'Yes, Mama, a perfectly good carriage that is full of worm holes and dust. And where is the team of four matching horses with which to pull it, pray? You know full well the only horse left in our stables is Grey Mist, and I will never part with her. I shall take the train.'

Defeated by this logic, her Ladyship conceded, but continued her ongoing demands of her son.

'It is over 60 miles to Lincoln's Inn in the city,' he complained. 'Reading would have been much nearer, but I shall go and collect those Deeds without delay. I'm damned if I will pay them another penny.'

'Geoffrey, why not leave it for now? Dear boy, there is no rush . . .'

'No, Mama,' replied Sir Geoffrey with great feeling. 'It is not in the least pleasant, and I do not in the least wish to go, but the longer the Deeds remain in their clutches, the more they will charge me for it. I shall leave in the morning. Apart from which, it is the Fortesecue's Ball next week and I wish to return in time for that.'

'Well you can be there and back long before that wretched Ball!' exclaimed her Ladyship in exasperation. 'Ungrateful boy. You show extreme discourtesy to your poor Papa's memory. I do not know how you can sleep at night.'

'I do not sleep at night, Mama,' sighed Sir Geoffrey, refusing on this occasion to be outwitted by her emotional blackmail. 'But that is because I lie awake worrying about the lack of money here, mainly thanks to Papa's inefficient way of running the estate.'

She chose to ignore this sally. 'And please don't be too long away,' she interrupted. 'I am not comfortable here on my own with just Dawkins and his wife, and a good-for-nothing kitchen maid for protection.'

'The place is like a fortress, Mama, I cannot think that any harm will come to you in my absence.'

'Just return as soon as your business is completed,' she commanded. 'There is no need to stay on in London enjoying yourself.'

'Mama, I have no funds to enjoy myself anywhere,' replied her son. 'Let alone in London.'

With a heavy heart he departed next morning. As his long-suffering parent had foreseen, however, even after executing his business with the solicitor promptly, he decided the journey had been tiring and he needed some respite. Despite her animadversions to the contrary, he stayed an extra few nights to enjoy the various pleasures of the flesh that were not yet to be found in Berkshire, met up with someone he knew, albeit slightly, drank too much and lost a large amount of money he could ill afford at cards.

Indeed, he stayed away so long it did not occur to him until he was on his way home and on the last leg of his journey, the precious Deeds safely stowed in his capacious pocket, that he was passing the Fortescue's home on the very evening the Ball was in progress. Sickened at the thought of missing it, frightened by his losses in London, and secure in the knowledge that he would undoubtedly recruit his finances at Sir Henry's gaming tables, he decided to go to the Ball in his travelling attire.

Sir Henry's sons had been his playfellows as a child; he knew the place almost as well as he knew his own home.

Briefly acknowledging that he was in no way dressed for a grand Ball, he decided he could skirt around the side of the house and enter through Sir Henry's large study windows, where the gaming tables were always set up every year, and no one there would care a jot that he was dusty and unshaven from his journey. He was also hungry and thirsty, and God alone knew, if anyone deserved to eat from Sir Henry's well-laden table, it was himself.

Patting his coat pocket, confident the precious Deeds were safe and secure, he changed his mind and entered the enormous dining room through the open French doors. Keeping a wary eye open for Lady Henry, and soon fortified by good food and too much drink, he moved on to the large but gloomy study and surveyed the scene.

'Geoffrey, m'boy!' exclaimed Sir Henry, astonished at the state of him. 'Are you well?'

'Yes, Sir, thank you, Sir,' replied Sir Geoffrey, no longer quite so confident that no one would notice his attire. 'Don't tell me,' said Sir Henry, who was a fond and understanding father, and had known Geoffrey all his life. 'You were passing on your way home and decided you could not miss our little get together?'

Astonished at his understanding, Geoffrey mumbled, 'Something like that, Sir,' but could not return his gaze. Realising the boy was the worse for drink, Sir Henry said kindly, 'Good to see you, m'boy, but don't let her

Ladyship see you dressed like that. Are you sure it's wise to play just now? Would you be better going home?'

Sir Geoffrey raised his voice and heads began to turn in their direction. 'Thank you, Sir!' he said stiffly. 'I am well enough to play. Your concern is unnecessary.'

Wishing to avoid a scene, Sir Henry gave in. 'Very well. What are you fancying tonight? Hazard? Whist? Poker?'

There were several card games in progress, and the stakes were already high. No matter, decided Sir Geoffrey. He would soon recover the funds he had lost in London, and then stop. Knowing when to stop was the key. He slipped unobtrusively into the nearest empty seat at one of the tables, waiting quietly until the current game ended, and received his cards for the following round.

Initially it went well. He gained confidence, and looked at the others seated around the table, most of whom he knew, but not all. The game continued, the stakes rose higher. Emboldened by drink and a few small wins, Sir Geoffrey knew he couldn't stop now. His winning streak had returned, there was no doubt he would soon recover the losses he had made in London.

The next hand he was dealt was proof, if proof were needed, that this was his night. A Royal flush! Nothing could beat that, his position was unassailable. In turn, the others dropped out. 'Knowing when they are beaten,' smiled Sir Geoffrey to himself. There were just two of them left in the game now. Himself and a stranger in an ill-fitting coat. He seemed as determined to continue as Sir Geoffrey himself, and raised the stakes once more. Silence descended on the room, and Sir Henry himself came over to watch.

Sir Geoffrey patted his pockets, knowing he had no more money on his person, but hoping nevertheless. Then he felt the rustle of the vellum Deeds in his pocket. Perfect! He dragged them out and cast them dramatically on the table. 'The Deeds to my home, Sir!' he exclaimed defiantly.

There was a murmur of remonstration. Even Sir Henry's impeccable manners did not stop him speaking. 'Geoffrey, are you sure? Is your hand so good?'

'Unassailable, Sir,' he replied, struggling to keep his speech coherent after so much to drink. 'Unassailable. My home is not at risk. Nothing can beat this hand!'

'Is it yours to hazard?' asked Tristram Sinclair, glancing at his own hand.

'Of course it's my property to hazard, Sir!' How dare anyone gainsay his decision? 'My father passed away over a year ago. It's only my widowed mother rattling around in it now, supported by too many cursed servants who are bleeding me dry. But that is not the issue, Sir! I believe my hand will best your own, and it is you who should be vouchsafing you are in funds to lose to me, not the other way around.'

'Then I will see you,' said Tristram quietly, and watched as Sir Geoffrey flamboyantly and triumphantly placed his Royal Flush on the table. Gently and slowly, almost apologetically, Tristram placed his cards on the table too.

Sir Geoffrey stared in disbelief. Drunk though he was, there was no denying that the stranger's hand beat his. How could that be? With Sir Henry watching him, and Sir Charles Worth standing behind his friend, he did not dare accuse the stranger of cheating. Not in Sir Henry's house. Sir Geoffrey slunk from the room, leaving the Deeds to his home on the table.

As Tristram sat in silence and watched him go, Charles leaned over his shoulder to pick up the Deeds. 'You know where this is, don't you?' he said to his stunned friend.

'No, indeed,' whispered Tristram, tearing his gaze from Sir Geoffrey's departing back to the vellum Deeds, and thence to Charles' face. 'I don't know anywhere around here. Where?'

'Brightwell Manor,' said Charles.

'Brightwell?'

'Yes, Brightwell.'

'The house we saw during our ride last week?'

'The very same.'

Evidently in shock, Tristram rose to his feet.

'I can't take this,' he said, gesturing towards the Deeds. 'He can't do that.'

'You can and he has,' said Charles quietly. 'Serves him right.'

'No, no, don't say that,' interrupted Sir Henry, their host, as the other players tactfully withdrew. 'He's a stupid boy to have played after drinking so much. I did try to stop him but he would have none of it. And he's even more stupid to have gambled the family home. I can't think how he came to have the Deeds with him. But it doesn't serve him right, Charles. God knows what his mother will say.'

Chapter 3

Unsurprisingly Sir Geoffrey's mother had a good deal to say, once she had recovered from her initial stupefaction.

It was not until her son flung into the dining room as she sipped her morning hot chocolate, that she knew anything was amiss. His coat was damp and he looked as if he had slept in it, goodness knows where.

'There you are at last, Geoffrey,' said his Mama before she took in any of these details. 'I particularly asked you not to stay away for long because I do not feel safe here without you, and you have been gone six nights. Six! You deliberately disobeyed me.'

When this sally met with no response, she at last looked up, and was immediately filled with consternation. 'My poor boy,' she cried, her hand paused in mid-air over the dish of sweetmeats from which she was making yet another selection. 'What has happened to you?'

'Mama!' Her son threw himself into the seat opposite her own. 'I have lost the house!'

'Lost the house?' she repeated, too bewildered to draw

any conclusion as to his meaning. 'What can you mean? You're in it!'

'What is there in that that is beyond your comprehension?' demanded her son, venting his anger on his unsuspecting Mama. 'I have lost the house, and its contents, in a game of cards.'

'A game of cards?'

'Yes, Mama, in a game of cards.'

'But . . . ' she was speechless. 'But how?'

'In the usual way, Mama. He had a better hand than I did.'

'Well I'm sure he didn't mean it. He can't take our home.'

'He can, Mama. He can and he will.'

'Who is he?'

'A friend of Sir Charles Worth, I believe. Tristram somebody. I have no idea.'

'Well he can't just . . . '

He interrupted her. 'He can! He will! He has the right.'

'But you can't just hand it over to him. What about the Deeds? He can't do anything without those.'

At last Sir Geoffrey managed to look guilty and crestfallen, rather than belligerent. 'Well he has them. I left them on the table.'

'Left them on the table?'

'I wish you would not repeat everything I say! I had them with me, did I not? I had been to London to collect them from that parasite solicitor, they were safe in my pocket.'

'Hardly safe, Geoffrey, if you gambled them away,' she said archly. 'And you left them on the table? Oh my dear Lord, what have you done?'

'I know.' He had the grace to feel sorry for her. 'I'm sorry. But it's done. There is nothing I can do to undo it. We will have to move out. Immediately.'

'Move out? Don't be ridiculous. I am not going anywhere.'

'We will have to, Mama. It is my fault, I am truly sorry, but there is no hope of changing it.'

'But where are we to go?'

'I have no idea. I might go travelling, although I have no funds.'

'Well where am I to go? And with whom? I cannot possibly live alone, without a chaperone.'

'Good God, Mother! A chaperone? What on earth do you want with a chaperone at your age?'

'I am a delicately nurtured female,' she said, mustering the little dignity that remained to her. 'Age has nothing to do with it. And I wish you would not blaspheme, Geoffrey. I have told you and told you . . .'

'Any man would blaspheme listening to you!' he said. 'How my poor Papa put up with you for so many years, I do not know.'

'Your poor Papa must be spinning in his grave to hear you speak to me so. And to hear you have lost the house at cards!'

'He has been dead over a twelve month,' he replied sourly. 'I doubt he is in a position to have heard anything. Where will you go?'

'I have no idea!' she said, tears welling. 'There is no one and no where.'

'Well don't you have a cousin in Hertfordshire? You must write to him and explain you are in need.'

'I don't want to go to Hertfordshire!' she protested indignantly. 'I don't know anyone in Hertfordshire and I don't really know my cousin. Apart from which, his wife is a difficult woman to get along with. She will not want me living there.'

'I'm not surprised,' replied her undutiful son, 'but one thing is certain, you cannot remain here. You need to make arrangements. And quickly.'

'Well, it won't be to Hertfordshire,' she said darkly. 'I refuse utterly to go to Hertfordshire.'

Eventually silence fell. They had said all they had to say and yet the situation remained the same. Brightwell Manor was lost and there was no going back. Into the silence a knock could be heard at the front door. Dawkins's shuffling feet echoed as he crossed the empty hallway, the door opened, muffled voices. 'It's him,' said Sir Geoffrey in resignation. 'He has come to evict us.'

'Mr Tristram Sinclair,' announced Dawkins in funereal tones, and went back to his kitchen. It was warmer down there. Slightly.

Two pairs of eyes turned towards Tristram as he entered, making him feel even more uncomfortable than he already felt. Sir Geoffrey rose to his feet looking terrible, still in the clothes he had been wearing the previous night. He chose to take refuge in sarcasm.

'So you have come to turn us out into the cold cold snow already, have you?'

Tristram blinked at this reception. 'It's May,' he replied, unprovoked. 'And the sun is shining.'

'Forgive me if I had not noticed,' responded Sir Geoffrey bitterly. 'Come to see your new home, have you?'

'No indeed not. Last night should never have happened.'

Her Ladyship let forth a loud wail.

'My mother, Lady Turnbull,' said Sir Geoffrey, belatedly remembering his manners. 'I don't know your name . . .?'

'Tristram Sinclair,' supplied Tristram, wondering whether to take her hand or to remain where he stood. He chose the latter course.

'No title?' she asked weakly.

'No title. Just Mister.' She emitted a groan.

'A commoner living in Brightwell Manor! After all these years.'

He ignored her rudeness and returned his attention to Sir Geoffrey. 'Last night should not have happened,' he repeated.

'But it has,' interrupted Sir Geoffrey.

'Yes, but it was too much to stake.'

'But I did. And you won it fair and square.'

'Yes. I know,' said Tristram, 'and I'm no doubt a fool, but how will you go on without funds?'

'To be honest,' said Sir Geoffrey, 'the place has been an horrendous drain on my resources. Servants bleeding me dry. Bills from here to Kingdom Come. I shall no doubt be better off without the cursed place.'

'But you said you have no income?'

'No, of course not. The estate used to provide but it has gone to rack and ruin during my father's illness. We just sold a painting or a piece of furniture when we needed money. I'm thoroughly ruined now, but the place hung around my neck like an albatross. I'm glad to be rid of it.'

Tristram pulled a paper from his pocket. 'I would like you to have this . . .' and handed a stunned Sir Geoffrey a Draft on his bank. 'The value of your home outweighed my own stake, and I would like to redress the balance.'

Sir Geoffrey glanced cursorily at it and then blinked. He looked more closely. 'Good God, Sir!' he said, 'Why? You won it fair and square . . .'

'I know,' said Tristram again, 'but I wouldn't feel right simply taking it from you so easily. Take that to help set up your new life, where ever it might be. It is to be used wisely. And stay away from the gaming tables,' he added, confident that his advice would not be heeded. 'You're not as good at the cards as you like to think you are.'

His words effectively destroyed any goodwill his actions might have engendered in their recipient. 'But that's more or less its full value!' exclaimed Sir Geoffrey, stunned.

'We don't know that,' replied Tristram. 'I don't suppose it's been valued in years. It seems fair.'

'Very generous,' allowed Sir Geoffrey, still managing to sound supercilious and ungrateful.

'I was wondering,' continued Tristram, 'how long your mother needs to vacate the premises? I do not wish her to be inconvenienced or uncomfortable.'

'She's not comfortable here!' said Sir Geoffrey sourly. 'It's cold. The roof leaks. We can't afford enough servants to make it comfortable. I wish you joy of it. We can be gone in a se'enight.'

'A se'enight?' blinked his Mama. 'A week?'

'Yes, Mama, a week. The sooner the better now. You can write to your cousin. With this Draft we can pay our way and hold our heads up high in the world again. We can be comfortable at last.'

'Maybe,' she said waspishly. 'But not in Hertfordshire. Nothing on God's earth will induce me to go to Hertfordshire.' She turned her eyes accusingly towards Tristram. 'You have stolen my boy's birthright!' she said venomously, and a muscle flicked in Tristram's jaw.

'Hardly stolen it, Madam,' he said stiffly. 'It was

offered to me on a plate and I have made a more than generous recompense for it. I trust your son will share it with you.'

'Steady on!' remonstrated her son. 'Not share it exactly. I will give her some of it . . .'

'That is between the two of you, Sir,' said Tristram, and turned on his heel. 'I will return in one week,' he tossed over his shoulder, 'Please see that you are gone by then.'

He paused and turned towards them again. 'Oh, and do feel free to take anything and everything you wish with you. I have no need of it. I'll see myself out.'

Sir Geoffrey needed one last word, and followed his guest to the front door. 'By the way,' he said, *sotto voce*, 'if some silly chambermaid comes looking for me, claiming I am the father of her brat, you don't know where I am.'

'Well, you're right,' said Tristram. 'I don't.'

Chapter 4

As Tristram approached Brightwell Manor for the second time, with Charles riding up the drive beside him, he was not sure what he would find. It felt strange to be knocking on his own front door, but no one had given him a key. He grasped the impressive door knocker representing cavorting dolphins, rapped loudly and listened to its echoes reverberating within.

Eventually the door slowly opened to reveal the extremely elderly retainer, who inclined his white head politely.

'Good morning,' said Tristram, wondering if the servant remembered his previous visit, and if he had been told of his own imminent arrival. 'You must be Dawkins? I am Tristram Sinclair and this is Sir Charles Worth. Is Sir Geoffrey at home?'

'No, Sir,' replied Dawkins, 'he left a few days ago. And Lady Turnbull has left too.' He opened the door a little further. 'We are expecting you, Sir.'

'Well that's a relief!' said Tristram to his friend, and they entered the large but gloomy hallway, littered with boxes and teetering piles of fabric and textiles, but very little besides. 'Was Lady Turnbull very shocked?'

'Yes, Sir, I believe she was. Extremely distressed.'

'Where have they gone?'

'I couldn't say, Sir,' replied Dawkins, leaving Tristram unsure as to whether he did not know, or was being misguidedly loyal to his erstwhile employer. Contradicting himself, the old man continued, 'Sir Geoffrey has apparently gone abroad, and her Ladyship has gone to live with a cousin in Hertfordshire.'

'So she went, did she?' said Tristram, with a grin. 'Objecting all the way, no doubt?'

'Well, yes, Sir.' Dawkins permitted himself the crack of a smile. 'As you say, Sir.'

'She was determined not to. Poor lady! Well, we are here now. Dawkins, can you show us around the house and grounds? What other servants are there here? Is there a Mrs Dawkins?'

'Yes, Sir, begging your pardon, Sir, she is indisposed.'

'I'm sorry to hear that,' said Tristram. 'What is wrong with her?'

Further questioning elicited the information that, begging your pardon, Sir, Mrs Dawkins had an ulcerated leg, and found it difficult to get about. It seemed the elderly couple had lived there for many years, and served the household faithfully. It became apparent that Dawkins did not approve of the son who had inherited his birthright just a year ago – and then lost it at cards. Dawkins had served Sir Geoffrey's father before him and brought Mrs Dawkins to the house as a young bride. The death of the Earl had saddened them deeply.

'But you remain?' asked Tristram.

'Begging your pardon, Sir, we have nowhere else to go. I am 82 and my good wife is 79. No one else would employ us now, and we have been unable to save when we were paid so little.'

Taking pity on the man, and his evident terror at being turned out of his home without notice, Tristram said, 'Well it looks to me as if it is time you retired, and Mrs Dawkins too. I believe I also own half a dozen or so cottages on the estate? You shall have one of those, Dawkins, when we have set it to rights, and a small stipend to tide you over.'

Dawkins looked as if nothing else on this earth could ever surprise him and, dismissed, went on his way rejoicing, bursting to break the glad tidings to Mrs Dawkins, who steadfastly refused to believe him.

'I expect you have it wrong again, Mr Dawkins,' she said. 'You never get anything right these days.'

There was also a kitchen maid lurking in the nether regions of the scullery, trying to hear what was being said in the hallway above her, without success.

'We will start in the kitchens!' Tristram told Charles, 'and work our way upwards.'

The kitchen maid heard this as they started down the stairs, and scuttled from her post behind the open baize door to the large kitchen table which she was supposed to have been scrubbing. Tristram entered and was surprised to see her, taking in her dirty apron and dishevelled hair escaping from beneath her cap. 'Aha!' he said, momentarily at a loss for words. 'What have we here?'

She looked round at the two gentlemen and bobbed a sulky curtsey. 'Prudence, Sir,' she said.

'There's no need to curtsey to me,' said her new employer. 'I'm a commoner, just like you! Is there any chance of a cup of tea?'

'Yes, Sir,' she said, somewhat confused by Tristram's honesty and forthright approach. The kettle sat on the hob and was soon persuaded into a singing boil, and tea was made in a large pot. Prudence was further scandalised when they pulled out chairs and seated themselves at the servants' dining table. Her hand trembled as she placed cups of tea before them. 'There is cake, Sir . . .?' she offered, still sulky but beginning to thaw.

'Excellent!' said Charles, and was surprised to discover that indeed it was. 'Who made this?' he asked, happily munching his way through a second slice of fruit cake.

'Well, Mrs Dawkins hasn't been well,' said Prudence defensively, 'So I made it, Sir. Mrs Dawkins said I could . . .'

'Well it's very good,' agreed Tristram, 'do you like to cook, Daisy?'

'Not particularly, Sir,' she said candidly. 'But there was no one else to do it, so I just got on with it. Lady Turnbull didn't eat very much and Sir Geoffrey was rarely at home.'

'Are there any other staff, Prudence? Apart from you and Mr & Mrs Dawkins?'

She looked at him. 'Not now, Sir, no. There was a chambermaid, Betsy, but she, er, left a while back.' She set her mouth, obviously unwilling to say more, and Tristram wondered if this might have been the girl Sir Geoffrey mentioned, who might come saying he was the father of her brat. He decided not to pursue it.

'Well we shall get you some help, Prudence, but I hope you will stay and continue to work for me?'

'Well, yes, Sir,' she said, considerably mollified, having obviously been afraid that she too might be turned off without notice and nowhere to go. 'I could do that, but the wages haven't been paid for some weeks now.'

Tristram laughed and told her she would go far. He dug into his pocket and handed her a sovereign to be going on with. 'We'll look into what you are owed, Prudence, and set it right, but take this for now. The tea and cake were very good.'

Fortified, he rose to his feet to continue his tour of the house and grounds. She gazed at his departing back in disbelief, and in her head she swore undying allegiance to this strange man who seemed to have no idea that servants were usually bullied, belittled and ignored, certainly not appreciated or encouraged with a kind word and a gold sovereign. She could not believe her good fortune.

Blithely unaware of the loyalty he had engendered in her breast, Tristram and Charles went in search of Dawkins, but could not find him anywhere. Unperturbed, they wandered at will, increasingly concerned by what they found.

'What on earth are all these fabrics and textiles in the hall?' asked Tristram. 'And what can we do to make it lighter in here? It is exceedingly gloomy.'

That was true of almost every room they visited. Tristram pulled back the heavy curtains from every window, brushed away cobwebs, shook off the dust, noted where improvements could be made. There were eight gloomy bedrooms, most with some furniture but not a full complement, and none with any sort of convenience added. There was a deep dark cupboard with a variety of hip baths stored within. 'Poor old Dawkins!' sympathised Tristram. 'Imagine having to lug enough hot water upstairs to fill one of those!'

There were china basins, jugs, chamber pots and ewers in plenty; guardrobes that had not been updated in years; no bathrooms whatsoever. 'Even Queen Elizabeth had a flushing lavatory!' laughed Charles. 'We certainly do. You have money to spend here, my friend.'

'Yes,' agreed Tristram. 'But won't it be splendid when all is done? Let's go and explore the grounds, that will be much more interesting.'

They escaped out of doors and Tristram immediately felt much happier. There were stables that had long ago fallen into disrepair; a long and narrow stone barn that needed a new thatched roof; a rank of cottages fronting on to the lane, one of which he had already rashly promised to Mr & Mrs Dawkins; even a sort of orangery, with much broken glass but warm in the mild sunshine and overgrown with ancient plants and weeds of all descriptions. Trees, bushes and shrubs had been allowed to run rampant unhindered, all was in need of husbandry or demolition.

Dismayed by the neglect, but excited by the challenge ahead of him, Tristram said, 'I need someone to manage the building and alterations. And staff to replace Mr & Mrs Dawkins – a housekeeper, a butler, a cook especially. Chambermaids; gardeners – several gardeners; grooms; stable boys. Where do I start, Charles? Where does one find good servants these days?'

'I believe Isabella uses some sort of agency,' said Charles. 'I think they interview applicants, and send only the most suitable for Isabella to meet. And she makes the final choice.'

They wandered happily across the grounds and empty fields, not entirely sure where his boundaries lay. 'I must take a proper look at those infernal Deeds,' acknowledged Tristram. 'And start the place paying for itself. Or at least supporting the people who live here. I need horses, of course, and some sort of carriage, but I would love to get some sheep and a few milking cows too. Oh and dogs. At least a couple of dogs.'

Charles laughed. 'It's a lifetime's work!' he said, and Tristram nodded in enthusiastic agreement. 'But it's not really habitable at the moment, is it? You really can't move in yet.'

'Well, Sir Geoffrey and Lady Turnbull managed it . . .' countered Tristram, 'but by his own admission, not comfortably. I worry that I will be wearing out my welcome at Tower Court. Your hospitality will be wearing thin . . .'

'Indeed no,' replied his host. 'It is good to see you again after so long. Isabella is more than happy to have you as a house guest a while longer, and the children have adopted you as their uncle already.'

Both men smiled fondly at the thought of James and Amelia, their boundless energy and how beautiful they were when they were asleep. Charles noticed his friend's smile too, and thought what an excellent father he would make.

'There is much to do here,' said Charles quietly. 'And much you need. But – I've said this before, Tristram – most of all, you need a wife!'

'I wish you well with that endeavour,' said Tristram

doubtfully. 'Why anyone would want to take me on, I cannot imagine, let alone Brightwell Manor in its current state.'

'Isabella will advise us on that head too,' said Charles, 'but surely you need someone who can make choices and decisions with you, together, a helpmeet?'

'Maybe I do.' Tristram still had his doubts. 'But at least give me time to buy some clothes that fit me properly! Is there a bespoke tailor in Reading? I desperately need a new coat and a pair of breeches of my own.'

Chapter 5

Once he had visited Charles's tailor in Reading, and had all he needed delivered to Charles's home near Newbury, Tristram was well on the way to setting up repairs and servants for his new home too. Isabella did indeed introduce him to the staff agency she used herself, and they were more than delighted to meet him, but he seemed to have discovered a limitless source of servants closer to home.

He had no idea how it had happened, but between them, the Dawkins and Prudence had put out the word, which had spread like wildfire, and once he had ridden Charles' horse Sylvester, now on almost permanent loan but still not for sale, to his new home each morning, there was almost always someone waiting to meet him, and offer their services.

His mill-owning father had trained him well in the care of his workers, and he realised that if he treated them with fairness, and took care of them, they would repay him in kind, and with loyalty. So as soon as he had found a Clerk of Works, Boddington, whom he insisted on calling his

Estate Manager, had found stonemasons, carpenters, plumbers to work the new lead on the roof, and even a man who claimed to be able to instal water closets, he first put them all to work on the rank of cottages in the grounds and the servants' quarters in the attics.

Charles thought him mad. 'Surely the leaking roof is priority?' he said.

'Yes, indeed, but that is part of the work on the attics too. If the servants are comfortable,' argued Tristram, 'we can move forward. I can't do anything there without them, not even feed myself. Oh yes!' He suddenly remembered, 'I need a cook and someone to work on the kitchens too.'

Prudence overheard this exchange, and spoke up immediately. 'Begging your pardon, Sir,' she said, having been trained diligently by Dawkins, 'but there is someone I know very good at kitchen work. Making improvements and such. And there's a very good chambermaid I know of as well.'

Tristram was intrigued as to how word travelled so quickly from so remote a place, because no sooner had he said, 'Thank you, Prudence, I should like to meet them,' than they appeared the following morning. And more often than not, he hired them. He was a good judge of character, and even one or two of the doubtful ones repaid his kindness and faith in them with loyalty and good service.

He was impatient to move in, as were his servants, but they had to wait until at least a few basic improvements were in place. Prudence's kitchen improver turned out to be an excellent craftsman, and did superb work, most of it at Prudence's instigation. 'After all,' said Tristram to Charles, defending yet another mad decision, 'Prudence has worked in that kitchen the longest, and knows what is good about it and what isn't.'

Once he seemed to be satisfied with the staff she had brought him, Prudence grew a little bolder.

'Begging your pardon, Sir,' she began, as always. 'Someone I know has just lost her husband, she's a widow, and needs to return to work. She is an experienced chambermaid, Sir.'

'Do we need another chambermaid, Prudence? How many do we have so far?'

'Only two, Sir. And even if you don't need them for ever, extra hands would be useful until we get everything clean and neat again.'

Tristram could see the wisdom of this, but he knew there was more to follow. 'Who is she, Prudence? Tell me abut her.'

'Well, Sir,' Prudence swallowed, hoping he had a short memory. 'Her name is Betsy . . .'

It rang a bell. 'And her husband has just died, but the thing is, Sir,' she hesitated and then finished all in a rush. 'She has a young baby, you see, Sir, but she's ever such a hard worker, Sir, and you wouldn't know it was here.'

Then Tristram remembered. On his first visit to the house, Prudence had mentioned a previous chambermaid by the name of Betsy having left recently. And he recalled Sir Geoffrey's cruel parting words. 'And if some silly girl comes looking for me, claiming I am the father of her brat, you don't know where I am.'

He looked at Prudence's earnest face and pleading eyes. 'How old is this baby, Prudence?'

'Well, it's only a few months, Sir, but it's very well behaved and it never ever cries.'

'But what would she do with it while she was working?'

Prudence had the grace to look crestfallen for a moment. 'Well, we could all help out, Sir. Taking it in turns, you know. And she has a perambulator for it, and could put the baby in it while she worked.'

Tristram knew Charles and Isabella would strongly disapprove and advise against it. It was against his own better judgement too. Until he heard himself saying, 'Well, why don't I meet her then?' and knew he was being weak.

'Yes, Sir!' Prudence beamed her gratitude. 'Thank you, Sir. You won't regret it, Sir.' Tristram knew he probably would. 'I'll let her know, Sir.'

'I'm not making any promises, mind.'

'No, Sir,' agreed Prudence enthusiastically. 'Of course not, Sir.'

Following that conversation, the hardworking Betsy and Sir Geoffrey's brat appeared so promptly that afternoon, Tristram suspected she might well have been on the premises already.

The perambulator was very fine and well looked after, and if he had only known it, recently liberated from the attics of Brightwell Manor. It had been lovingly dusted and washed, and the baby within was wrapped in rags, but they were clean rags.

Betsy looked at him anxiously as she entered his study, and cast a glance at her baby, willing it to remain asleep and silent.

'Hello,' he said, feeling slightly nervous himself, but refusing to show it. 'Betsy, isn't it?'

'Yes, Sir.' She nodded too, for good measure.

'And this is . . . ?' He indicated the very fine perambulator.

'This is Millicent Victoria, Sir.'

'A girl.'

'Yes, Sir.'

'How old?'

'Six months, Sir. She's very good, Sir. You wouldn't know she was here. She never cries.'

'Never, ever?'

'Well.' Betsy hesitated. She was not going to lie. 'Only when she's hungry, Sir. But then I feed her, and she stops.' Tristram hid a smile.

'What would you do with her while you were working?'

'She would sleep in the perambulator, Sir. I would keep her beside me.'

'What about if you were working upstairs? As a chambermaid, you would be needed in the bedchambers, would you not? And going up to the servants' quarters in the attics at night . . .?'

'Oh well, we brought it downstairs easily enough . . .!' She stopped suddenly, realising what she had said, and blushed furiously.

'Brought it down?' queried Tristram. Light dawned. 'Oh! You brought it down from the attics, did you?'

'Well, I'm only borrowing it, Sir. I shall return it when she grows too big for it.'

She could see that Tristram had a good heart, and even felt that he would like to help her if he could. She decided to be honest with him but it took every ounce of courage she possessed.

'It wasn't stealing, Sir,' she said stoutly. 'I always meant to return it when we were finished with it. No one else had need of it. And you see, Sir . . .' Tears welled in her eyes but she hastily brushed them away. 'Prudence said, considering who the father was, Millicent Victoria had every right to use the perambulator really.'

Not for the first time, Tristram thought that Prudence would go far. Pleased by her honesty, Tristram raised a quizzical eyebrow. 'Sir Geoffrey?'

Betsy swallowed hard. 'Yes, Sir. But it wasn't my fault, Sir. I swear I didn't know . . . '

'So you're not a widow, then?'

'Not exactly, Sir. No.'

'How old are you, Betsy?'

'Fifteen, Sir. But I'm strong too, Sir. I work hard. I wouldn't let you down.'

At that point, Millicent Victoria began to stir. Hastily Betsy took the handle of the very fine perambulator and gently jiggled it up and down. 'I could start straight away, Sir. Now, if you like.'

Tristram smiled, realising she was desperate. 'Alright,' he said, and she gasped in relief. 'Let's give it a go, shall we? How about a month's trial?'

'Yes, Sir. Thank you, Sir.'

Millicent Victoria let out a little wail.

'And I tell you what, Betsy. Instead of dragging my very fine perambulator up and down to the attics every night, why don't you live – temporarily, mind – in one of the cottages when they are ready? Mr & Mrs Dawkins will be next door, they might even help with Millicent Victoria on occasion.'

Hearing her name mentioned, Millicent gave another little wail. And then another. Betsy jiggled his perambulator ever harder.

'Yes, Sir, thank you, Sir.'

'And why don't you ask Prudence to help you and see

if I have a cradle in my attics as well? Then you could have her near you while you are chambermaiding.'

Betsy swallowed hard. 'You are very kind, Sir.'

Kinder than she could have dreamed. Finally Tristram withdrew another golden sovereign from his pocket and handed it to her. 'Take this and buy Millicent Victoria some clothes,' he said. 'We can't have her dressed in rags if she is to live at Brightwell Manor, can we?'

Such kindness and generosity completely unmanned Betsy, and she burst into deep sobbing, so relieved she was unable to control herself. By the time she wheeled the perambulator out of the room, Millicent Victoria was yelling lustily too.

'I expect she is hungry,' said Tristram drily, making Betsy giggle in between the sobs. 'You'd better feed her before you start work.'

Later, just as he had prophesied, Charles and Isabella were horrified when he confessed to them what he had done. 'Sir Geoffrey's by-blow?' exclaimed Charles. 'You must be mad.'

'How could I turn her away, Charles? She is fifteen years old and desperate. She will work hard and remain loyal, I know she will.'

'Yes,' interjected Isabella. 'But she'll also get very tired and the child will take her time and attention. She won't be able to drag it round in your perambulator for ever.'

'I'm very glad to hear it,' said Tristram. 'Well, I've

taken on everything else of Sir Geoffrey's that needs fixing. Why stop now?' They smiled grimly. 'And besides,' looking Charles in the eye, added, 'I might want it back one day.'

This effectively put a stop to further conversation and Millicent Victoria was never again referred to as Sir Geoffrey's by-blow.

Chapter 6

It was perhaps fortunate that just a week later, Isabella's agency sent him a highly qualified couple, the husband an experienced butler, the wife an equally experienced housekeeper, Mr & Mrs Nesbit. They had the highest credentials and excellent references. Tristram was highly relieved as it meant, once appointed, they would be responsible for interviewing and hiring all the other household staff he needed, including a new cook.

The Nesbits weren't too happy at inheriting Betsy and baby Millicent Victoria, but they soon took to the little mite and their initial reservations were quickly forgotten.

Once relieved of his duties, Dawkins felt relief and jealousy in equal measure. Someone taking over the duties he had proudly performed for so many years was a hard cross to bear. His attempts to 'train' and to interfere with the new butler were met with stony silence, and once he saw that his domain was in capable hands, he was content to leave them all to it.

Tristram took more interest in finding the outdoor staff himself, despite the fact that the excellent Boddington, the new estate manager, was more than capable. Gardeners, it seemed, were ten a penny, and he soon acquired six, and a young lad, Chedworth, for them all to bully, and to rush hither and thither while telling him he was a lazy little so-and-so, and would not have lasted ten minutes in their day.

Some of them were intended to be temporary, just until the grounds were back under control. Once he had glanced at the infamous Deeds, however, and discovered the full extent of his land, he kept them on and kept them all busy.

Once the stables had been restored and repaired, he found an excellent groom named Jeffreys, and allowed him to hire the stable boys he needed. Once all was in place, he realised time had been passing and it was August already. Tristram knew it was time to buy his horses.

'Charles,' he said next morning as they ate breakfast together, knowing Tristram would not be able to move into his new home until he had transport. 'Would you have time to accompany me to Tattersall's one day soon? I'm ready to by a horse or two now, and need a carriage and possibly a curricle as well.'

'Yes, indeed!' replied Charles with enthusiasm. 'I haven't been to Tattersall's in years. I would love to come.'

'You are probably a better judge of horseflesh than I am,' said Tristram, a look of sadness crossing his face. 'I shall miss Sylvester,' he confessed. 'A wonderful mount in every way. Are you sure he is not for sale?'

'I'm sure, Tristram. Sorry. Can't be done. Shall we take your new groom along as well? He seems to know horseflesh even better than we do between us.'

'I hope he will advise me as to carriages as well,' said Tristram. 'I need some sort of conveyance, but there are quite a lot of new ones available of which I know nothing. I will also need somewhere to store them. That barn that needs re-thatching will be useful, but it's rather a strange shape. And I think it could be a little larger. Maybe I need an architect to advise me.'

Into all this frenzied activity, Charles and Isabella had occasionally been allowed to interject a little social entertainment. They had been invited to another Ball, not quite as grand as Sir Henry's, and Tristram had been enthusiastically included in the invitation.

Despite having Lady Anne for his mother, Tristam was not of the aristocracy but he was comfortable in their company. Having been left his fortune by an Aunt in America did him no harm, and being undeniably handsome besides, he was an amiable guest and popular with the men as well as the ladies.

He avoided the gaming tables on this occasion, and remained in the ballroom, dutifully dancing with the young ladies his hostess brought his way, but to their everlasting disappointment, only once each. One of them he took against surprisingly strongly, dismissing her to

Charles later as a Simpering Miss. Then he looked at her mother and knew it could not have been otherwise. The other ladies appeared to have made little impression.

'They are all so young,' he complained, 'and prattle about such inconsequential matters.'

'You probably make them feel nervous,' said Isabella.

'I can't think why,' he said irritably, but she could.

There were invitations a-plenty. Word had travelled quickly about the handsome, single and wealthy new owner of Brightwell Manor. Everyone also seemed to know of his kind heart, and all about Betsy and baby Millicent Victoria.

'If it had been anyone else,' said Charles, 'it would have been a scandal. But because it's you, everyone thinks it charming.'

Several fond Mamas, hopefully parading their daughters for his approval, had even lost some of their best servants to his employ, but no one held it against him. They were only too glad to have him in their midst. Apart from his own manifold merits, Sir Geoffrey had not been popular.

He was friendly and polite and charming, danced just once each with a seemingly endless stream of empty-headed prattling young ladies, not one of whom won his heart.

Most evenings, how ever elevated the company or sophisticated the entertainment, he would soon start yawning, and long for his bed.

'I'm meeting a new contractor in the morning,' he would say. Or 'There is a large delivery arriving at 10 o'clock tomorrow, I must be there to check it all before it is unloaded.'

Charles and Isabella would take pity on him and bring him home.

One of these early appointments was with the new architect Boddington had found, who needed to be shown around and briefed as to exactly what improvements Tristram had in mind. Mr Samuel Cunningham of Samuel Cunningham & Sons, Architects, had been highly recommended, and sounded suitably illustrious. They were due to meet at 11 o'clock next morning.

As usual Tristram had ridden over on Sylvester, revelling in the final moments he had with this wonderful stallion, dreading having to get to know an unknown replacement all over again. Dismounting, he turned to see Mr Samuel Cunningham, Architect, driving a carriage up the drive, with a very smart lady beside him.

'Good morning!' Tristram hailed them, and introduced himself. 'Tristram Sinclair.'

'Pleased to meet you, Mr Sinclair,' replied Mr Cunningham, shaking his hand with crushing strength. 'Samuel Cunningham at your service, and my daughter, Miss Grace Cunningham.'

Tristram was intrigued. He bowed toward Miss Cunningham, but directed his comments to her father.

'But your Company name is Samuel Cunningham & Sons, Sir?' he said with a smile.

'You are right,' agreed Mr Cunningham comfortably. 'And indeed I have two fine sons in the firm, Henry and Matthew. But my daughter here has a remarkable aptitude as well. In fact, my boys feel almost overshadowed by her on occasion. She has a good eye, Sir, and you will find her highly professional. But I can hardly allow her to attend an appointment on her own, can I now?'

'No, indeed you cannot, Mr Cunningham. That would not be at all appropriate.'

Miss Cunningham laughed. 'Pray do not encourage him, Mr Sinclair,' she begged. 'I am for ever telling him it would be perfectly alright, but he will not allow it.'

'I'm afraid I must agree with your father, Miss Cunningham,' said Tristram apologetically. 'It would not be wise at all.'

'And I can hardly re-name the firm Samuel Cunningham & Sons & Daughter, can I?' asked Mr Cunningham. Tristram considered the matter. 'It would be a little unusual,' he said judiciously, 'but it would be the truth.'

Miss Cunningham's lovely eyes sparkled. 'It was ever thus,' she said, with the lilt of laughter in her voice, and a teasing glance at her Papa. 'We women have always been repressed, suppressed, and ignored, and I do not anticipate that will change in the foreseeable future, despite having a Queen on the throne again.'

'I give you my word, Miss Cunningham,' said Tristram mock seriously, 'I will never repress, suppress or ignore you or your architectural recommendations.'

She laughed again. 'Then we shall deal very well together, Mr Sinclair. You have a beautiful home here. Can we see what it is you have in mind?'

'Yes, indeed,' he said, 'come this way.' And he led them through the gardens at the side of the house and along to the large stone barn that was sadly in need of re-thatching. 'As far as I know, the stonework is sound and solid. When the roof is re-done, I intend to use it for vehicles – I will shortly be acquiring a coach and possibly a curricle. But as you can see, it is long and narrow, and to use it as it is, I would need to park them one in front of the other, and remove one if I need the next.'

'That would be inconvenient,' agreed Mr Cunningham, 'but it is a fine barn.'

'It is indeed,' agreed his daughter. 'In fact, it looks to me as if it might have been here before the house. It seems to belong to a much earlier period.'

'That's interesting,' said Tristram, intrigued by her knowledge and confidence. 'I am considering extending it in some way, so that it is considerably wider. As you see, it is very near the stables, so it would be ideal if one could drive into the barn, turn the vehicle, unharness the horses, and lead them straight across to the stables. No reversing, no changing the order. The problem is, I cannot think how best to build an extension to achieve that, and I do not know if we can obtain matching stone. Which is why I have been recommended to call upon you.'

Miss Cunningham appeared to be considering the barn from all angles. She walked away from it towards the stables; she turned and studied it in its entirety; she squinted along the length of its walls; she went inside and looked up at the sky through the shreds of remaining thatch. Finally, she nodded, and returned to the two gentlemen watching her in anticipation.

'Would it be sensible, Mr Sinclair, to open up the longer side facing the stables, and use the stone to fill in the doorway on the shorter end? That would effectively make it wider, and allow you to store your vehicles across the width of it, rather than in the depth of it. We could put large double doors across the new opening, there is enough space to open them outwards without obstructing the stables. And it would require minimal re-building. Which would save you a lot of money. And give you the matching stone you need to fill in the shorter end.'

He stared at her in disbelief and admiration. 'But of course!' he said, with rising excitement. 'That is the obvious solution and it had escaped my notice entirely. And Boddington's too!'

'I told you she had a good eye, Mr Sinclair,' said her father proudly. Privately Tristram thought she had two beautiful eyes, but refrained from saying so.

'We would need a very long beam to support the roof over the new wider opening,' said Miss Cunningham, thrilled by his enthusiasm and seeking refuge in practical considerations. 'But we could easily remove the three or four courses of stone above it, insert the beam, and then re-build the three or four courses back over it. That would avoid any risk of it collapsing. Might you have any oak trees already felled on your land, that would be suitable?'

'I'm not aware of any at the moment, but I haven't had time to explore it all fully. I must make the time to do so.'

'Of course. We need to take some measurements, and to have it properly surveyed by one of my brothers who specialises in the technicalities. But it seems to me that would be the simplest solution. It could be done quite quickly, with minimal manpower, and would be the least expensive option too.'

'Yes, indeed,' agreed Tristram, simply amazed by her knowledge and ability to consider so much in so short a time. He turned to include her father in his remarks, but was careful not to exclude or repress Miss Cunningham at the same time. 'Can I ask you both to proceed, and do all that is necessary towards making this come about? It is beautiful in its simplicity! I am quite shocked that it did not occur to me.'

She allowed her father to answer for them both.
'We will indeed, Mr Sinclair. I can see you would like it done as soon as possible.'

'Yes, I am hoping to buy new vehicles and my horses next week. Transport is the only thing stopping me from moving into my new home. It has taken most of the summer to get the place cleaned up and into some sort of habitable condition. There is still much to do, but I have found some good servants, who have made an enormous difference.'

'In the meantime,' added Miss Cunningham, 'perhaps you can survey your land further, and see if there is a felled oak tree suitable for the beam? Even a fallen oak would be acceptable, as long as it is not diseased. As the roof is thatched, we could possibly use green oak, as thatch is flexible and there would be no risk of cracking. But it would be preferable if you have some that is well seasoned. If there is enough, we could use it to make the new double doors too.'

Truly excited by this new project, and the backing of such an excellent firm as Samuel Cunningham & Sons & Daughter, Tristram was keen to see it executed with all speed.

'Can I offer you refreshment before you leave?' he asked.

Miss Cunningham would love to have seen inside the house, but unfortunately they had to decline.

'We would like that, Mr Sinclair,' said her father, 'but we have to see another client a short drive from here, and time is pressing. Perhaps next time?'

'Yes, indeed,' said Tristram, and escorted them back to their carriage. 'I hope it won't be too long. What will happen next?'

'My brother will contact you, Mr Sinclair,' said Miss Cunningham. 'He will arrange a date and time to visit and to do his survey, and take all the measurements we need. He will also be able to give you an estimate of the costs involved and how long it will take. We can also recommend a thatcher when you need one.'

'That is excellent news,' said Tristram, shaking her hand warmly, and risking another finger-wringing pumping from her Papa. 'I shall look forward to it.'

He watched until their carriage was out of sight and remained for sometime, trying to sort out his teeming thoughts and feelings.

Chapter 7

Since his meeting with Mr Samuel Cunningham and daughter, Tristram became steadily more impatient to move in to his new home. Everything except transport and horses was now in place, and he was spending almost all his time at Brightwell except for sleeping. His servants were in residence, including a new cook, Mrs Hatton, and there was now little reason except transport to stay away.

'Charles,' he said one evening at dinner. 'I need horses and some sort of conveyance. I do not wish to wait until the barn has been converted, as that could take some time. Could we go up to Tattersall's very soon?'

They agreed on a day the following week and, accompanied and advised by the highly capable Jeffreys, they soon found almost all they were looking for.

Following Jeffreys's advice, Tristram bid on a fine pair of glowing chestnuts to draw a coach or curricle, which Jeffreys said had good mouths, and later he bid on one of each of the conveyances as well. By late morning they had found all they needed, except a steed for Tristram.

Having grown to love Sylvester so much, nothing he saw at Tattersall's could compare.

'I'd like another grey,' he said, 'like Sylvester, the same size, the same sweet temper.'

'There doesn't seem to be anything to match that description today, Sir,' said Jeffreys.

Then Tristram spotted a pretty grey gelding that reminded him of Charles' mount. He was young and fit, about 14 hands, compared to Sylvester's 18 hands.

'That's more of a lady's ride,' advised Charles, and Jeffreys agreed. 'I don't think she would take your build, Sir. Too short in the leg.'

'I know, I know!' said Tristram. 'But is he healthy? I think he's lovely.' He was picturing Miss Cunningham mounted sidesaddle, accompanying him on Sylvester, surveying his land and looking for felled oak trees.

'He might come in handy,' he said as nonchalantly as he could manage.

'A nice ride for a lady, I should imagine,' confirmed Jeffreys. 'Very sweet tempered,' and Tristram bid on him until he won. Charles simply watched without comment, puzzled.

On the way home, Tristram confided, 'I don't know where we will store the conveyances until the barn is ready, but it will all be delivered very soon.'

'We can manage for now, Sir,' said Jeffreys. 'There are other outbuildings large enough to take a single vehicle each. Not ideal, but we can manage for a time. The stables are ready for the horses, which is good.'

'Once the horses are delivered, I shall move in,' said Tristram, and Charles knew better than to contradict him. 'Very well,' he agreed. 'Perhaps you should send to Halifax for more of your effects?'

Tristram spent that evening writing a letter to his brother Hugh, revealing all that had been happening to him, and telling him his news of a new home. He hoped Hugh and his family would come and visit soon, and see it all for themselves, but having seen how committed his father had always been to staying at the Mill all day every day, he was not optimistic.

Tattersall's agreed to deliver all three horses, the carriage and the curricle on the Tuesday of the following week and Tristram decided moving day would have to be on the Wednesday, the day after they arrived.

He invited Charles and Isabella to accompany him, and the children too if they thought it appropriate. He deeply regretted not having been able to find a mount for himself, but he would keep his eyes open. No horse, how ever fine, could replace Sylvester, and his excitement at moving in to his new home was tempered by the sadness of having to return Sylvester's reins to Charles so that he could lead his beloved mount back home.

He had asked one more time if Charles would consider selling Sylvester after all, and even told him to name his price, but Charles refused yet again. 'Sorry, Tristram, can't be done,' he said, and changed the subject.

At last the longed-for Tuesday arrived, and Tristram rode Sylvester over early in order to be there when Tattersall's arrived. He kicked his heels all morning, growing steadily more impatient. At about 2 o'clock when they had still not come, he gave up and went indoors for some luncheon.

Just as he'd left, the little cavalcade of horses, the curricle, his coach and no less than four of Tattersall's best grooms, came slowly up the drive. Jeffreys sent Stebbins racing up to the house to let Tristram know they were here, and much to Mrs Nesbit's consternation, he abandoned his meal and dashed out of doors.

They had come from London to Reading by rail, loaded onto stock cars by Tattersall's staff as carefully and tenderly as if they had been new-born babies, and on arrival at Reading station, driven out to Brightwell Manor. The young groom that had ridden the grey gelding had quite fallen in love with him, and was loath to dismount. 'He's a fine little horse,' he said. 'One of the best.'

Jeffreys was there to welcome them too, and led the cavalcade round to the stables. Everything was carefully checked over, and once satisfied, the groom had the curricle and coach in their respective outhouses. The pair of chestnuts were installed in their freshly prepared stables and given a welcoming haybag, water and extra oats after the trauma of their journey. Tristram welcomed the little gelding personally, and taking his reins, led him over to Sylvester, who's head could be seen over the top of his half-stable door, curiously watching the new arrivals. He introduced the two, and noted with huge satisfaction that they were both an almost perfectly matched grey, just as he had suspected and hoped.

Tristram thanked the grooms, delighted them by giving each one a hefty tip, and sent them up to the house to find Mrs Nesbit and take some refreshment before their return journey. He remained in the stables admiring his new horses and transportation, and spent a happy afternoon with the grooms and stableboys, wishing he could stay and sleep in the stables alongside them. However, he needed to ride back before dark to Charles and Isabella for a final night at Tower Court, before moving in to his new home tomorrow. Hunger finally drove him away, much to the relief of Jeffreys and Stebbins, who were beginning to think he would never leave.

Wednesday dawned bright and clear, and Tristram and Charles rode beside the carriage conveying Isabella and the children. Nesbit already knew he would be arriving that morning, and asked if Mrs Hatton could prepare a light luncheon for the five of them.

All this time Tristram had been impatiently awaiting a letter from Samuel Cunningham & Sons & Daughter to let him know when the younger Mr Cunningham would be coming to Brightwell to do his survey. It had been almost a week since Mr and Miss Cunningham's visit, and he was trying to curb his impatience regarding that too. He didn't yet feel ready to divulge to Charles that his new architect was in fact a lady, because he knew what he would say. And think. And imagine.

As they approached the house up the long drive, Tristram led the way, followed by the carriage, with Charles to the rear. At the door he dismounted, and allowed himself a moment to go to Sylvester's head. Although Charles and his family were staying for the afternoon, Tristram knew this was goodbye to his lovely borrowed steed. He leaned his head against Sylvester's neck, and to his surprise and delight, Sylvester turned his head and nuzzled his own neck in return, as if he too knew this was farewell.

Charles dismounted and, after helping his family down from the carriage, allowed Tristram to place Sylvester's reins into his hand. 'Before we go indoors, Tristram . . .' said Charles, and Tristram looked up at him inquiringly. 'We have a housewarming present for you.'

'A present?' said Tristram, genuinely surprised, and looked towards the carriage to see if there was a parcel there. Charles smiled and, taking his friend's hand, pressed Sylvester's reins into his palm. Bewilderment was writ large on Tristram's face, and then puzzlement as he looked in turn at Charles, then Isabella. They were smiling broadly. 'The reason Sylvester was not for sale,' explained Isabella, 'was because we wanted to present him to you as a gift.'

Disbelief then realisation flitted across Tristram's face. 'A gift? You can't give me a gift so valuable, so wonderful, so beautiful! Sylvester is worth rubies . . .'

'Yes,' agreed Charles, 'he is. And that is why we are happy for you to have him. We have our own favourites, and we know Sylvester will have a good home here.'

Tristram was overcome, bereft of words. 'I can't believe it,' he said at last. 'You . . . you're too kind. Are you sure?' And when Charles only nodded, and Isabella beamed, and the children laughed at his confusion, all he could say was, 'Thank you. Oh Charles, thank you a thousand times over. Thank you so much.'

One of his grooms had reached the front of the house by then, and took Sylvester's reins to lead him to one of the newly refurbished stables. Another groom took Charles's mount and followed Sylvester to the stable yard, where both horses would be fed and watered.

A young stable lad remained to hold the heads of the pair pulling the carriage, waiting until Jeffreys returned to lead them to the stable yard too, until the family had dined and were ready to return home. Without Sylvester. Tristram still could not quite believe it.

'Come in! Come in!' he said, recovering his manners,

and leading them all in through the front door. 'Are you hungry?' Both children enthusiastically said they were, and Tristram led them into his new dining room, where a light luncheon would be served and he would entertain guests for the very first time.

After lunch, they explored the other rooms and outbuildings, and Charles was amazed at the changes and improvements that had been made since he had seen it on their previous visit.

'It looks wonderful!' he said, 'you have worked wonders.'

Isabella, seeing it for the first time, was less fulsome in her praise. 'Not quite yet a real home, but it is a fine house, Tristram. When you have had more time, it is going to be splendid.'

Delighted with their praise, he was not sorry when Charles said it was time for them to leave. He escorted them round to the stable yard where Charles's mount and the carriage were ready for departure. Sylvester was in his own stable, with hay in the manger, water in his trough, and he looked out over the half-stable door, to see his erstwhile master leave. Charles went to him and patted his neck affectionately. 'Goodbye, old friend,' he said, 'look after Tristram for us.'

The children wanted to see Tristram's other horses, and before climbing back into the carriage, they visited the grey gelding which was in the stable next to Sylvester's.

Looking across at them both, Charles was struck by how similar the two horses were. 'Apart from size,' he said, looking quizzically at Tristram, 'they are almost a match.'

'I suppose that is why I was attracted to the gelding,' said Tristram, with an air of innocence. 'He reminded me of Sylvester, and I was so sad at the thought of parting, I wanted something to remember him by.'

'Yes,' said Charles. 'Even if it was a momento you could not ride!'

'Thank you again, Charles,' said Tristram, shaking his hand, his arm across his friend's shoulder. 'This is a wonderful day, and Sylvester is a wonderful gift. You are the dearest of friends. I will never forget this moment.'

On the way home, as he rode beside her carriage, Isabella said to her husband, 'There's more to this than meets the eye. That gelding is definitely a lady's mount. And almost identical in colour to Sylvester, an unusual silver grey. I suspect something is afoot.'

Charles was more sanguine. 'Nonsense, my dear. Where can Tristram have met a lady for whom he would want to buy a gelding? If he had, we would surely have known.' Isabella was not so certain.

Having waved his dearest friends off down the drive, Tristram turned and went inside. Pausing to take a deep breath, he was not sure what to do next. As he stood in the large and still empty hallway, his butler approached, with a folded letter on a silver salver.

'This arrived for you this morning, Sir,' said Nesbit, 'but I thought you would prefer to wait until your guests had left before opening it.'

Reaching out to take it, Tristram said, 'Thank you, Nesbit. Most thoughtful of you.'

'There is a fire in the drawing room if you have need of it, Sir,' said Nesbit. 'The evenings are turning chilly now.'

Tristram entered the drawing room and Nesbit withdrew. Unfolding the letter, Tristram was delighted to discover that the younger Mr Cunningham would be arriving the following morning to survey the barn and take the necessary measurements. He had moved into his new home at just the right moment.

Chapter 8

That evening Tristram dined well but alone at the long and newly polished oak table in the dining room. A new footman named Clements served him with due ceremony, which both participants felt to be entirely unnecessary.

Tristram tried to make a little light conversation, but Clements was unaccustomed to such civility and his responses were awkward. He had heard that Mr Sinclair was inclined to give out golden sovereigns for no apparent reason, and was keen not to do anything to impair his chances of receiving such largesse.

After Tristram had replaced his knife and fork on his empty plate, and quaffed the last of his wine – had he asked for wine? He thought not – Clements stepped forward and said, 'There are two kinds of pudding, Sir.'

'Oh God,' said Tristram, 'is there really? I'm not sure I want anything else.'

'Very good, Sir.'

'I'm sure the others in the kitchen can eat it?'

'I'm sure we can, Sir!' said Clements, with the ghost of a smile.

'Tell the cook it was all very satisfactory. And thank you too.' Clements watched his retreating back in amazement.

After his meal Tristram escaped to the stables, and went to visit Sylvester. The year had progressed almost without his noticing, and it was growing dark, but still just light enough to see his way. The stable boy was bedded down in straw for the night, and leapt up in alarm at the sight of Tristram.

'It's alright, Stebbins,' said Tristram hastily. 'I just came to see Sylvester. He's more company than I have indoors at the moment.'

Stebbins laughed. 'Yes, Sir,' he agreed. 'Horses are the best company in the world.' Not sure he entirely agreed with that, Tristram was nonetheless grateful for someone confident enough to talk to him in comfort. 'He's a lovely animal, Sir.'

'The best,' agreed Tristram. 'And now you have gone from none to looking after four!'

'We'll be fine, Sir,' reassured Stebbins. 'Mr Jeffreys and me, we're both accustomed to a lot of horses. In Mr Jeffreys last employment, they hunted too, and there were loads there.'

'Things will pick up,' said Tristram, hoping this was true. 'It's all a bit new at the moment, but we'll get busier as time goes on. I'm hoping to get some sheep and maybe a few cows later on.'

'Any dogs, Sir?' asked Stebbins hopefully. 'I love dogs. I've always had dogs, Sir.'

'Yes, indeed. We must have some dogs.'

'A Collie would be best if you're having sheep, Sir. Obedient.'

'You know about dogs, do you?' asked Tristram. Fearing he had said too much, Stebbins modestly consented. 'Well, a bit, Sir.'

'That will be useful when we get round to it,' said Tristram. 'Goodnight.'

There was nothing left for it but to return to the house and go to bed. It was dark now, and there was not much of a moon, but he found his way without difficulty.

Ever since he had received the letter from young Mr Cunningham saying he would be coming to survey and measure the barn on the Thursday morning, Tristram had been hoping that Miss Cunningham might accompany her brother. He was not disappointed. As their carriage came to a stop at the head of the drive, he stepped forward and opened the carriage door.

'Good morning, Miss Cunningham!' He smiled as she stepped down from the carriage, offering his arm, should she have need of it. Apparently she did.

'Good morning, Mr Sinclair,' she said, returning his delighted smile. Her brother followed her, and turning, she said, 'May I introduce my brother, Mr Matthew Cunningham?'

'Good morning, Mr Cunningham!' beamed Tristram, offering his hand. 'Tristram Sinclair.' They shook hands. 'Good morning,' said Mr Cunningham in his turn, 'that's a fine looking house you have there.'

This was immediately the way to Tristram's heart. 'Thank you, yes, indeed.'

'Built around 1680, if I am not mistaken,' he said. His sister agreed.

'Yes, Matthew, I think you are right. Certainly during King Charles II's reign. A lot of Royalists had followed him into exile, Mr Sinclair, and seen a little of Europe. When they returned home, they tried to include some of that architectural influence, but fortunately in the case of Brightwell Manor, not too much.'

'Indeed,' agreed Matthew, 'building houses was still quite a humble affair in the 1600s. It didn't get competitive until the eighteenth century, when people added false chimneys and grand facades in order to display their great wealth.'

Tristram looked at them both in amazement. 'I didn't know any of that!' he exclaimed.

'Well, you haven't really had time to find out yet,' Grace sympathised.

He laughed. 'No, I have been a little busy. Maybe you would like a tour of the house? It is much improved now, and at least clean. I should love to hear more about it.'

Matthew Cunningham spoke for both of them.

'I am sure my sister would be delighted, Mr Sinclair, but I need to get on.' He dived back into the carriage and lifted out a case heavy with equipment, most of it for measuring, thought Tristram. 'Where would you like me to start?'

Remembering the matter in hand, Tristram said, 'Come this way,' and they followed him through the gardens at the side of the house to the stone barn and stables beyond. Mr Cunningham looked at the barn with interest. 'Unusual to have built the entrance on the short wall,' he said. 'I wonder why they did that?'

'I suggested to Mr Sinclair that the barn might be older than the house itself, Matthew,' said Miss Cunningham to her brother. 'What do you feel?'

'Very possibly,' he replied. 'I will know more when I have had a better look . . .' He was obviously keen to get started, and to be left in peace.

'Would you really like a tour of the house, Miss Cunningham?' asked Tristram.

'Indeed I would, Mr Sinclair,' she said, with genuine enthusiasm. Tristram glanced nervously at her brother. He already knew how closely Mr Samuel Cunningham liked to chaperone his daughter. 'Would that be alright, Mr Cunningham?'

Young Mr Cunningham was not so assiduous as his father in his dealings with his sister. 'Yes, yes, of course,' he said. 'She will love it, and she will bore you to death with her immense knowledge of all things historical.'

She laughed at this brotherly remark, and said composedly, 'I will indeed, Mr Sinclair, are you sure you wish to take the risk?'

Tristram could not believe his good fortune. He was keen to learn all he could about his new home, and he was obviously in expert hands. As they left her brother behind them, already oblivious to anything other than the fine stone barn and the work before him, she said more seriously, 'Are you sure you have time, Mr Sinclair? I can easily occupy myself . . .'

'No indeed,' he hastened to reassure her. 'I have now taken up residence here – at last! – and I was almost bored last night. I've been accustomed to my friends Charles and Isabella, and their two little ones. They were excellent company and last night I dined alone with one rather grand footman to wait on me. I was completely overwhelmed.'

'It sounds positively dreadful,' she said, with the tantalising lilt in her voice that suggested she was on the brink of laughter.

As they walked back round the side of the house to the front door, he told her about Charles's gift of Sylvester, and she could hear in his voice the joy and surprise this had brought him. 'We've also been to Tattersall's and bought the other horses I need for now. And a carriage and a curricle. Do you ride, Miss Cunningham?'

'Oh yes, Sir, since I was in short petticoats! I believe my Papa first put me on a horse when I was two years old. I was riding at the age of three.'

As he opened the front door for her to precede him, he said, 'Well, let us have our tour of the house, and when we return to see if your brother has finished his work, I can take you to the stables en route, and introduce you to Sylvester.'

'That would be delightful,' she agreed, as she stepped into the hall, 'but my brother will be hours yet. He is very thorough.'

She glanced around. 'My word, you are starting with a blank canvas in here,' she said.

'I'm afraid that is true of the entire house,' said Tristram, with a rueful glance.

'It has beautiful proportions,' she said kindly. 'There is a great deal you could do to make it quite beautiful.' Tristram was at a loss to think of anything. 'And look,' she indicated the walls. 'You can see where paintings have been hanging for many years, but have since been removed.'

Tristram had not noticed this before. 'Probably sold off one by one as the family needed money,' he said. 'Sir Geoffrey said as much. And some of the furniture too, I fear.' She had already heard elsewhere how he had won the house at play, and she knew of Sir Geoffrey Turnbull by name and reputation, but had not met him.

They continued into the inner and grander hall where an elegant staircase rose to the next floor. He opened the door into the main drawing room and interrupted Betsy laying a fire in the magnificent fireplace. She looked up guiltily, even though she was doing nothing wrong.

'Oh, beg pardon, Sir, I will come back later . . .'

'No, no, Betsy, you carry on. We are only looking round the house. We will be gone in a moment.'

Betsy glanced up and noticed he was accompanied by a very smart lady, whom she later described downstairs as being 'more beautiful than you realised'.

'Yes, Sir,' she said meekly. Hoping to reassure her in her confusion, Tristram said, 'How is Millicent Victoria getting along?'

Betsy allowed herself a radiant smile at mention of her daughter. 'She is doing very well, Sir, thank you. She is with Mrs Dawkins in the cottage next to mine. They have taken to each other, and get along famously.'

That was exactly what Tristram had hoped when he suggested the arrangement, relieved both for himself and for Betsy, as well as satisfaction in knowing that Mrs Dawkins had something important to do in her retirement, and to think about other than her failing health. 'Do you have everything you need in your cottage?'

'Oh yes, Sir!' said Betsy, in raptures. 'It is quite wonderful. We have everything we need and more.

I bought Millicent Victoria some new clothes with the sovereign, thank you, Sir.'

Miss Cunningham listened to this artless exchange in some surprise, but said nothing, and turned her attention to the fine wainscoting on the walls and the beautiful view beyond the windows.

'A lovely room,' she said, when he returned to her side, 'and that wainscoting is original. I like it very well, it is lighter in colour than is customary for the period.'

They discussed it in some detail, and the beautifully decorated ceiling too. As they were leaving the room, a thought struck Tristram. 'Betsy, could you ask Mrs Nesbit to come and see me, please?'

'Yes, Sir, of course, Sir,' replied Betsy, and fled downstairs to do as she was bid.

Tristram and Miss Cunningham moved on to the dining room, and from there to the library, which was where Mrs Nesbit found them.

'Ah, Mrs Nesbit, yes,' said Tristram, and introduced the ladies to each other, describing Miss Cunningham as his architect. 'May I ask you to escort Miss Cunningham upstairs and show her the bedchambers? And,' he added with pride, 'possibly the newly appointed bathroom? She is having a tour of the house and I would like her to see all of it.'

The ladies withdrew and left Tristram wondering what to do during their absence. He knew Miss Cunningham's

Papa would not approve of his daughter being shown the upstairs rooms by her host, so was relieved to have thought of his housekeeper and such an appropriate solution.

So was Miss Cunningham, who would be delighted to see the newly appointed bathroom for more reasons than one, but would never have dreamed of asking. What a kind and thoughtful man he was. Mrs Nesbit understood this too, and provided fresh soap and a small hand towel, and waited for Miss Cunningham to re-join her on the wainscoted landing.

'There are eight bedrooms in all, Miss Cunningham,' said Mrs Nesbit, 'so you may not wish to see every one of them.' In this tactful way she considerately avoided showing her Tristram's room, and his dressing room. As they entered the last and smallest of the bedchambers, which was almost entirely bereft of furniture, Miss Cunningham could contain her curiosity no longer.

'Mr Sinclair seems to be on good terms with all his servants?' she said enquiringly.

'Yes, indeed,' agreed Mrs Nesbit with enthusiasm. 'He has been kindness itself to all of us. It has occurred to me that he is not perfectly accustomed to having servants at his beck and call. He always asks us so nicely if he wants anything done, and makes a point of thanking us afterwards. We all feel very privileged to work for him.'

'I had that impression,' said Miss Cunningham,

gently prompting her to continue. 'We met Betsy in the drawing room, laying the fire.'

'Oh, Betsy!' exclaimed Mrs Nesbit, needing no further encouragement. 'Betsy most of all. The poor girl worked here previously, before the Earl died and, shortly after his passing, she found herself to be increasing, and was turned away without a penny.'

Miss Cunningham maintained her silence, hoping Mrs Nesbit would continue. She was not disappointed.

'If Prudence had not befriended the poor girl, she would have starved. When Mr Tristram became the new owner, he needed new staff, and Prudence suggested taking on her friend. Having given birth to a daughter, Prudence thought it expedient to describe Betsy as a widow. But Mr Tristram was not taken in, and Betsy soon confessed that Sir Geoffrey was to blame.'

Miss Cunningham was not surprised to have her suspicions confirmed. She had heard nothing good of Sir Geoffrey, and was not sorry when she heard he had lost the house during a game of cards, and had since gone abroad, abandoning his poor Mama in the process. She had not realised at that time, of course, who Mr Sinclair was, or that he would be in need of anyone's architectural services, let alone that he would be recommended to contact her father's firm.

'Once he knew the truth,' confided Mrs Nesbit, 'he not only gave her back her old place as a chambermaid, but allowed her to live in one of the estate cottages as well, so that she would not have to carry the baby upstairs to the attics for sleeping. And,' said Mrs Nesbit, pausing for breath for maximum dramatic effect. Miss Cunningham raised her eyebrows in anticipation. 'And, he gave the girl a gold sovereign in order to buy the little mite some clothes. She was in rags before that.'

Suitably impressed, Miss Cunningham felt their absence must by now be noticeable, and suggested they return to the Library where they had left Mr Sinclair.

'Yes, indeed,' agreed Mrs Nesbit, as they walked down the beautiful wide staircase. 'And you must be getting hungry. Has Mr Tristram invited you remain for lunch?'

Miss Cunningham was becoming exceedingly hungry, and thought this an excellent suggestion. 'My brother is here too, conducting a survey of the old barn for conversion, and I think he would probably like that very much.'

On finding Tristram in the Library, relieving his boredom by scanning the few books that lined the shelves, Mrs Nesbit said, 'Were you planning to invite your guests to remain for some luncheon, Mr Sinclair?'

He immediately saw the wisdom of this idea, and addressed Miss Cunningham. 'Yes, indeed, if you can stay, Miss Cunningham? And your bother too, of course. He must be getting quite hungry by now.' When she agreed with him, he turned back to Mrs Nesbit. 'It is rather short notice, Mrs Nesbit, is that alright?'

'Yes, of course, Sir,' she said, feeling almost motherly towards the pair of them. 'It will only be something simple, but I am sure we can provide.'

'Something simple will be ideal,' said Miss Cunningham, and as Mrs Nesbit bustled away on her mission, she turned to Tristram saying, 'Perhaps we should go and find Matthew? The morning has passed so quickly!'

'Yes, I am keen to see how far along your brother is with his investigations and surveying,' suggested Tristram, as they went out through the front door again. 'Will he need to continue his work after lunch? What time is your father expecting your return?'

'Oh, he knows Matthew will take for ever! He won't be concerned until mid-afternoon, but of course we need to be home before dark.'

'Well, we must make time for you to meet Sylvester and the other horses too,' said Tristram, and led the way through the gardens at the side of the house in their search for her brother.

He heard their steps on the gravel and turning, called out in some excitement, 'This barn was originally built as a church!'

'A church?' repeated Tristram in some astonishment.

'But of course!' exclaimed Miss Cunningham. 'That explains why the entrance is on the short wall, and why it is built to be long and narrow. How clever of you, Matthew. What made you realise?'

Matthew grinned at her but spoke to Mr Sinclair. 'Have you had time to look into it properly yourself, Mr Sinclair?' When Tristram shook his head, Mr Cunningham continued, 'There is a great deal of debris and rubbish and even some sort of sheeting,' he said. 'But underneath it all I found some old organ pipes. Rusting now, of course, but still with some of the design visible.'

He led them to the far end. 'And this wood that you can barely see, seems to have been part of a pulpit. It is a very hard wood, which is how come it has survived. I'm not an expert on pulpits but I would date it to around 1650, which is about the time Charles II was exiled in France. So it probably dates from the reign of Charles I. How it came to be here I cannot imagine.'

Miss Cunningham seemed to be more excited than Tristram himself, who felt self consciously ignorant, worried that the significance of it all was rather lost on him. Noticing his diffidence, Miss Cunningham took pity, and addressed her brother. 'Matthew, we have been so absorbed in visiting all the rooms in the house, we hardly noticed the time. But then we realised we were quite hungry, and knew you must be too, so Mr Sinclair has kindly asked his housekeeper to provide us with a simple luncheon.'

'That is splendid news,' agreed Matthew, wiping his hands on a cloth. 'I'm starving. May I leave my tools here, Mr Sinclair? I will need to continue my work afterwards.'

'Yes, do,' agreed Tristram, 'but come and meet Sylvester quickly before we go indoors again. I am longing to see him myself.'

They entered the stables and Sylvester nuzzled Tristram's pockets, secure in the knowledge that there would be an apple or a carrot for him there.

'What a beautiful grey!' said Miss Cunningham. 'He is one of the finest I have seen.'

Thrilled by her appreciation of his mount, Tristram said, 'Thank you. Now come and meet the young gelding I bought from Tattersall's, whom I believe matches him perfectly. My friend Charles and my groom, who came to Tattersall's with me, said I would have no need of him but, because he was an identical silver grey, I couldn't resist.

'Miss Cunningham, perhaps you would do me the honour of riding him, and accompany me when I ride through the park in search of a suitable oak as a lintel for the new opening in the long wall of the barn?'

Glancing across at the pretty little gelding, Miss Cunningham said, 'I should be delighted!' and a blush deepened the rose of her cheeks. Fortunately her brother was looking back at his handiwork, and did not notice. He had heard what they were saying, however, and added,

'Yes, indeed, Mr Sinclair. We will need a lintel as soon as possible. And more oak to make the double doors for the widened entrance, I think. I will give you the measurements by day's end.'

Chapter 9

After the simple luncheon, served in the dining room, which young Mr Cunningham also admired very much, he left them again to return to the old barn, now almost convinced it had originally been a church, and Tristram suggested Miss Cunningham might like to take a turn around the outside of the building. Young Mr Cunningham raised no objection, so they set off, inspecting the outside walls carefully as they went.

'Take care here,' Tristram said, as they negotiated some rough and stony ground. He offered his arm, which she was glad to take. Once they were safely past the stony part without mishap, he held her arm for an imperceptible moment longer than was strictly necessary, loathe to let her go.

Content to leave Matthew to his work, they walked a little further, and then Tristram suggested they should return to the house for some tea. 'We mustn't leave Matthew too much longer,' she said. 'We will need to leave soon, and he will not notice the time.'

'Have some tea first,' said Tristram, leading her back to the house, and Clements, the footman, brought them a tray and placed it on a low table before the unlit fire.

'Shall I put a light to it, Sir?' asked Clements, but the day was warm, and both Miss Cunningham and Tristram were happier admiring the view through the window.

'I wanted to ask you one further question,' said Tristram, watching her pour his tea for him.

'Milk?' she asked, reaching for the little jug.

'Yes, please.'

'Sugar?'

'No thank you.'

Returning to her seat facing him, she said, 'And what did you want to ask me, Sir?'

He laughed. 'Oh, please don't call me Sir!' he admonished. 'The servants do it all day long, at least once in every sentence, and I have come to dislike it very much.'

'I am sorry!' she smiled, 'I will refrain. What was your question?'

'I've been wondering how much the house would be worth today? If it were to be offered for sale, I mean.'

She looked her concern. 'You're not planning to sell?'

'No no,' he said hastily. 'Not at all. But I should like to have some idea of its value, that is all. Having won it at cards, I have absolutely no idea.'

She considered for some moments, and then said,

'Well, our other brother, Henry, is the one that does

the valuations. You would be better asking him.'

'But he isn't here!' said Tristram, unwilling to wait for a formal appointment. 'I can see you are very experienced in your father's firm, you must have some idea?'

'Well, indeed, but I am not expert, please do not quote me,' and she named a figure.

'Really?' said Tristram, pleasantly surprised. Then he remembered the sum he had persuaded Sir Geoffrey to accept the morning after the card game, and divulged the figure to Miss Cunningham.

'But why?' she exclaimed. 'Why would you do that? You won the house in a game of cards, fair and square. Why did you feel the need to pay him money he did not deserve?'

Tristram shrugged. 'He had the Deeds with him that evening because he had been to London to collect them from the Solicitor who had kept them safe all these years. After his father died, he was so short of money, he objected to paying for even that small service. He had no other way of increasing his stake on the game, and he truly believed he had the better hand.'

'But he didn't, did he?' she said.

'No, he didn't. And I had admired the house from the hills during a ride with Charles just a few days previously. So I was glad to win it, but Miss Cunningham, he was literally penniless. Taking his home meant he had nothing, not even the price of a week's lodging.'

She seemed unsympathetic. 'Well, he should have considered that before he gambled it away,' she said. 'And it wasn't just himself he rendered homeless, it was his poor Mama too.'

'Precisely,' agreed Tristram. 'I was told that after he left, and I felt sorry for the pair of them. I think he had come to loathe the place because it was a drain on what little he had left. He said several times it was bleeding him dry. I discovered when I came to visit that first time, the servants had not been paid for some weeks. There were only three of them – Mr & Mrs Dawkins and Prudence – but they had not left because they had no money, and nowhere else to go.'

'What a sorry state of affairs,' she said. 'So you called on him next morning, and insisted he accept payment too?'

'Yes,' agreed Tristram, 'that's exactly what I did. And he said what you said. 'Why? You won it fair and square!' And it's true, I did, but I couldn't see him turned out of his home with nothing, could I?'

'Other men would have done so.'

'Maybe. Anyway, I gave him a Draft on my bank. I expected him to share it with his mother, but I very much doubt that he did so.'

'Well, if my figure is not too far out, you are still in profit.'

'I genuinely had no idea what it might be worth,' he said again. 'It was just a guess. Not too wide of the mark, as it turns out.'

A terrible thought struck Miss Cunningham, and she frowned. 'Mr Sinclair,' she said, pausing while the enormity of the idea unfolded in her head. 'Please tell me you dealt with all the relevant paperwork as the result of this exchange?'

'What paperwork?' said Tristram innocently. 'The only paperwork was the Deeds, and I have those safe.'

'The conveyancing paperwork!' Miss Cunningham told him. 'There is a lot to deal with, and a lot to be signed. By both parties. Did you at least get a receipt for the money?'

'No, I didn't think to ask him for a receipt. I gave him a Draft on my bank, and when he presented that, they would retain it in exchange for the money. They have no doubt returned it to me by now. I haven't checked yet.'

'Well that is something, I suppose,' said Miss Cunningham, not in the least mollified. 'Mr Sinclair, I am seriously concerned that if the relevant paperwork has not been signed, the house might not be legally yours.'

He refused to become alarmed. 'It's fine,' he said, as much to reassure himself as Miss Cunningham. 'I have the Deeds, and I will have the Draft. Surely that is evidence enough for anyone. And he has left the area. Possibly gone abroad. We shall not be seeing him again.'

'Well, I very much hope you are correct,' she said doubtfully. 'But are you not concerned that one day he too might realise that the legal paperwork was not completed correctly, and return to reclaim his birthright?'

'Oh, he couldn't do that,' said Tristram, dismissing the idea. But when she did not vouchsafe a reply, he added, 'Could he?'

'I don't know,' she said quietly. 'I will ask Papa about it for you. And Henry. They are both more knowledgeable than I am. But if he has disappeared for now, there would seem to be no way to make it legal without him.'

'There were plenty of witnesses that evening.' Tristram seemed to feel the need to defend his actions. Or lack thereof. 'There can be no doubt . . .'

Something else seemed to have occurred to her. 'It's a good job Betsy's baby is a girl and not a boy! A boy could inherit, whereas a girl won't, of course.'

Tristram wished very much that they had not started this conversation, and began to drink his tea which had grown quite cold. She did the same, and then rose to her feet. 'I am so sorry to have mentioned something so horrid,' she apologised, 'but it will be getting dark soon, and Matthew will have to stop his work, whether he has completed it or not.'

Tristram stood up too, and longed to possess himself of her hand, but knew he could not.

'Please do not worry,' he said stoically. 'It is my mistake if indeed a mistake has been made. I would be grateful if you would ask your Papa about it, and see what his advice is.'

'Indeed I will, Mr Sinclair,' she said, wishing too that he would take her hand as a token of forgiveness at her tidings but, like him, knew propriety would forbid it.

'If you are anxious about the return journey, I would be more than happy to accompany your carriage on Sylvester.'

'You are very kind, Mr Sinclair, but I will have Matthew with me and the coachman, I am sure all will be well if we leave very shortly.'

Matthew must have been of the same mind, for they found their horse already harnessed between the shafts, and the coachman, who had spent a pleasant day in the stables with Jeffreys and Stebbins, ready to go.

Matthew came to shake Tristram's hand, and congratulated him on having such a fine church on his premises. 'Grace's suggestion that we create a double-door opening on the long wall, and use the stone to fill in the entrance on the short wall is very sound,' he said, with a glance at his sister. She was thrilled by his praise. 'I'll need to return and take some more measurements, and you will need to find a lintel long enough in your parkland. It is all moving forward most satisfactorily.'

'Thank you both for coming,' said Tristram, already feeling forlorn at their departure. He knew Miss Cunningham would tell her brother all that they had discussed over tea, and said, 'I hope your father will come and visit too, and reassure me that all is well with the paperwork.'

The coachman twitched the reins, the horse started forward, and Tristram watched as they departed down the drive, a prey to many misgivings in more ways than one.

Chapter 10

After a sleepless night, Tristram was seated in the dining room awaiting the arrival of his breakfast when there was heard a lengthy hammering on the front door. Unsurprisingly his early morning visitor turned out to be no less a personage than Mr Samuel Cunningham.

Tristram arrived in the hall just as Nesbit, his butler, opened the door, and had the happy idea of inviting Mr Cunningham to join him for breakfast. This was well received by the corpulent Mr Cunningham, and Tristram asked the butler to let Mrs Nesbit know they would be two for breakfast, not one. And to bring extra coffee as soon as she possibly could.

Mr Cunningham settled himself comfortably into the chair indicated by Tristram, and said, 'I hope I'm not too early?' Tristram manfully replied that he had timed it very well, and his footman, Clements, brought them all the vittles they could need, and more.

Once Clements had left the room, and Mr Cunningham had amassed a hefty plate before him, he said,

'My daughter told me all that transpired yesterday,' which caused Tristram to look up in some concern.

'I would like to take a look at your barn,' he continued, 'Matthew thinks it might be a church. As Grace says, that would explain why it is long and narrow, but we can decide when we see it.'

'I'd be delighted to escort you there immediately after breakfast,' said Tristram, and poured more coffee. Mr Cunningham allowed himself to be momentarily diverted from his purpose. 'Nice to see you enjoying coffee,' he said. 'It is still quite new in some quarters.'

'I acquired the taste for it in America,' confessed Tristram. 'It is quite usual over there. They are ahead of us in many ways.'

Mr Cunningham cleared his throat, returning to one of the other reasons for his visit. 'My daughter tells me she had a tour of the house, and that you invited your housekeeper to escort her to the upper floor.'

'I thought it more appropriate, Sir,' said Tristram, anxious that this had not displeased his guest.

'Very proper,' agreed Samuel. The architect in him seemed to take precedence over his being a protective father. 'She tells me you have a bathroom and one of the new water closets?'

'You are welcome to see that too, Sir,' said Tristram with a smile. 'It is very new, it may be that it requires further development one day.'

'They both came home full of their day,' said Samuel, returning to the matter in hand, 'but the reason I am here so early,' he stabbed another slice of meat and hefted it onto his plate, 'is the matter of the legal ownership of this house.'

'Yes, Sir,' said Tristram. 'I did say I would welcome your opinion. It is very good of you to come so promptly.'

'I imagine you are somewhat concerned, Mr Sinclair?'

'Yes indeed. I had little sleep last night.'

'My Grace feared as much. She was regretting having spoken on the subject, and wished me to come here at the first opportunity to reassure you.'

'But are you able to reassure me, Sir?' queried Tristram. 'It seems I have shown a marked lack of perception in the matter.'

'Well, after this excellent repast, let us take a look at the Deeds, and the Draft on your bank. My Grace was correct in saying that there is a great deal of paperwork for the conveyance of ownership, but if Sir Geoffrey stays away long enough, it might serve the purpose.'

'How so, Mr Cunningham?' asked Tristram, not yet reassured.

'Well, they do say possession is nine-tenths of the law. They also talk about squatter's rights, which doesn't quite apply, but could be fashioned to do so.'

'Squatter's rights, Sir?' said Tristram, painfully aware that it must sound as if he knew very little about anything.

'Yes, indeed,' said Samuel, pleased to have an appreciative audience who knew less than he did. 'It was of major consideration during the Peasants' Revolt in 1381 and again for the Diggers in the 17th Century, peasants who cultivated waste and common land, claiming it as their rightful due. I'm sure if Sir Geoffrey were to return, and knew his rights, which seems entirely unlikely, we could fashion a case around that. Anyone in their proper mind would see that you are in the right of it.'

Somehow Tristram did not find this entirely reassuring. 'Well, if we are talking squatter's rights, the Talbots have been here for 250 years!' He hoped Mr Samuel Cunningham would enlighten him further, but for now he longed to be out of doors and showing his guest the barn. 'Can I offer you more coffee, Mr Cunningham? Or more of anything else?'

'No thank you, Mr Sinclair. I am well fed after my early morning ride. Let us go out to the barn first and see what my Matthew has discovered.'

Both gentlemen were pleased to escape to the outdoors, and Tristram led the way. As they walked through the now much-improved gardens at the side of the house, Mr Cunningham said, 'My Grace tells me you have a lovely grey?' Tristram was more than happy to make a detour to the stables, and introduce him to Sylvester.

'She also tells me you have a matched gelding, and that you have invited her to ride him?'

Tristram looked anxiously at Mr Cunningham, his countenance blandly innocent of all emotion.

'Well, yes, Sir, I did mention it in passing. Young Mr Matthew Cunningham tells me we will need a good length lintel if we are to make a wider entrance on the long wall of the barn, I mean church. And wood for the double doors too.

'I planned to ask your permission first, Sir, whether it would be alright for your daughter to accompany me when I ride across the park searching for an appropriate oak? Her knowledge and experience far outstrips my own in such matters.'

'No need to worry, Mr Sinclair,' said Samuel. 'I can see you have conducted yourself most properly towards her, and I am sure she would be safe enough. Matthew will be here too, overseeing the building works, and I might come along myself on occasion. But you are welcome to invite Grace along on the search for a suitable oak lintel. You are right, her judgement is as good as mine.'

Tristram's spirits rose, and relief sounded in his voice. 'You are very good, Sir. I hope you feel you could trust me to the ends of the earth with your daughter. I value her opinions and knowledge enormously, and am grateful to have her expertise at my disposal, as well as your own.'

'Is there no more to it than that, Mr Sinclair?' asked Samuel, with a fond smile. Tristram looked at him and hoped they understood each other.

'Since you mention it, Sir,' he glanced at the ground, but resolutely returned his gaze to Samuel's face. 'Since you mention it, I would seek your approval to, er, perhaps pay my addresses to your daughter?'

'Do you mean to court her, Sir?'

'Well, it is very early days, but I have a respect for her that I have not felt for the other ladies to whom I have been introduced.'

'She's not a Simpering Miss, if that's what you mean, Mr Sinclair.'

Tristram smiled in acknowledgement, but vouchsafed no reply.

'Just give her a little time, Mr Sinclair. My Grace is a very unusual young lady,' continued Samuel proudly. 'Her mother died when she was very young. I did not set out to educate her particularly. Women are rarely educated today, as you know. It is a common belief that an educated female might deter possible suitors.'

'Really, Sir?' asked Tristram, surprised. 'But that is one of the very things I find so appealing about her. What could be more tedious than to be shackled to a wife with no conversation? And no opinions?'

'I agree, Mr Sinclair, I do agree, but I must confess her education was not a deliberate policy of mine. It just so happened that I had the firm, and my sons were learning all the time. Grace simply absorbed it all along with them. And reading, Sir! Always had her nose in a book.

Always wanting to know what and how and why. And she is blessed with a very good memory, Mr Sinclair. Almost better than her brothers. Once she has read something, she remembers it well.'

'I had noticed it, Mr Cunningham,' enthused Tristram, delighted to have someone with whom he could discuss the object of his growing affections. 'If you consider me suitable, Sir, I would very much like to court your daughter. But only with your permission and approval.'

'Others have asked for it,' revealed Samuel, 'and even though she is 25 years old, I have had to tell them no. She always says her feelings are not engaged, so it is not simply a question of whether I approve of them myself,' he paused, and Tristram looked searchingly into his eyes. 'It is also a question of whether Grace herself considers them worthy. And I think perhaps on this occasion, she does, Sir. Her latest excuse is that she is now beyond marriageable age! Do give her time.'

Tristram's heart soared. 'You are very kind, Sir. I am very sensible of how you would like your daughter to be treated and protected, and I will always have that in mind, throughout all my dealings with her.'

'I feel I can trust you,' replied Samuel. 'And I feel she can trust you too. As you said, it is early days, but it does not take long to know when someone is right for you, does it? I knew the moment I met my wife, Grace's mother. After our first meeting, no other would do.'

'I feel that is possibly the case here too, Mr Cunningham. Maybe this is the moment to reassure you that I am more than able to support a wife.'

'I had guessed as much, Mr Sinclair. Your feelings do you credit, and you are welcome to invite my Grace to ride with you when you go in search of Matthew's precious lintel. She is interested in the gelding you have bought too. From what you have told her, she seems to think he will make a fine mount.'

A prey to doubts as to whether Miss Cunningham was more interested in the gelding than himself, Tristram was nonetheless euphoric after their conversation. 'But for now,' said Samuel, 'let us go and see Matthew's church. He tells me he found some organ pipes and possibly a pulpit. These I have to see.'

Comfortable in the knowledge that they had now satisfactorily dealt with the most important business of the day, and the real reason for Mr Cunningham's early visit, they set off with one accord, able at last to turn their minds to other things.

Happy now to leave the stables and visit the barn, Mr Samuel Cunningham stood still to study it from a short distance. Before entering, he walked the outside perimeter of the building, thoroughly inspecting every wall, nook and cranny.

'You can see from the outside where the windows were,' he said at length. 'Filled in now, of course, to make it suitable for use as a barn. Someone made a very skilled job of it.'

Finally he ventured inside. He merely glanced at the organ pipes: 'There's no way to be certain if they are here because there was an organ, or if they were simply stored here because there was space.'

He moved on to look more thoroughly at the pulpit, now lying flat on its side upon the floor. 'Again, it's not attached to anything. There's no way of knowing if it was actually used here, or if it was just dumped here, along with the organ pipes. It's not conclusive.'

Then he began a minute search of the walls. At last he pounced. 'I was wrong!' he exclaimed, 'Look here, Mr Sinclair. It is possible to see where a pulpit has been attached to the wall. The outline matches perfectly.'

Not yet quite satisfied, he subjected the walls to still greater scrutiny, and pointed aloft. 'Yes, look. As I thought. There were windows, but they have been skilfully filled in with matching stone, so that it hardly notices. Not as many windows as I would have anticipated, but they were there.'

He relapsed into silence then, and Tristram studied the walls himself, but could discern little difference. It barely showed. At last Mr Cunningham felt able to deliver himself of an opinion.

'I think my Matthew was almost correct,' he said, 'but I think this was more likely a chantry chapel.'

Tristram wondered if any of the Cunninghams would ever raise a subject with which he was familiar. '

'A chantry, Sir?'

'Yes, they were popular very early on, priests were employed to chant for the soul of the departed owner of the property. He would have left funds in his Will to cover their employment, and they would have continued their chanting until sufficient time had elapsed for his soul to go through Purgatory, and arrive in heaven.'

'Oh,' said Tristam, somewhat nonplussed.

'Yes, Sir, Oh indeed,' agreed Mr Cunningham with a smile. 'Henry VIII did for most of them when he was knocking down the Monasteries. But it suggests there was a very grand house here before this one, to have had its own chantry chapel. And a very wealthy and probably important owner. We might learn more from your Deeds, but at least for now it explains why there were so few windows.'

Feeling somewhat overwhelmed by all this history, Tristram asked what he considered to be the most pressing question. 'So is there anything to prevent our going ahead with Miss Cunningham's suggestion of opening up a double entrance on the long wall, and using the stone to fill in the entrance on the short wall?'

'No, Sir,' beamed Mr Cunningham, 'nothing at all. We can make a start on that as soon as you wish.'

'Well then, please let's just go ahead and make it all happen. I need the barn before winter, and we must begin our search for the lintel we need, and for the double doors too.'

Having received permission to proceed, and sounded out Mr Sinclair on the subject of his daughter, Mr Cunningham felt it was time to take his departure. Returning to the stables to collect his horse, he said, 'I will take a look at your Deeds another day, if I may. We seem to have run out of time. One thought occurs to me, Mr Sinclair. In view of the circumstances, why not lodge your precious Deeds with your bank or a good solicitor? They will put them in a vault and keep them very safe.'

'That is good advice, Mr Cunningham,' replied Tristram, pleased with the suggestion. 'I do not have a solicitor myself. Do you have one you can recommend?'

'Yes, indeed. We have used Henderson's Reading branch for many years and they have served us well. They have several offices, including one in London, I believe, but Reading is the most convenient to you.' And so saying, he mounted his horse and bade Tristram farewell.

Delighted with developments, but relieved to be on his own at last, Tristram asked Jeffreys to saddle Sylvester. It had been too long since he had ridden him, and both were ready for some exercise. He went indoors to change into riding dress, and returning to the stables, sprang into the saddle. He would ride over to visit Charles and Isabella, and the children. There seemed to be a great deal to tell.

Chapter 11

Once Tristram had handed over the Draft on his bank, and left the house, Sir Geoffrey spent a few moments taking it all in. He remained at the front door, and watched Mr Sinclair riding down the drive on a beautiful grey.

Placing the Banker's Draft in his pocket, he closed the front door. He needed time to think, and make plans, but he knew if he returned to his mother in the drawing room, he would not have the peace or the opportunity to do either. Suddenly realising how hungry he was, he tugged at the bell pull that eventually brought Dawkins into the hall.

'A large breakfast, please, Dawkins,' he said. 'As soon as possible.'

Despite having had no sleep, he suddenly felt a great deal better than he had in a long time, and leapt up the stairs two at a time to change into dry clothing. Dawkins watched him in some surprise, wondering what on earth had happened, and ambled down to the kitchen to tell a stunned Prudence of the master's orders.

Eating his breakfast, hardly noticing what it was, Sir Geoffrey was able to mull things over and decide what he was going to do. Leave the country was first on his list, but before that he needed to ensure his mother would vacate the premises without delay. Fortified by his repast and able to face her with the determination that was necessary in his dealings with his Mama, he returned to the drawing room. She remained seated on the sofa, apparently in some shock, and merely raised reproachful eyes to his face.

'Yes, I know you don't like it, Mama,' he said, unsympathetically. 'But it is done, and cannot be undone. We must shift for ourselves as best we can.'

'But it's our home, Geoffrey,' she wailed. 'My home! I have lived here since I was a bride . . .'

'Yes, we know all about that,' said Sir Geoffrey, revolted. 'And now you can't. I know you don't want to go to your cousin in Hertfordshire, but do you have any other suggestion?'

She sulked for a moment, and then said, 'Well, I've hardly had time to consider the matter, have I?'

'What is there to consider, Mama? It seems to me that is your only option.'

'Where are you going?' she asked. 'Can I not come with you?'

'Hardly!' said Sir Geoffrey, stung that she should realise he had no particular plans either. 'I am planning to kick the dust of this country from my heels as soon as possible. Once you are provided for I will be gone.'

'What?' It seemed to be one shock after another. 'Will I go to my grave without ever seeing you again?'

'Of course you won't, Mama. I will send you my address as soon as I am settled,' he insisted, but they both knew he meant 'if and when I am settled' and perhaps not even then. 'I'm only going abroad,' he added hastily. 'I am not going to disappear off the map altogether.'

That, however, was what he was hoping to do. It would suit him very well to disappear completely, not only to avoid facing people who knew him, and knew of his shame, but also to avoid any further repercussions there might be after having turned Betsy off without a reference, knowing she was pregnant with his child. It would be to his considerable advantage if she did not know where he was either.

His mother was in little doubt of his motives, and allowed a tear to roll down her cheek.

'I don't know what to do,' she said pathetically. 'How am I to reach Hertfordshire if I do go?'

'You can go on one of the new trains, Mama,' said her son, trying to generate some enthusiasm. 'You haven't been on a train yet, have you?'

'No,' she said, with some asperity. 'And I am not going to start now.'

'As far as I can see, there is little option. I will go to

Reading and enquire about trains at the station. I am sure there must be one to Hertfordshire.'

A thought struck him. 'Where is Hertfordshire, anyway?'

'I have no idea, Geoffrey,' said his Mama waspishly. 'I would have thought it would hardly matter to you, since you obviously have no plans to visit me there.'

This sent Sir Geoffrey from the room, saying, 'There is no talking to you when you are in such bad humour, Mama,' conveniently forgetting that it was entirely his fault that she was in such a mood, and was in fact somewhat justified. He was glad of the excuse to leave, and went straight to the stables, saddled his horse, and rode off to Reading.

On arrival, he was hungry again, but had no money to eat at the inn, and immediately sought out Tristram's bank. His father had always used Coutts Bank in London, so he was not known here. He handed the Draft over to the cashier, and demanded to cash it in immediately. The cashier took one look at the amount, and went straight to the Manager. In turn the Manager looked at it in some surprise, and left his office to shake hands with the gentleman who had presented it.

'Good morning, Sir,' he said, 'can I invite you to step into my office?'

Sir Geoffrey followed him, and took a seat as he was bid. 'Is there a problem?'

'No, indeed not, Sir. We can accommodate your

request, of course, but it is rather a large amount, and you may have caught us unawares. We usually require a little notice for large sums.'

'Why?' demanded Sir Geoffrey rudely. 'Do you not have sufficient funds in your vault?'

Simpering at this, the Bank Manager said, 'We do indeed, Sir, but you would hardly want that amount in sovereigns, surely? It would be very heavy. And the notes are of a rather large denomination, which would not only make you conspicuous, and vulnerable to robbery, but most tradespeople would be unable to provide change for such large sums.' Sir Geoffrey had not considered this. God, why did everything have to be so complicated?

'First things first, though, Sir, I will need your name and address, and some sort of identification.' Sir Geoffrey unwillingly divulged his identity and home.

'May I suggest to you, Sir,' continued the Bank Manager, refusing to be impressed by the revelation that his customer's address was Brightwell Manor, 'that you might care to open an account with us, and keep the money safe there? It would be available on demand, any time at your convenience during opening hours, and you could withdraw smaller amounts at a time.'

'That's no good,' replied Sir Geoffrey impatiently. 'I am going abroad, and I need to take it all with me. Now.'

All this began to seem rather odd to the Bank Manager; a stranger requesting a large amount of funds and then leaving the country? He was wary of how to proceed, and cleared his throat.

'Might I enquire how you came by this Draft from Mr Tristram Sinclair, Sir? Is he perhaps a benefactor of yours?'

'Anything but!' exclaimed Sir Geoffrey, and could see the Bank Manager's dawning suspicion. 'I lost my house to him at cards,' he said, not meaning to sound quite as belligerent as he did. 'And he has given me this sum in recompense. He said my stake was disproportionate to his own, and wished to redress the balance.'

'That was very generous of him, Sir,' said the Bank Manager, making a resolution to check with Mr Tristram Sinclair before paying this strange and rude young man anything at all.

'Yes,' agreed Sir Geoffrey grudgingly. 'I suppose it was.'

'Well, Sir.' The Manager took a deep breath. 'As I said, you have caught us unawares, and we usually require some notice before being able to pay out such a large amount. I can have it ready for collection on Thursday.'

'Good God, man! But today is Tuesday.'

'I'm sorry, Sir, it is the best I can do. What denomination notes would you like on Thursday?'

Sir Geoffrey was struggling to hold on to his temper. 'I don't care,' he said, 'what ever you think appropriate. But you have to give me at least 100 guineas of it now. I need to buy vittles, I've had nothing to drink since this morning. And I need to purchase railway tickets.'

Despite his rudeness, the Bank Manager took pity on him. 'Sir Geoffrey,' he said, 'I do not have to give you anything.' He considered the matter. 'Very well, Sir,' he agreed at last, 'I can give you 100 guineas now, and the remainder on Thursday. Will you please sign here.'

After Sir Geoffrey had left, the Bank Manager considered all the facts very carefully. Knowing Mr Sinclair was still staying with Lord and Lady Charles Worth at Tower Court, he decided he had better ride over to see him the following day, and to check that things were as Sir Geoffrey Turnbull had presented them.

As it happened, however, this turned out to be unnecessary. Customer after customer in the Bank that day was full of gossip about how Brightwell Manor had been lost at play just a few nights previously, and to a commoner at that.

Relieved, the Bank Manager realised Sir Geoffrey Turnbull had been telling the truth. And he should have his money on the Thursday, as promised. God knew he had tried his best to help the young man, but now it would be up to him to keep his money safe. He obviously did not realise how heavily such a sum would weigh upon him, in more ways than one.

Irritated, frustrated and hot, Sir Geoffrey left the bank, relieved to be in funds at last, and headed straight for the Inn where he called for ale and a large plate of food. After this he felt better, and continued on to the railway station, where he enquired about trains to Hertfordshire. The railway clerk was tired and irritable too, and not inclined to be helpful.

'How often are there trains to Hertfordshire?' he asked.

'None from here, Sir. Paddington only.'

'Well, how does one get to Hertfordshire?'

'Line ends at Paddington, Sir. You would need to get over to Euston and get a train to Hemel Hempsted.'

'How does one get from Paddington to Euston?'

'I couldn't say, Sir. The Electric Underground might go there one day, I don't know.'

Sir Geoffrey could not see his Mama coping with the Electric Underground, now or in the future.

'How far is it? From Paddington to Euston?'

'Not my job to know, Sir.'

'Well I would have thought it was your job to know!' said Sir Geoffrey, his frustration increasing.

'It's not far, Sir. A couple of miles, I believe.'

'So one could take a Hansom cab?'

'I would have thought so, Sir. I don't really know. I could never afford to do that myself, Sir.'

'I'll buy tickets for Friday's trains.'

'Would that be a return or a single, Sir?'

'A single,' said Sir Geoffrey with some pleasure. 'Does it tell you the times of the trains on the tickets?'

'No, Sir. There's a timetable on the wall to your right.'

Sir Geoffrey raised his eyes to heaven, paid for the

tickets, and went with some dismay to study the timetable. It was enormously complex with footnotes and too much small print, but he eventually found what he was looking for, and hoped he would remember it all until he arrived home to tell his Mama what he had arranged for her.

He was not looking forward to this exchange, and rightly so. She was irate and distraught in turns.

'How can I possibly travel on a train on my own?' she said. 'And take a Hansom cab from Paddington to Euston. Don't be so utterly ridiculous, Geoffrey.'

'Mother,' he said sternly. 'You don't seem to realise the straits you are in. You have to be out of this house by Friday. You cannot stay here. You should write to your cousin immediately, and tell him to meet you at Hemel Hempstead railway station on Friday at seven o'clock.'

She let out a shriek. 'Seven o'clock?' she screamed. 'Seven o'clock in the evening? I will be travelling all day?'

'Yes, Mama,' he said. 'Can you not see it as an adventure? An excitement? To be getting out into the world? Better than dying here of suffocation, I would have thought. Here are the tickets. I have done my best for you, Mama. I suggest you write to your cousin without delay, and I will put it in the penny post for you in Reading first thing tomorrow morning.'

'And how I am supposed to get to Reading station?' she asked. 'If I decide to go at all.'

Having overlooked this point himself, and having no idea, he said, 'I will arrange something, Mama. I will arrange it tomorrow.'

Overnight he had an opportunity to give more thought to himself, and where he would go. Realising it was an adventure, an excitement and an opportunity for him to get out into the world as well his Mama, he decided to head for the nearest port and pondered whether to take a ship to Europe or possibly America. The Atlantic could be rough, he knew, and would take a lot longer than the shorter voyage to Europe.

However, neither France nor Holland appealed to him; Italy would be ideal if this was a Grand Tour, but it was hardly that. He didn't profess to know a great deal about any of these countries, but none appealed as much as the land of opportunity, America, and he decided going West might be preferable. He thought the Civil War there was pretty much over, was it not? He had not heard, but surely it would not drag on this long?

At last it was Thursday, and he could return to the Bank to collect his money. He rolled a change of clothing into a blanket, intending to strap it behind his saddle, ate a large breakfast, and gave his mother a hasty farewell kiss on her dry cheek, ready to leave the house.

'You have the railway tickets safe, don't you, Mama?'

'Yes,' she said, 'but I have no money. What am I to do without any money whatsoever?'

He had forgotten that, and hastily emptied his pockets and gave her what remained of the 100 guineas. 'Will that be enough?' she asked doubtfully.

'I hope so, Mama. It is truly all I have at the moment.'

He set off again for Reading and posted the letter his mother, giving in to the inevitable, had unwillingly written against her better judgement. He was assured it would arrive the following day, and devoutly hoped this would be the case. It would be bad indeed if his mother arrived at Hemel Hempstead railway station and there was no one there to meet her.

He returned to the Bank and was again invited into the Manager's office. Anxious for a moment that there was some mistake, and he would not receive his money after all, he was flooded with relief when the Manager produced it from his safe. The man had been right, it was rather a lot to carry around in his pockets. No matter, he would soon be on board ship and that surely would be safe enough. He thanked the Manager, who wished him well, and stowing it carefully in both coat pockets, left the building.

Having studied the railway timetable on the wall again, he sought out trains to either Tilbury Docks or Southampton. Tilbury was not mentioned, so he bought a ticket to Paddington and onwards to Southampton. He was sure there would be a ship at the Docks going somewhere that appealed to him.

Leaving behind his horse cost him a small pang, and he patted her neck in farewell. What to do with her? It was too short notice to sell her, and he had had need of her until now. He looked about him outside the station, and spotted a young man of fourteen or fifteen begging on the corner. 'Here,' he called him over. 'Can you take care of my horse? I won't be needing her again, but I'd like her to have a good home.'

He fished in his pocket and drew out a sovereign. It was rather more than he had intended, but he handed it over to the lad. 'Take this towards her keep. And be good to her.'

The young man stared after him in astonishment as he disappeared into the cavernous entrance of Reading railway station. No one was ever going to believe this. He could hardly believe it himself.

Chapter 12

Completely unaware of all that had befallen the previous owner of his home, Tristram rode happily to Tower Court and looked forward to seeing not just Charles and Isabella but their two delightful children too.

'Tristram!' exclaimed Charles, looking up from his desk when his imperious butler, Fletcher, showed Tristram in to his study. 'My dear man!' He stood up quickly to shake hands, adding, 'We wondered what had become of you.' Turning to Fletcher, he asked for refreshments to be brought.

'We'll have a drink together,' he said, 'and then we'll go and find Isabella and the children. They will be delighted to see you.'

'As I will be to see them,' said Tristram, sitting down in the chair indicated by Charles and making himself comfortable. 'A great deal has happened since we last met.'

Tristram went on to tell his friend of the developments with the barn that had turned out to be a church, or possibly a chantry chapel, and had filled-in windows you could barely discern. On joining the family, Tristram was called upon to repeat himself, and to his delight, Charles's son James, now aged 6, was also interested in the building project. When Tristram mentioned having to find a new oak lintel to place over the widened entrance to the barn, James wanted to know how this was to be achieved.

Tristram looked evasive. 'I think it's to do with a block and tackle,' he admitted, having no very clear idea what that might entail. But James knew, explaining kindly that it was a system of ropes and pulleys which could pull a heavy item into place. He further informed Tristram knowledgeably that he would probably need at least two and maybe three for such a wide doorway.

Tristram was much obliged to him, and when James asked to be allowed to come and watch on the day, Tristram promptly agreed, remembering just in time that he must first ask his Papa and Mama.

Out of James's hearing, Tristram asked Charles how on earth his son knew about such things. Charles laughed.

'I have no idea,' he confessed. 'James loves anything mechanical. I think we have a future engineer in the making.'

'Or an architect?' said Tristram. 'They seem to know all about everything.'

He then admitted to having been highly fortunate in finding a very good architect, Mr Samuel Cunningham, and that his son, Mr Matthew Cunningham, had discovered why the barn was long and narrow. He even revealed that there was another son, Mr Henry Cunningham. Strangely he neglected to mention that his architect also had a daughter, who was very knowledgeable too. And altogether wonderful. In almost every way. It didn't seem to be the right moment to talk about that.

On the ride home he wondered why he had omitted to mention her; he longed to talk about her, indeed, he longed to see her again. The thought of her filled him with such joy, and Charles would have been the very person to share it with. Maybe he simply was not yet ready to share his joy. It was indeed early days.

He reckoned without Isabella's feminine instincts. 'There is something different about him,' she observed to her husband, after Tristram had left. 'You are right, my dear,' Charles had agreed. 'I noticed it myself. I suppose he is excited about the changes he is making to his home, and the barn in particular. He told me work will be starting on that very shortly. He can hardly wait.'

'I think you might find, Charles,' said his wife, looking at him levelly, 'I think you might find there is a lady involved.'

'A lady?' echoed Charles, taken aback. 'No, surely not? He would have said so.'

'Maybe he is not ready to share his news just yet. It must be very early days.'

'No!' exclaimed Charles in disbelief. 'He would have said. And in any event, where would he have met a lady without our knowledge? He has had no opportunity.'

'I do not know, my dear,' she replied, smiling fondly. 'But I think your Tristram is in love!'

The subject of their conversation rode blithely home and, suddenly noticing the beautiful views, the changing colours of the utterly lovely trees, and acutely aware of the purity of the birdsong around him, was rapidly coming to the same conclusion.

Jeffreys came out to the stable yard to greet him on his return, and was also struck by the change in his master's demeanour. 'Good evening, Jeffreys!' exclaimed Tristram. 'What a beautiful evening!'

'It is indeed, Sir.'

He dismounted, and went across to the gelding's stable.

'He seems to be settling down well enough,' he said, with a disproportionate amount of excitement in his voice.

'He is indeed, Sir.'

'He is a perfect match for Sylvester.'

'I am sure you are right, Sir.'

'What shall we call him? We need to think of a name.'

Jeffreys cast him a lagubrious look. 'Eunuch, Sir?'

Tristram laughed. 'I think not, Jeffreys. Hardly suitable for a lady to ride a mount named Eunuch.'

Ah, thought Jeffreys, so it was for a lady. He had suspected as much.

At last the longed for day arrived when work on the barn was to begin, and with it not only Mr Samuel Cunningham and Mr Matthew Cunningham but, to Tristram's relief and delight, Miss Grace Cunningham too. They spent the day receiving deliveries of various materials and equipment, which they referred to as 'plant' to Tristram's further bewilderment, and all seemed to be moving forward with great speed.

Various other craftsmen appeared on the scene, were introduced to Tristram, and then given a careful briefing as to what would be required of them. This included the careful dismantling of part of the long wall for the new double entrance, which made finding a felled oak in the parkland even more urgent.

Tristram went in search of Miss Cunningham. 'Come and see the new gelding again,' he invited her, and she was touched by his excitement. 'You must meet him properly this time.' Only just remembering not to take her by the hand in his enthusiasm, he conducted her to the stables and officially introduced them. Sylvester could be seen watching the proceedings with his head over the half door of his stable, and she glanced across at him.

'You were quite correct, Mr Sinclair,' she said. 'Look how well matched they are.'

Just to be sure, Tristram asked Jeffreys to bring Sylvester over to meet the new arrival too, and as they stood beside each other there was no mistaking it.

Even Jeffreys had to admit his master had shown excellent judgement.

'Would you like to ride him tomorrow, Miss Cunningham?' asked Tristram. 'We really do need to go in search of the felled oak for the lintel and doors without further delay.'

'We must indeed,' agreed Miss Cunningham, both parties happily convincing themselves that there was no time to be lost. 'I shall come in my riding habit. Oh! Do you have a side saddle?'

Tristram glanced helplessly at Jeffreys. 'We do, Sir,' he reminded his master. 'The gelding came with his own bridle and side saddle, if you recall. What he doesn't have is a name, Sir. Not that we know of, anyway.'

'Yes indeed,' said Tristram, who had forgotten about the side saddle but was hugely relieved to hear it. 'And you must think of a name for him, Miss Cunningham.'

'That is an honour!' she laughed. 'I shall give the matter my utmost consideration once I have ridden him.'

Returning to the barn and all the activity going on there, Tristram confided, 'Your father has already given permission for you to ride with me.'

She nodded, having had a similar conversation with him herself. 'Yes indeed,' she replied. 'I've said there really is no need to worry. He and Matthew will both be here anyway, overseeing things. I shall look forward to it immensely. And to choosing his new name.'

Tristram's impatience was finally rewarded. The next day dawned and he was up bright and early, dressed in his new riding breeches and coat, ready to escort Miss Cunningham around his parkland. He had only ridden that part of the estate once or twice himself, so he was looking forward to exploring it all, and finding a suitable fallen oak, as much as he hoped she was.

When the Cunningham contingent arrived, Jeffreys had Sylvester and the matching gelding ready for them. He led the smaller horse over to the mounting block, where Miss Cunningham elegantly mounted, and professed herself ready. They set off demurely enough, but once she was sure she was out of her father's sight, she asked if she could put her mount through his paces.

'Of course,' agreed Tristram, assuming she meant trotting or even a canter. 'Let's see what he can do.'

Looking relaxed and barely making any movement herself, she began with a series of manoeuvres that reminded Tristram of dressage, which he had seen demonstrated by the military, after years of training. It was like watching a ballet, she even had him walking sideways and turned him on the spot. She looked across at Tristram, as surprised as he was. 'I think he has been trained,' she said at last. 'He wouldn't do this simply at my command. Not the first time.'

Tristram did not know whether she was being modest, and wondered how she knew dressage herself. She simply leaned forward, patting his neck, praising and cajoling at the same time, then urged him to a trot.

Half way across the park she gave him slight pressure with her heels and he seemed glad to have the chance of a canter. Turning him expertly as they approached a hedge, she gave him his head and galloped back across the lush grass towards Tristram, slowing to a trot as they approached.

As they came to a halt beside him, Tristram could not hide his admiration. Whether it was for the horse or its rider, she could not tell.

'Bravo!' he exclaimed, smiling his pleasure. 'Well done!'

She took a mock bow. 'Thank you, kind Sir,' she laughed, 'he goes like the wind! How would you feel about calling him Pegasus?'

'I'd like it very much,' he said. 'An excellent choice.'

She gave a little nod of satisfaction and turned her mount to fall in beside him as he allowed Sylvester to move forward. 'And now let us start looking for felled oaks,' he said. 'We can't go back with nothing to report.'

'No indeed,' she said, 'failure is not an option,' and they headed towards a wooded area where a variety of trees still grew in abundance, some fallen and rotting, but none deliberately felled.

Further into the parkland there was a fine stand of oak trees, growing tall and straight towards the sun.

'These would have been intended for building the tall sailing ships,' she said, looking at them approvingly, 'but we need seasoned wood. They were planted close together so that they had to fight for the light, and grow tall and straight.'

'Clever,' said Tristram, and again she was uncertain whether he meant the men who had planted them or herself for knowing of it. He pulled slightly ahead.

'And look here!' he exclaimed in excitement. 'Felled oaks by the dozen!'

'Oh my word!' she said. 'These are splendid. Do you think they might have been felled for Nelson's ships during the Napoleonic wars? He was killed at the Battle of Trafalgar in 1805 so it was relatively recently. Perhaps the wars ended before they were needed . . .'

'We're spoilt for choice for one lintel!' said Tristram.

'Yes indeed,' she said, as excited as he was. 'And almost all of them plenty long enough for the purpose. Take your pick! There's even enough for the double doors and frame.'

They soon identified the best of them, and Tristram calculated their position so that he would recognise them again. 'Wonderful,' he said, more than satisfied. 'And now I suppose I should return you to your Papa. He will be wondering where we are.'

'Yes,' she agreed, with some regret. 'Can we just have one last canter back across the park?'

He heeled Sylvester into a canter, glad to give him his head, and Pegasus was beside him every stride of the way.

Chapter 13

They walked the horses back to the stables in companionable silence. Tristram was deep in thought. He remembered with crystal clarity the advice Mr Samuel Cunningham had given him on the one occasion he had broached the subject of wooing his daughter.

'Give her time, Mr Sinclair,' he had said. 'She's an unusual sort of girl. I've had several offers for her hand over the years, and she has persuaded me to decline all of them. She said her feelings were not engaged, and nowadays she insists she is past marriageable age.'

Tristram had laughed at that. 'She must be considerably older than she looks then, Mr Cunningham!' Samuel sent him a comical glance. 'Aye, Sir, she's all of 25 years old. And she says men don't care for a knowledgeable or educated female. It puts them off.'

Tristram had merely raised an eyebrow, and decided he must be an unusual sort of man then, because in his current situation, with a house to repair and refurbish, he found her knowledge indispensable, and her being educated, and virtually self-educated at that, most appealing. As he had told Charles more than once, he wasn't interested in a Simpering Miss, he wanted a wife with whom he could have an intelligent conversation, about things that interested him. And her too, of course.

He glanced across at her as Pegasus walked beside him, and thought again how beautiful she was. More beautiful than you realised, he decided, unconsciously echoing Betsy's report to the kitchen staff downstairs. She would make him a perfect wife.

However, he reluctantly decided he must take her father's advice and give her time. It would not do to rush things, or make her feel pressured. He would devote himself to wooing her, and endeavouring to engage her feelings towards him. He even dared to hope that process had already begun. As far as he could see, they dealt famously together.

It had been worrying him that once the work on the barn was completed, and the Cunningham's professional services as architects were no longer needed, there would be no excuse to see her again. Well, he would wait until the barn was finished before plighting his troth. As long as she accepted, that would ensure he would continue to see her again for the rest of their lives. He was now anxious to know how long the work might take.

Arriving at the stables, Jeffreys greeted them, solicitously enquiring whether all was well.

'Yes, indeed, thank you, Jeffreys. Miss Cunningham and the gelding seem to have taken to each other extremely well. She has suggested we name him Pegasus.'

'A very good name for a horse, if I may say so, Sir,' said Jeffreys. And without a glimmer of humour, he added levelly, 'Better than my own suggestion, Sir.'

'Yes indeed, Jeffreys. Significantly better.'

'What was Jeffreys' suggestion?' asked Miss Cunningham as she dismounted. Tristram longed to tell her, he knew she too would find it amusing. 'I'll tell you another time, Miss Cunningham.' And with that she had to be content.

She went to Pegasus's head and gave his neck an affectionate pat. 'Thank you for a wonderful ride, Pegasus.' He lowered his head to nuzzle her pockets, and she produced an apple which he ate with relish.

'Good gracious!' said Tristram. 'Sylvester does that. How amazing that they both have the same habit.'

Miss Cunningham laughed and glanced across at the groom. 'I suspect all horses have that habit, don't you think so, Jeffreys?'

'I couldn't possibly say, Madam,' responded Jeffreys, sure she was right but unwilling to appear disloyal to his employer.

Standing beside Tristram she inspected her palms. 'Mr Sinclair, I wonder if I might bother your housekeeper? I would very much like to visit your wonderful bathroom and wash my hands.'

'Of course,' said Tristram, wondering why he had not thought to suggest it himself. They hurried around the side of the house to the front door and, admiring the gardens as they went, he ushered her inside. Clements the footman had stationed himself in the hall anticipating just such an eventuality, and Tristram asked him to summon Mrs Nesbit, who came all-abustle feeling very important, and took Miss Cunningham upstairs, producing fresh towels and a new piece of soap on the way.

On her return, Tristram suggested if she was ready they should hasten straight away to the barn, and let everyone know they had been successful in their search and had found the perfect lintel for the new double doorway. Glancing about the hall as they left, Miss Cunningham said, 'You have had little time to make very much more progress indoors.'

'You are right,' he replied. 'I much prefer to be outdoors anyway, and with the barn project taking all my attention, I have given little thought to what else needs doing inside. I have managed to get enough work done to stop the roof leaking, and instal the bathroom, of course, but the rest of it is a little outside my expertise.'

'Yes,' she agreed lightly, as they turned again into the gardens beside the house, back towards the stables from whence they had come. 'It needs a woman's touch.'

She had spoken without thinking, merely agreeing with him, but on realising what she had said, she blushed to the roots of her hair. 'Oh!' she said, looking somewhat flustered. 'I didn't mean . . . I simply . . . !'

Charmed by her confusion, Tristram stopped and took her elbow, drawing her into the privacy of the hedge, which obscured them from view in either direction.

'Please do not be embarrassed,' he reassured her. 'You are absolutely correct, that is exactly what it needs. Miss Cunningham,' he went down on one knee. 'Would you do me the honour of being that woman? My wife?'

Blushing more than ever, Miss Cunningham said,

'Oh, Mr Sinclair, please get up! That isn't what I meant at all. I wasn't making hints, I promise you. I wasn't being serious . . .'

'I know you weren't, Miss Cunningham.' He rose to his feet and dusted off the knees of his new riding breeches. 'But I am. I would very much like you to be my wife, and to help me with this place, which I believe you have come to regard as I do. And I would very much like you to call me Tristram, and to be allowed to call you Grace, Miss Cunningham.'

Regaining her composure, she smiled warmly, and said, 'Not in my father's hearing, I believe, Mr Sinclair! I would very much like to become your wife, Sir, and I would be delighted to call you Tristram and have you call me Grace. But could you bear to mention it to my father before we do either? He is rather a stickler for the proprieties, you see.'

Tristram longed to take her in his arms then, and to kiss her, but reluctant to do anything to pre-empt her father's goodwill, he refrained. 'You have made me the happiest man alive, Miss Cunningham,' he said, and she smiled her happiness back, deep into his eyes, longing to be kissed too.

He led her beyond the house then, past the stables and towards the barn.

'Ah, there you are at last!' said Mr Samuel Cunningham. 'We were wondering what had become of you.'

'Well, Papa,' said his daughter, trying not to look too guilty, 'I rode Pegasus for the first time, and couldn't resist putting him through his paces. We think he may have been trained in dressage by his previous owner. And then we went in search of the lintel, which we have found, and after our return, I needed to go indoors to wash my hands.'

'Oh yes,' said her father benignly. 'The famous bathroom.'

'Yes,' she said, more than happy to change the subject. 'I've suggested to you before, Papa, you must go and see it, and we could instal one at home. It would be so much more convenient.'

Undeceived, Samuel noticed the glow in her cheeks and the gleam in Mr Sinclair's eyes, and knew it was not because they had found the best lintel in the length and breadth of the country. But he allowed himself to be distracted. 'So, you have found a good lintel for us to use, have you, Mr Sinclair?'

'Yes, indeed, Sir,' replied Tristram hastily, and launched into a detailed description of the virtues of this particular tree trunk above all others, which copse it was to be found in, how he had marked it, and asked how it was to be brought to the site.

Mr Cunningham humoured him for some minutes, discussing the whys and wherefores, confident that his Grace had helped him make the correct choice, and described how two shire horses with the correct harness would easily pull the felled oaks to the barn.

Seeing that his daughter had decided to leave them to it, and had nonchalantly wandered over to see her brother Matthew, to discover how he had been getting on, Samuel Cunningham took Tristram's elbow and led him further to one side. Tristram looked at him in concern, wondering what he was about to say.

'A blind man could see the two of you are made for each other, Mr Sinclair. Go ahead and ask her. You have my blessing.'

Chapter 14

The following day Tristram became aware that Miss Cunningham's Papa had been appraised of his proposal, but fortunately allowed to remain in blissful ignorance as to its timing. He had asked to be allowed to concentrate on the project in hand, the conversion of Tristram's barn, before making it official, or making any arrangements for a wedding. His daughter was glad to comply with this, as it gave her time to consider the forthcoming change in her life, and to adjust to a turn of events she had never seriously anticipated.

Progress on the barn continued apace, and as soon as a date for the hoisting of the lintel was confirmed, Tristram rode over to Tower House to ask if James, and indeed Charles and Isabella, and Amelia too, would like to come and watch the spectacle. James's enthusiasm far outweighed that of his parents or, indeed, his little sister, but served to persuade them that such an event was not to be missed.

Once they had arrived and were comfortably ensconced at a safe distance, the workmen were just getting the three blocks and tackle into their positions (James had been right!) and work soon began. The little boy watched fascinated. When he remembered, he provided a brief commentary for the benefit of his Papa and Mama as to what would happen next, and on each occasion he was proved correct. Charles and Isabella were inordinately proud of their son, and considered him to be a budding genius from that day forward.

Afterwards, it fell to Tristram's lot to introduce his friends to the Cunninghams. 'Mr Samuel Cunningham, my friends Sir Charles and Lady Worth from Tower House near Newbury.' They shook hands and Samuel made the slightest of bows, as befitted the occasion.

'And his son, Mr Matthew Cunningham.' Again the handshake and an incline of the head. 'And, er, this is Mr Cunningham's daughter, Miss Grace Cunningham.'

His heightened colour and lingering glance on Grace's lovely face immediately told Isabella all she needed to know. Not so Charles, who simply shook her hand with appropriate politeness, and proudly introduced James, who was bursting to ask a million questions and wanted to know all there was to know about blocks and tackle.

On their way home in the carriage, Lady Isabella looked at her husband with great satisfaction and a knowing nod. 'So, my dear, it would seem I was right.'

'About what, my dearest?' he asked, genuinely unaware of what she was referring to.

'Why Miss Cunningham, of course!' she said, and laughed indulgently.

'Who, the daughter? In what way? It is certainly unusual to have a female on a building site.'

'Oh Charles! Do you never notice what is under your nose? Tristram is madly in love with her!'

Charles stared. 'No!' he said. 'Do you really think so?'

'Dearest, I know so!' replied his wife without hesitation. 'She is perfect for him. We spoke briefly after we were introduced, she is a charming girl, and very knowledgeable too I think. She is part of the family business, and a highly valuable part too, I would say.'

Charles was utterly non-plussed; he thought he knew his friend, but had not noticed anything other than what he assumed to be his delight with his newly-orientated barn. 'They were very discreet,' he said lamely, in his own defence.

'Yes, dear, you are right. They were,' agreed his dutiful wife with a fond smile, wondering how anyone could not have noticed the pride and glowing looks Tristram cast in Grace's direction, and how she responded with dignified delight. 'I think we might hear wedding bells in the not too distant future.'

The following weeks passed in something of a haze for Tristram. He was invited to the Cunningham's home, Malvern House, which was more modern than he had anticipated, but without benefit of any conveniences as far as he could see. His proposal to Miss Cunningham became openly acknowledged and, once work was completed on the barn, a notice was placed in the local newspaper.

A date was set for the nuptials, and preparations were put in hand, of which Tristram remained blissfully unaware. Now that they were officially betrothed, Miss Cunningham was allowed to visit Brightwell Manor to discuss repairs within the house itself, decoration and improvements. Fortunately her taste was excellent and her requests reasonable and restrained, because Tristram was happy to provide anything she asked for, and to indulge her slightest whim. She showed more wisdom and discernment than any other female he had ever encountered, his beloved home blossomed under her touch, and he loved her all the more.

'Tristram,' said Grace one morning when they were planning the furniture and what should go where in their new home together. 'If Papa permits it, would it be alright if I bring a few books with me?'

'Yes, of course, my dear,' said Tristram with enthusiasm. 'We have a whole library to fill, there are precious few books left there at the moment. And I am unlikely to add to it greatly myself.'

Her Papa was also enthusiastic in agreeing that Grace was welcome to take all her books with her to Brightwell Manor. 'I shall be glad of the extra space,' he teased her.

'And will at last have room for my own collection of reference books.'

When the packing cases began to arrive, Tristram laughed at what she had called 'a few books'. There were boxes and boxes of them, and Grace had a wonderful time sorting and cataloguing them all and arranging them on the shelves in what quickly became referred to as Grace's library.

At last their wedding day dawned, a watery winter sun appeared, and although a little nervous before the ceremony, the happy couple soon emerged from the church as husband and wife, and a vast number of family and friends repaired to Malvern House to celebrate their future.

They had discussed the possibility of a honeymoon, and Tristram had offered his bride a choice of anywhere in the world, but in their heart of hearts they simply wanted to return to the home they loved, ride the horses they adored, and to get on with their lives. They did escape briefly for a few days to Malvern, where Samuel Cunningham had taken his bride many years previously, and why their home was so called.

On their return, Tristram took his new wife tenderly in his arms and carried her joyfully over the threshold.

'There you are, Mrs Sinclair,' he smiled tenderly, setting her down gently upon the elm floorboards that had been cleaned and polished just a few short weeks previously. 'You are at last where you belong.'

They looked up in some embarrassment to discover that Nesbit had assembled the entire domestic staff in the hall to welcome their return. Tristram briefly introduced the new Mrs Sinclair to her servants, each of them in turn, which surprised them. He then delighted them all further by asking Nesbit to pay each of them an extra silver shilling to celebrate his marriage.

Not long after their return from Malvern, Tristram remembered Mr Samuel Cunningham's advice to lodge his Title Deeds with a bank or Solicitor, and realised he had not done so.

'Dearest,' he said one morning at breakfast, broaching the subject. 'I think I had better go today. Do you care to accompany me or shall I go alone?'

'I would love to come,' she said, 'I have a little shopping I would like to do. But I would also like to see the Title Deeds, Tristram. Have you ever read them yourself?'

'Well no,' he confessed, feeling a little sheepish. 'I haven't. And your Papa said he would take a look at them, but he hasn't had the opportunity to do so either. I would be glad for you to cast your eye over them. They are rather fine, written on vellum.'

'Vellum?' she echoed in surprise. 'Is that not unusual for a property built as late as this one? Matthew and I believed it to be in the 1680s, if you recall. Vellum was certainly used earlier, from the Reformation onwards, as far as I can remember, but I am almost certain it was customary to use parchment or good quality, hand-made paper by the 1650s.'

'You are so knowledgeable, my dear,' replied her husband, glazing over slightly at so much history. 'Maybe you can solve the mystery when you read them. I will fetch them from their hiding place and you shall see them immediately after breakfast. Perhaps we should postpone our visit to the Solicitor until tomorrow instead?'

'That might be wise,' she answered him, and looked forward with excitement to reading what most people would consider a very boring old document.

As soon as he placed the vellum pages before her, she was engrossed. He made his excuses and took himself off to the stables, while she found some paper and a pen of her own, and made copious notes. When he returned in the mid-afternoon, he was surprised to discover she had only just finished her self-imposed task.

'Have you solved any mysteries, my dear?' he asked lightly, confident there were none.

'Well, it certainly made interesting reading,' she said evasively, 'I have learned a great deal.'

'So shall we take them to Reading tomorrow, and lodge them with your Papa's solicitor?'

'Yes indeed, if you think that is for the best, dearest.'

'It was what he recommended, and he knows better than I about these things. I am happy to take his advice.'

'I shall look forward to our expedition tomorrow,' she said, and let the matter rest.

The visit was completed to their mutual satisfaction. They met Mr Harold Henderson Senior who seemed somewhat surprised but assured them their Title Deeds would be placed in a safe box in the enormous company safe, and would be as secure as they could possibly be.

Afterwards Tristram accompanied his wife to several of the shops where she completed her purchases, and they returned home late in the afternoon, pleased to be back again after the bustle of the busy town.

Life continued in a state of sheer bliss for the pair, and just when Tristram felt he could not be any happier, she shyly told him the she was with child, and his joy was unbounded. 'Grace, my darling, we are so blessed.'

Fortunately Millicent Victoria, now almost two years old, no longer had any need of his fine perambulator or his crib, and they had been returned to their place in the attic long since. So these were brought downstairs once again, thoroughly cleaned and returned to their former glory.

Grace spent many happy hours knitting and sewing, preparing a layette worthy of any one of Queen Victoria's eight children. During the last few months before her confinement, Tristram treated her so gently and carefully, she was forced to protest.

'Tristram, I am not ill!' she said one day when he would not allow her to stoop to pick up a dropped ball of wool. 'I am merely increasing!' and she laughed teasingly at him, full of love for her husband, and he for her.

To their delight, the child was a boy and they named him Hugh Samuel after their respective fathers. At about this time, as Tristram informed Jeffreys of the happy news, the stable boy, Stebbins, stepped forward and said hopefully, 'Begging your pardon, Sir,' (Dawkins lives on! thought Tristram), 'but my Jess has just delivered a litter of six puppies, and you said you might like one?'

'Oh, yes!' said Tristram with enthusiasm, 'I would indeed and this will be a good time, but we'll keep him in the stables with you, if that's alright. With a new baby in the house, that's best for now. Let me know when they are ready to leave their mother, and I will choose one.' He added, much to Stebbins's surprise, 'How much are they?'

'I don't know, Sir,' said Stebbins, and named a random figure that he considered to be a fortune, and that Tristram thought eminently reasonable. 'We might have to have two at that price! I'd definitely like a male,' he added, and told Grace they might be getting a puppy soon, and she would have to think of yet another name.

'What is the mother's name?' she asked.

'Jess.'

'Well then,' she said immediately, 'Let's call him Jester.'

Hugh Samuel Sinclair turned out to be a very well behaved baby, easily managed by his mother. Two years later, when a second son appeared, they christened him

Jack, who was well named, devil may care and with a wonderful sense of humour.

Later, a daughter, Harriet, followed, named after Tristram's aunt who had made all this possible. She was a bossy little thing, and expected both her elder brothers to do her bidding, which they mostly did.

Tristram and Grace both took great joy from their children, whom they brought up to be safe, happy and secure. On the occasion of each birth, Tristram thanked his wife from his heart, for three wonderful children and a sublimely happy marriage, and each time he said, 'We are so very blessed.'

Then, in 1888, all that changed when for a fourth time, Grace shyly told her husband they would soon be blessed once again, and another child was on its way.

Chapter 15 – 1888

Frederick Leonard Sinclair thrust his way into the world, indignantly bawling loud enough to wake the dead. The serving midwife said, 'He's a lusty one,' cleaned up, cleared up, claimed her payment from Tristram waiting anxiously on the landing outside, and left the premises.

Assuming he was allowed in now, Tristram entered his wife's bedchamber and smiled fondly at her. 'How are you, my dear?' he said, wincing slightly at the screams emanating from the bundle in her arms.

Grace had never had any problems giving birth, and the moment Tristram returned to her side to see each tiny baby almost as soon as it had arrived had been the proudest of moments for her. This time she raised her cheek for his loving kiss as usual, but then grimaced at the new arrival's furious red face.

'I wonder why he is so angry?' said Tristram, and watched as Grace offered her nipple, only to have the little face turn one way and then the other, and carry on screaming. 'Is he in pain?'

Grace looked up at him helplessly. 'I don't know, Tristram. The midwife checked him over in the usual way, and said all was well. Perhaps Mrs Nesbit . . .?'

Mrs Nesbit was summonsed, and came bustling but, having had no children of her own, was unable to offer any constructive help. 'Betsy had her Millicent Victoria,' she proffered hesitantly, 'perhaps she might know something?'

So Betsy was sent for, unnerved because she usually entered the bedchamber to clean and polish, lay the fires and empty the chamber pots. Being needed in the guise of consultant was a new experience for her. She peeped round the massive bedchamber door to be greeted by the wails emanating from the bed.

'Come in, Betsy,' said Tristram above the din, relieved at the sight of her. 'Do come in. We need your help! As you know, we have had three babies before, but they have all been as good as gold. But Frederick here seems to have other ideas.'

Betsy shyly edged towards the bed and peeped down at the furious baby. 'Should I take him, Ma'am?' she offered hesitantly. Grace was glad to offer him up to her, and lay back exhausted from the effort. The moment Betsy held him, and rearranged his shawl around him, silence reigned. Betsy looked as non-plussed as any of them, and stood stock still, afraid to move lest he should start bellowing again.

As Frederick Leonard Sinclair remained silent in her arms, she gained confidence and began to jiggle him up and down on one hip, cooing to him gently, oblivious of his parents nearby. Almost immediately he fell asleep, and his exhausted mother fell asleep too.

'Try laying him in his crib, Betsy,' whispered Tristram. Very gingerly, and with great stealth, Betsy lowered the little bundle into the curtained crib, and gently withdrew the arm caught beneath him. Apart from a gusty sigh, Frederick did not stir, and slumbered on.

'Well done, Betsy!' whispered Tristram. 'You must have a magic touch.'

She smiled. 'It comes from keeping Millicent Victoria so quiet when I first came here,' she whispered back. 'I told you she never cried, so I had to keep her quiet.'

'Thank you so much,' he said, escorting her to the door.

Grace had always taken great pride in looking after her own babies, and feeding them herself too. The thought of a wet nurse was alien to her, and the contentment of the three previous offspring seemed to be evidence that she had done a good job. Tristram had suggested hiring a governess later on when their first born was five years old, but the government had recently brought in an Act saying children must attend school until the age of 10, and were in the process of building a school in most villages and towns.

Tristram remained seated beside his wife, watching her sleep, and gazing lovingly at her face, beautiful in repose.

She was tired out, this birth had been more trying than the others, and although he loved each one of his family, he very much hoped this would be their last child.

Having slept for over an hour, Frederick woke suddenly, and started bawling immediately. Inevitably this woke Grace, and Tristram lifted him carefully from his crib and placed him in her arms. She offered her breast again, and this time he took it, suckling the nipple with great energy, even though the milk would not come in until later.

'Dearest,' said Tristram hesitantly, concerned his suggestion might not be to her taste. 'It seems Frederick might be quite a demanding child. And the others are still very young. Would you like a little help this time round?'

'Yes, Tristram,' she replied, not taking her eyes from her new son's face as he sucked greedily at her breast. 'I think you may be right.'

'I am pleased to hear it,' he said, relieved. 'Would you like me to contact Isabella's agency, or do you think Betsy might be suitable?'

'If Betsy is willing, I think she would be entirely suitable. She could watch over Millicent Victoria at the same time. And it will be much easier to find a new chambermaid to replace her in that role than it will be to find someone new, to whom we would be willing to entrust our children.'

'I will speak to Mrs Nesbit myself,' said Tristram,

'and Betsy too, of course. I will tell her it is a promotion, and offer her an increase in wages.'

When he did so, Betsy professed herself delighted and thought she would be happy to do it for nothing. So it was quickly arranged and Prudence soon put her grapevine into operation and produced a replacement chambermaid, subject of course to Mrs Nesbit's approval.

Reporting these developments to his wife, who was still inclined to remain in bed during the mornings, Tristram smiled proudly at her above his new son's head. He indulged himself in the thought that their troubles were over, but never was a man more mistaken.

Chapter 16
1888 – 1898

Hugh, Tristram's first born, and Frederick, his fourth, were not destined to get on well together. Frederick's wit and charm, even from a young age, did not fool Hugh, who had enjoyed his parents' approbation and undivided attention for almost five years, until Frederick came along and spoiled it all.

Jack and Harriet had been Hugh's great playfellows, and respected their place in the sibling hierarchy, defaulting to Hugh, as befit their station, even if Harriet was a little bossy on occasion. (She would only get worse!) Hugh felt his youngest brother got all the attention, which was true, but he was too young to realise it was for all the wrong reasons.

Frederick perplexed them all. Jack coped with him best, laughing at his peccadilloes and ignoring his taunts and teasing. Jack thought Hugh was too easily riled and should simply shrug it off. Harriet quickly learnt not to take sides and, being three years older than Frederick, even displayed some motherliness towards him, which was not in the least welcomed or tolerated.

For Frederick was a law unto himself, and rarely played by any rules except his own. His behaviour led to many uncomfortable interviews in Papa's study, but to Hugh's disgust, never led their father to resort to the slipper or the cane, since Tristram possessed neither. Frederick always emerged from these interviews looking not in the least chastened.

'It's not fair!' became Hugh's ongoing refrain, which was not attractive, but his Mama's requests that he desist did not sway him, even when Frederick fell out of the apple tree and broke his arm at the age of seven. The doctor was sent for, came quickly, re-set the arm and put it in a sling. And instead of being told off as Hugh believed he would have been had he climbed the apple tree, Frederick was heaped with praise for being a brave boy. All Frederick said was, 'Didn't hurt!' even though Hugh could see it jolly well did.

Even worse, in Hugh's opinion, was that the staff all adored Frederick too. They had once adored Hugh, Jack and Harriet, and continued to do so to some degree, but now it was all Frederick this and Frederick that. Betsy was partly to blame, because she adored him most of all, and regaled the kitchen staff with hilarious tales of what Frederick had been up to that day. They all looked upon him indulgently, and waited in anticipation to hear what he would be up to next.

Because Betsy had been involved in helping with

Frederick from birth, he became her favourite, and Millicent Victoria his devoted friend. Hugh thought girls were very silly, and Millicent Victoria's allegiance toward his youngest brother was yet another thorn in his side. When Frederick began to learn to talk, he could not pronounce 'Millicent Victoria', but did manage to call her MillyVic. So after almost seven years of being respectfully called by her full names, she became MillyVic to one and all except her mother, and found she liked it.

In a word, Frederick could do no wrong, and Hugh was jealous. He felt Frederick never got his just deserts, and that that really, truly, genuinely was not fair. Hugh spent his life being good, and no one took any notice. Frederick spent his life being naughty, and on occasions downright bad, and as far as Hugh could see, everyone loved him for it.

'You don't need to be jealous of Frederick,' explained Grace to Hugh many times. 'He is the youngest, and he doesn't know any better. He will grow out of it. You are our first born, and it is you who will inherit Brightwell Manor one day. Jack, Harriet and Frederick will have to make their own way in the world, but your future here is assured. Please don't be jealous of your little brother.'

Her words were meant well, but it only added fuel to Hugh's fire of burning indignation. 'Don't make excuses for him!' said Hugh, and to Grace's frustration, slipped quietly from the room.

Tristram was concerned about Hugh too, and noticing his growing interest in the animals and wildlife he was discovering in the grounds of Brightwell Manor, he sought to encourage his son by finding a gamekeeper. He mentioned the idea to Boddington, but said, 'I know gamekeepers typically raise birds for shooting and that sort of thing, but I don't want that. I simply want someone who will protect the wildlife, encourage breeding, increase the amount of fish in the stream, and who can manage the woodland areas for the benefit of the birds, deer, fish and wildlife in general.'

Finding a man with the right sort of philosophy was important to Tristram, and the search took a while, until one day Jeffreys surprised him by suggesting Stebbins, the stable hand, who had been right under his nose all along. Tristram was much struck with the idea.

'Yes, indeed!' he said. 'Stebbins loves animals, and has been breeding dogs for many years now.'

'He has a lot of knowledge altogether, Sir,' agreed Jeffreys. 'Why not have a word with him?'

So Stebbins was sent for and entered the interior of the house for the first time in his life. He was very impressed and rather nervous, wondering what he had done wrong. He was relieved and delighted by Tristram's suggestion, thrilled by the prospect of an increase in salary and, having been wooing the newest chambermaid, Lilly, for sometime, overawed by the offer of taking on one of the estate cottages in which to live.

'Oh yes, Sir!' said Stebbins, who had always been one of the few staff able to have a normal conversation with his employer. 'That would be wonderful. Would there be any objection to my getting married and bringing my wife to live there with me?' he asked.

'No objection at all, Stebbins,' replied Tristram, smiling his delight. 'It sounds ideal.'

And so it was that Stebbins and Lilly were married, moved into the cottage, and the estate had its own gamekeeper. It also needed a replacement chambermaid for Lilly, and Mrs Nesbitt, with prompting from Prudence, quickly found a suitable candidate, Faith, for Mrs Sinclair's approval.

Initially this arrangement worked well. Hugh took an interest in all the new gamekeeper was trying to achieve, did a little fishing but on Stebbins' advice always threw them back, and began to think of ways in which the grounds could be used in future for the benefit of all.

Frederick too, being a precocious rider and having his own pony, Dobbin, at an early age, had always got on well with Stebbins. He spent most of his time outside school hours with the new gamekeeper, who was happy to impart as much of his knowledge as Frederick was interested in.

Everyone remonstrated with Frederick about his pony's name. Tristram protested to his wife. 'But he's a fine, lithe animal, a lovely first mount. Dobbin suggests a plodding old nag destined to become glue!' Grace only laughed.

'I think it might be my fault, dearest,' she said. 'I have been reading him a story about just such a horse, and his name is Dobbin.' Tristram sighed in resignation and gave up the cause.

Frederick was growing up and needing to assert his authority. He hated going to bed so early, especially in summer when it was still daylight. 'But I'm not tired!' he would say, when Grace mentioned the subject.

'Maybe not,' she said wisely, 'but you will be tomorrow if you don't go to bed when you are told.'

'You can't stock up on sleep,' he argued, with irrefutable logic. 'You should sleep when you're tired, and eat when you're hungry. And you are always wanting me to do it at all the wrong times.'

Tristram looked up at him. 'Frederick,' he said in a stern voice. 'It is your mother's opinion that you should go to bed now.'

So Frederick went, protesting all the way. 'Why are only grown ups allowed opinions?' he asked. 'Why am I not allowed opinions?'

'Very well then, my son,' said Tristram. 'What are you opinions?' Frederick was so surprised, he immediately forgot what they were.

It was at about this time that great excitement was caused by a letter from Tristram's brother Hugh, who wrote to say that he was proud to have a son he could trust (temporarily and short-term) with the running of the Mill, and was seriously considering retirement. As a test run, he thought he could at last accept Tristram and Grace's longstanding invitation to come and visit, but only for a week.

The new trains made the journey much easier and shorter than when Tristram came to visit Charles and Isabella some years previously, and Grace mustered the servants to clean the house from top to bottom, and to prepare the best guest chamber for their visitors.

Brother Hugh arrived with his wife, Miriam, who immediately took to Grace and spent many happy hours telling her all about her own wonderful offspring and, despite their being considerably older, favourably comparing them with Tristram's four. Even Frederick seemed to behave himself for the week, which was something of a relief to Grace, who had briefed him carefully before the visit.

Charles and Isabella had invited them all to Tower Court for lunch on one of the days, and as their week's visit was drawing to a close, Tristram and Grace gave a special luncheon the day before they were due to return home, and invited Charles and Isabella in return.

It was a warm sunny day, so once they had finished dining and quaffing some of the finer wines from Tristram's cellar, they went out through the tall French windows to take a turn around the gardens. They said they would take coffee later, on their return, and dismissed Clements to go downstairs to eat his own lunch with the other servants.

This unfortunately meant that the table was not cleared immediately, as it normally would have been, and gave Frederick the opportunity to go round it unnoticed, sampling the wines left in the glasses. This began out of curiosity, and continued because no one came to stop him. He soon noticed there were even a couple of opened bottles on the sideboard still a quarter or so full, and Frederick sampled those too.

Not too much later, Clements returned to the dining room, and was alarmed to discover Frederick looking very much the worse for wear. He took one look at the empty glasses before him, and the equally empty bottles, and was somewhat alarmed. He hurried back down the stairs looking for Betsy, and hastily summoned her to the dining room.

'Oh, you silly boy!' said Betsy, and helped Frederick to his feet. The world rocked, and Frederick said, 'Gonna be sick!' and promptly was. This did not please Clements, who immediately went to find someone else to clean it up. Betsy thought quickly and decided the best thing to do was to get Frederick to bed. This was not easy; he leaned heavily upon her, was inclined to laugh hilariously while groaning intermittently, and begged her not to tell Mama.

Somehow she got him onto the bed and took his shoes off. She gave him a bowl in case he was sick again (which he was), and said, 'Of course I must tell your Mama. You have made yourself very ill and she would wish to be told.'

So she left the room and went out into the gardens in search of Frederick's mother. 'Might I have a word with you, Mrs Sinclair? I'm sorry to bother you when you have visitors, but it is rather important.'

Realising Betsy would never interrupt unless it was a matter of life or death, Grace followed her indoors.

'What is it?' she asked, somewhat concerned.

'It's Frederick,' said Betsy when they were out of earshot of the rest of the party. 'He has made himself rather ill, I'm afraid.'

'Ill?' said Grace, in growing alarm. 'What has happened?'

'He has been sampling the left over wine in the dining room, Mrs Sinclair, and has been rather sick. I have put him to bed . . .'

'Oh the wretched boy!' said Grace, and immediately went upstairs to see her son.

Wretched was the right word for him. He lay on his bed groaning, and holding on to the counterpane, afraid he might fall off. 'Oh, Frederick!' admonished his Mama. 'What have you done now?'

'I'm sorry, Mama.' Frederick wasn't apologising, he was feeling very sorry for himself. 'I didn't know it would feel like this. Why do people drink it if it makes you ill?'

'Well, we don't drink quite as much as you appear to have consumed, Frederick. What ever made you do it?'

Frederick merely groaned. 'I think the best thing is for you to stay here and sleep it off. Drink some water when you can,' she said, and poured him some from the jug standing on the dressing table.

'Are you going to tell Papa?' he mumbled from the pillow, almost asleep.

'Of course I shall tell Papa,' she answered. 'But I shall tell him you have inflicted sufficient suffering on yourself, and that is punishment enough.'

The next day, Frederick remained in bed nursing a hangover, and their guests left, none the wiser. Grace carefully avoided telling Miriam, who would no doubt have delighted in letting her know that her own children would not have dreamed of doing such a thing at Frederick's age.

Tristram paid his son a visit in his bedchamber, and could see that his headache, thirst and ongoing nausea were indeed punishment enough, as Grace had said.

'What induced you to do such a stupid thing?' he demanded of his son. 'You've effectively poisoned yourself.'

'I had no idea it would make you feel like this!' groaned Tristram. 'I can't think why grown ups drink it.'

'Well anything to excess is harmful. Most grown ups, your mother and I at least, drink it in moderation.'

'Well, grown ups are silly. I shall never drink ever again!' said Frederick, and drifted back to sleep.

So Tristram left the room thinking that was no bad thing, and if this unfortunate episode had put Frederick off drinking for the rest of his life, it might have served a useful purpose. Once recovered, Frederick re-emerged, blinking in the daylight and, to Hugh's indignation, the incident was never referred to again. So on yet another occasion, thought Hugh bitterly, Frederick had been very naughty and come through it unscathed.

Chapter 17
1898 – 1901

Even from a very young age, Grace was keen to instil into the children her great love of books. She read them stories every evening and taught each of them in turn to read. Harriet took to it immediately, and could read well by the age of four.

Hugh and Jack took it in their stride. Frederick enjoyed being read to, but announced that learning to read yourself was 'for girls and sissies'. This was calculated to include Hugh, who read well, without calling him by name, but his brother knew it was a shaft aimed at him.

As each child turned five years old, they were duly enrolled at the new village school, which was now compulsory for all children, including MillyVic who revelled in it. She was bright and intelligent and loved going off to school each morning, practising her letters on her slate with white chalk.

The teacher, Miss Goddard, who seemed to be very old but smelled wonderfully of vanilla and musk, delighted in her bright pupil, and being older, on occasion allowed MillyVic to teach some of the younger ones their letters in turn.

It did not go down well with Frederick when his turn to go to school arrived. He would have preferred to be outdoors, riding his horse, being indulged by the various servants and watching the wildlife from the undergrowth.

As much to his own surprise as anyone else's, Frederick did enjoy learning his sums, and excelled where the other children were not so competent. Grace even asked him one day to help his eldest brother with a particularly thorny mathematical problem, which did not suit Hugh's consequence at all.

Tristram and Grace watched all these developments closely. Grace was worried that Tristram might wish to send his sons off to boarding school, but he calmly said, 'Let's wait to see which of them shows the most aptitude. If they wish to go, then of course they can. And to University later on, if they wish, but let them find their feet and see in which direction they choose to go.'

Grace was relieved and endorsed this wisdom, but as a mother she knew early on how things would turn out. Harriet would make an excellent teacher, she was sure, and she encouraged her daughter in every way. They raided her library together, where Harriet read voraciously, and discovered for herself that reading opened up a whole new world.

Attending school together, Harriet and MillyVic became close, almost like sisters, and Harriet always insisted on sharing everything with her friend. To her, it made no difference that MillyVic lived in a humble cottage in the grounds with her Mama and no Papa, and she lived in the big house with both. She simply accepted MillyVic for who she was, someone as intelligent and curious as she was herself, the sister she had never had.

Frederick made a new friend at school too. Gregory, universally known as Greg, was a local farmer's son, and he was often invited to come and visit Brightwell, sleeping on a truckle bed in Frederick's room, his horse sharing Dobbin's stable, and they would go off exploring the world together during almost all the daylight hours, returning only when dusk was falling, much to Grace's relief.

She was never quite sure what they were up to, but at least they came to no harm, returning safe and sound, and voraciously hungry. They would come into the house via the kitchens, and Mrs Hatton took delight in feeding them her excellent homemade cake before they went upstairs for high tea.

If Grace had known what they were doing during their time together, she would not have been so sanguine. One day as they were walking the length of the stream Greg put out a hand to stop Frederick in his tracks, and silenced him. 'Look,' he whispered, gazing down into a still part of the water. 'See that trout? Well, just its tail really.' Frederick peered into the shallows but could see nothing. 'They have been swimming upstream, and have come out of the current under those stones for a rest.'

Very stealthily, Greg went down on his knees and then lay full length on his stomach, and Frederick followed suit. Then the farmer's son slowly dipped his hand into the water and began tickling the length of the trout's stomach. As he reached its gills, he made a grab, and was suddenly holding the trout aloft in triumph. Frederick was deeply impressed and demanded to have a go. After a couple of false starts, he managed it too, and was extraordinarily proud of himself.

He picked up the two unsuspecting fish and carried them to the kitchen where he gave them to the cook, Mrs Hatton. He was a favourite of hers too, and she accepted the trout saying, 'They'll do nice for your Ma and Pa's supper tonight. I was wondering what to give them.'

However, even such a fond mother as Grace could never have anticipated Frederick's latest exploit, which was very much beyond the pale.

Once the school holidays were over and life at Brightwell resumed its usual pace and rhythms, the autumn term began and the children returned to school, Frederick protesting all the way. He had loved his freedom, being out of doors with Greg and following their own pursuits. School was a torture to him, and to his great chagrin, in 1898, when he was ten years old and looking forward to leaving, the government passed a new Act that extended the school leaving age from 11 to 13, and he had to do an extra two years.

Hugh laughed at his discomfort, and said the government had brought in the new rule especially for Frederick because they knew how dim he was. Frederick swore he would get his revenge, both on his older brother and on the system responsible for this extended two-year sentence.

Tristram had learned to ignore their bickering, but it did cause him some distress. His favourite time of day was when the children had had their high tea and were going about their business, and he could sit down with his wife for their evening meal, and have her all to himself.

'Mmmm,' he said one evening, 'this is very flavoursome trout. The cook must have acquired a new supplier.' On other occasions he commented about the tasty game and rabbit, and wondered why he had not noticed it before.

It was at about this time Stebbins approached him in the stables looking worried and said, 'Might I have a word with you, Sir? I am beginning to think we have a poacher.'

Tristram was immediately concerned and asked what made him think so.

'Well, I found a trap hidden in the woodland yesterday, Sir, and I have even heard a shotgun being fired a few times. At first I thought it was the new clay pigeon shooting they have on our neighbouring lands, but since then it seems to be closer. The dogs found the body of a pheasant deep in the woods too, and that had been shot dead. I have no way of keeping count of the wildlife of course, but I cannot think of any other explanation.'

'Any suspects, Stebbins?' asked Tristram, 'Anyone local who would do that sort of thing?'

'Not really, Sir. It is strange it has started now, after all these years.'

Tristram discussed the matter with Grace later, and it happened to be in Frederick's hearing. He merely grinned to himself but said nothing.

Mrs Hatton continued to accept Frederick's spoils at the back door, blithely unaware that he was doing anything wrong, and glad to have the opportunity to show off her prowess to the other kitchen staff at plucking, skinning and drawing freshly killed birds and animals. He did suggest she should perhaps keep her source to herself, and having such a soft spot for the lad, she did so without giving it very much thought. Food from the wild had more flavour and could only be a good thing.

His trapping and shooting became more successful and as he grew more confident, he consequently took more risks. As the incidents appeared to increase, Stebbins maintained his vigil. He even slept in the woods one night, but nothing happened, not while he was awake anyway.

Then, early one morning, as he walked quietly through the woodland, he caught sight of movement in the undergrowth. He also thought he saw the flash of sunlight on the barrel of a gun, so he dropped to his stomach and remained where he was. He had learned early to never approach a poacher with a gun in his hands, but he peered through the trees trying to see who it was. Once he realized, he was very shocked and could not decide what to do.

He discussed it with his wife, Lilly, and she was certain. 'Honesty is the best policy,' she said. 'You have to tell Mr Sinclair. If you do not, when the truth comes out, as it assuredly will, it will look bad on you too.'

So Stebbins once more lay in wait for Tristram in the stables, and asked haltingly if he might have a word.

'I'm very sorry to have to tell you this, Sir . . . I wondered whether I should or not, but Lilly thinks it for the best.'

His preamble went on for so long, Tristram hid a smile and said, 'Well, spit it out, man.'

'I think I might have discovered who our poacher is, Sir.'

'Good!' some Tristram firmly. 'We shall pursue him with due diligence. He cannot get away with it. Who do you think it might be?'

'Well, Sir, I'm sorry to say, Sir, but I think it might be, er, your son, Sir.'

Tristram looked thunderstruck. There was no need to ask which son! Yet while he could believe it of Frederick, doubt remained.

'But how on earth could Frederick have acquired a gun?' he demanded.

'I don't know, Sir. I am very sorry, Sir, but I made certain it was him before I spoke.'

Tristram immediately abandoned all thought of his morning ride and went in search of Frederick. He met him coming round to the front of the house from the direction of the back door. Suddenly light dawned, and Tristram realised where all the flavoursome game and fish had been coming from – his own land! And even worse, his own son.

'Frederick!' said Tristram, as cordially as he could muster. 'I wish to have a word with you. In my study.'

Frederick knew this was not good news and followed his father into the house in some trepidation.

'Is there anything you wish to tell me?' asked Tristram, hoping his son would be honest with him. Frederick decided to play the innocent and deny everything.

'No, Papa,' he said, effecting injured surprised. 'What sort of thing had you in mind?'

'Have you acquired a gun recently?'

'Yes, Sir,' he said stoutly. 'I suppose I have.'

'But from where? There are no guns in this house, there never has been, and there never will be.'

'Well there is now,' said Frederick, growing bolder. 'It's a fine sport. Many gentlemen enjoy hunting, shooting and fishing.'

'Not under my roof!' said Tristram, rather more loudly than he had intended.

'Well, no, indeed,' said Frederick, hoping a little humour might lighten the mood. 'Outdoors, naturally.'

'Don't get clever with me, young man!' said Tristram sternly, and Frederick realised he had made matters worse. 'Where did you get it from?'

'Someone at school, Sir.'

'What? At school! Greg, I suppose? I can't believe it.'

'Yes, Papa, Greg. He lives on a farm and they have guns there all the time. He sold it to me.'

'Sold it to you? And where did you get the money, pray?'

'Saved it up. From my allowance.'

Tristram was horrified.

'But why do you have to shoot everything in sight?' he demanded. 'I thought you loved animals and wildlife?'

Perceiving this as a rather ineffectual response to the situation, Frederick felt he could yet rescue himself.

'Well you've been enjoying the results, Papa!' said Frederick defiantly. 'Where do you think all those delicious pheasants, partridge, rabbits and trout have been coming from?'

'You could've killed someone! Or yourself, you stupid boy. Have you no sense?'

An awful thought struck him.

'Frederick, tell me you have only been shooting on our own land?'

'Well, yes, Papa. For the most part.'

'I certainly hope so. It was not long ago that shooting rabbits was a hanging offence!'

'So turn me in, Papa,' said Frederick insolently. 'Report me. Perhaps I'll be deported to Australia with all the other convicts.'

'A few years ago that could have been a distinct possibility! Fetch the gun immediately,' commanded Tristram. 'I shall get rid of it for you.'

All Tristram could do was stop Frederick's allowance for the foreseeable future, confiscate the gun, and forbid Greg from visiting Brightwell Manor ever again. He hoped such measures would instil some sense of the seriousness of the crime in his son, but very much doubted it. Frederick merely went to visit Greg's farm instead, where they had even more freedom to shoot and fish, and no one said a word. It was quite normal to hunt, shoot and fish there.

Having confiscated the firearm, he was then at a loss as to what to do with it. In the end, he went back to the stables and handed it over to Stebbins for safe keeping.

'Thank you for telling me the awful truth,' he said to his loyal gamekeeper. 'I realise it was difficult for you, but you did the right thing.'

Once he returned to the house, Grace could immediately see he was distressed, and indeed, trembling slightly.

'My dear!' she said. 'What has caused you to be so upset?'

Tristram rolled his eyes to heaven and said one word. 'Frederick.'

'Oh dear,' she said. 'What now?'

Once Tristram described to her what had happened, she was angry too, but was able to remain calm and dignified. 'You have dealt with the matter just as you should, dearest. What else could you do? I will have a word with Mrs Nesbit, and ask her to instruct the cook in no uncertain terms that she is not to accept any more produce from Frederick.'

'If you would, my dear,' said Tristram. 'I had not thought of that. Perhaps if he discovers he is out of favour with her too, and has nowhere to bring his offerings, he will cease.'

'You don't think he will acquire another gun, do you?' said Grace in alarm. 'I can hardly bear to think of him handling a firearm with no training. It was totally irresponsible of that farmer's son to sell it to him in the first place.'

'I had not thought of that aspect of it, Grace,' said Tristram, his face still grim. 'Perhaps we should allow him to have some training, so that he will at least learn to respect the weapon. If he has discovered an interest in them, he will no doubt have even better access in the future, and we should at least have him taught how to protect himself. And others too.'

So a professional gamekeeper was found who visited Brightwell Manor two or three times in order to teach Frederick some respect for his weapon.

Hugh was incensed when he heard of the plan. 'So not only has he done something even worse than usual,' he complained, 'you are rewarding him with lessons to do the very thing you do not wish him to do! Where's the punishment in that?'

Chapter 18 – 1902

When it became time for MillyVic to leave school, Miss Goddard said to her, 'If I can get funding, would you care to stay on and teach the younger ones?'

'I'd love to, Miss Goddard!' replied MillyVic, surprised and delighted by such recognition. 'But I have no training, no qualifications.'

'You're a natural,' said her teacher in return. 'You know more than they do, and I need some help. Leave it with me.'

MillyVic told her mother, Betsy, and they speculated with excitement about her new life. 'My daughter a teacher!' exclaimed Betsy to Mrs Sinclair. 'Imagine! Not in service! Who'd have thought it? I don't know where she gets it from! Not from me, that's for sure!'

When Miss Goddard came back to MillyVic saying she had the mysterious funding, and permission, MillyVic's future was assured. 'It will be good experience for you too,' said Miss Goddard kindly. 'You might just get to University one day, now that they are considering allowing women in, and this will set you in good stead.'

MillyVic merely smiled, but knew in her heart that she would never get to University, even if women were allowed in one day, because her Mama simply could not afford such a thing. She did not know then about Scholarships, and she reckoned without Harriet's determination.

Hugh was next to leave school, and his future was already assured. He had chosen to go to agricultural college, and learn more about the running of the estate, and perhaps introduce farm animals, making it even more profitable. His place at Cirencester Agricultural College in Gloucestershire had been reserved some years previously, and he went off full of hope and good intentions.

Jack too was already decided about what he wanted to do. All things nautical had always appealed to him, and he wanted to go into the Navy. Arrangements for that too were in hand, and Tristram went with him to HMS Dartmouth to get signed up, and left him 'on board', even though Dartmouth was an extremely beautiful building in the middle of Devon. Hugh called him 'Jack Tar' but with affection, and they did manage to keep in touch with sporadic letters over the next several years.

Partly because Frederick was growing up too, and partly to compensate for all the excitement for his brothers and MillyVic, Tristram decided to buy his youngest son a new horse. 'You're getting a bit too big for Dobbin now,' he said as he proudly revealed the lovely new chestnut in her stable.

Frederick was thrilled with his gift and promptly named the animal Black Beauty.

'But she's a chestnut!' protested Tristram, and Grace laughed. He looked at her accusingly.

'Another book?' he asked

'I'm afraid so, dearest,' she confessed. 'By Anna Sewell this time. 1877. A lovely story.'

With a long-suffering sigh Tristram said, 'Perhaps Frederick is colour blind? At least when you've stopped reading to him, and it seems unlikely he will be reading many books for himself, perhaps he will name his horses something sensible in future.'

MillyVic spent three happy years teaching the youngest new entrants to the village school, until it became Harriet's turn to leave, and her Papa had already arranged for her to go on to boarding school.

'You are so lucky!' confided MillyVic as Harriet talked, full of her plans. 'After boarding school you will be able to go on to University, and get proper qualifications, and become a proper teacher.'

'But you're a proper teacher!' said Harriet loyally. 'You teach.'

'Yes, indeed, and I love every minute of it, but I don't have any qualifications so I'll never be able to advance.'

Harriet looked thoughtful and sought out her Papa.

'MillyVic should be allowed to come with me,' she told him. 'She will make an even better teacher than me!

She is a natural, Miss Goddard told her that. And she is gifted too.'

'But her Mama cannot afford the fees of a private boarding school,' Tristram told her indulgently, to which she immediately replied, 'No, Papa, of course not. But we can. I'm not going without her!'

Tristram seemed a little stunned by this idea. 'It may be too late for her,' he said hopefully. 'You are the right age for this year's in-take, whereas MillyVic is three years older.'

Seeing his daughter's crestfallen face, he said he would look into it. Because the boarding school was a private one, and income paramount above all else, they kindly agreed to overlook the fact of MillyVic being older than the norm, and were delighted to give her a place. She had aptitude and experience, and indeed, two lots of fees were better than one.

'You know what this means, don't you?' said Tristram to Grace darkly. 'Harriet will expect us to pay for MillyVic to go to University too, when the time comes.'

But he too had reckoned without Scholarships, and when the boarding school saw just how gifted MillyVic was, they arranged it all. Harriet did not qualify for a Scholarship because her Papa had means, but so it was that the two girls went off to University together. The Dean even said age was irrelevant, and that they welcomed students of all ages.

It was Grace's turn to be envious. 'They are so lucky!' she said. 'I would love to have gone to University. They didn't allow women to attend University in my day.' As an afterthought she added, 'They've only just started allowing it now!'

'You did perfectly well without it, my dear,' said Tristram, hoping to comfort her. 'You were self taught, which was a greater achievement in its way.'

Grace merely sighed, and reflected that had she gone to University, she might never have met Tristram, nor had her beloved children, so all had turned out for the best.

This put her in mind of Frederick. During all this excitement and comings and goings, Frederick had quietly left school and remained at home, enjoying the company of Stebbins, the gamekeeper, and going off on his own mysterious pursuits from time to time, generally keeping a low profile. He frequently came home late and next morning would say nonchalantly to his father, 'I find myself a little short in funds, Papa. Could I possibly have an advance on my allowance?'

Tristram would remonstrate, and ask what he had done with the previous advance on his allowance, but they both knew he would hand over more notes if Frederick pursued the subject long enough.

Trying to think of an appropriate career for their wayward son, Grace asked Tristram, 'What is Frederick good at?'

'Causing trouble!' he replied with feeling, and considerable justification. 'I shall have to have a chat with him.'

So Frederick was summonsed to Papa's study for the umpteenth time in his life, and sat down cheerfully, no longer in trepidation.

'I suppose there is little point in asking if you would like to go on to boarding school?' began Tristram.

'None whatsoever, Papa,' said Frederick cordially.

'Have you not considered though,' pursued his father, 'when you are old enough, we could set you up in a business. And it would be easier to run, and become more successful, if you had a little more education behind you. Boarding school would be excellent preparation for life.'

'I'd only run away, Papa,' said Frederick, sympathetic towards his father's naiveté.

'Yes,' said Tristram, giving in gracefully. 'You would, wouldn't you?'

'It would be a waste of my time and your money.'

Tristram gave a rueful grin. 'It's not often anyone thinks about that!' he confided. 'But you can't just kick your heels here at home, Frederick. You have to make your own way in the world. Boys a lot younger than you are out working, helping to support their families. They are in the mills, down the mines, being sent up chimneys . . .'

'I'm a little large to be climbing up chimneys, Papa,' said Frederick with a grin.

Tristram knew it was a lost cause. 'Well,' he continued, 'can I ask you to at least give some thought to the sort of business you might like to run one day? Something you would enjoy doing.'

'Well, Papa,' said Frederick, trying to break things to him gently. 'By the time I'm old enough to run a business, I think the new motor cars will have become popular. They are the future.'

Tristram was stunned, not only by the thought that the motor car could ever replace the horse as a mode of transport, but that Frederick had genuinely given the matter some thought. And, furthermore, that he had come up with an original idea.

'If I get in at the beginning of it,' continued his son, unusually enthusiastic, 'and learn to fix engines, repair bodywork, and even sell petrol, which everyone will need, I'd be ahead of the game. I'd be offering a service no one else was yet able to offer. I can see the day when farmers will have agricultural machinery too, and that will need maintaining and fixing as well.'

Tristram had his doubts about that. Horses had been pulling the plough since time immemorial, but he did not want to discourage his on.

'I think you might be on to something, Frederick,' he said, trying not to sound too surprised.

'Bicycles too,' added Frederick, not dissatisfied with the effect all this was having on his father. 'They are few and far between at the moment, but I think they will catch on one day. If I can fix them, and build a wheel, when no one else can, they'd all have to come to me, wouldn't they?'

Tristram could not see the deeply uncomfortable bicycle catching on at all, but he did not want to dampen his son's enthusiasm.

'Well, yes indeed,' he hedged. 'Probably less so than the car, but yes, another string to your bow. And viable on the same premises as a garage.'

Frederick was beginning to feel his father's burgeoning interest and decided to strike while the iron was hot.

'With so much business coming my way,' he added, 'I probably wouldn't be able to do all the work myself, and would need to hire people to do it for me. And train them in it too.'

'Well, yes indeed,' Tristram said again. 'But where could you go to learn these skills yourself? I don't know of any courses available yet. And I don't know of any garages around here at the moment, where you could go as an apprentice.'

And a good job too, decided his son, who didn't want to go on any courses or do a poorly-paid apprenticeship. 'No there isn't,' agreed Frederick, 'not yet. But there might be one soon, I could keep an eye open and go and ask. But the mechanics of all this are quite simple and straightforward, Papa. With my aptitude, I am sure I could take an engine apart and put it back together again quite easily. And learn that way. Mama was self-taught and look how well she did. Trust me,' he added as his final volley. 'It is coming, I know it is.'

Tristram nodded, still feeling a little shell shocked at this turn of events.

'Maybe if I bought a bicycle to start off with?' queried Frederick hopefully. 'I could practice riding it and fixing it and possibly improving the design of it. I could be an expert by the time it starts selling well. And I could sell them too! There would be good profit in selling them.'

'If you think so . . .' said Tristram, a little doubtfully.

'I'll go to Reading soon,' Frederick reassured him, 'and see what I can see.'

He did not mention money, which further surprised Tristram, and he smiled.

'Let me know if I can help,' he said and his son smiled back, unable to think of any way Papa could help other than financially, but he was glad of the offer which he took to be permission to get started on his new career.

In the meantime, Harriet and MillyVic were settling down to University life and beginning to enjoy it. Until one day Betsy went to the Post Office and was given a very unsettling letter from her daughter. Over the years, MillyVic had taught not only the younger children at the village school to read, but her own mother as well. So Betsy read the letter standing outside the post office with mounting horror and hurried home. After a short period of indecision, she knew she must show it to Mrs Sinclair.

'I'm sorry to trouble you,' she said later, finding Grace in the Library.

'What is it, Betsy?'

'Well, I've had a letter from Millicent Victoria.' She was the only person that continued to call her by her full name.

'That's nice.'

'No, Mrs Sinclair, it isn't nice at all.'

She handed the missive over to Grace who glanced at Betsy's troubled face and began to read. She soon reached the paragraph that was causing Betsy such distress.

'The first I knew of it,' wrote MillyVic, 'was when one of the other students came to find me, and said my Papa had come to visit me. Obviously I was surprised and said but I do no have a Papa. But they insisted, and said he was waiting to speak to me in the Great Hall. He was an ugly little man but obviously very wealthy. And he said although we had never met before, he was my Papa, and he knew my Mama, Betsy, and Mr Sinclair and all about Brightwell Manor.'

Betsy watched her mistress scanning the letter, and saw the colour drain from her face. She did not speak, but continued reading.

'He said he used to live there, and he wanted me to find some papers at the house that rightfully belonged to him. Of course I realised then who he was, and that it must be the Deeds he wanted. So I said I am sorry, Sir, but I do not live there any more, and the papers he referred to were not there any more either, but lodged safe with Mr Sinclair's solicitor in Reading . . .'

Grace emitted a groan. Betsy knew which part of the letter had dismayed her so much. It had dismayed her too.

' . . . and would he please go away and leave me alone and never come back.'

Grace had turned quite pale. 'May I keep this to show Mr Sinclair?' she asked, and left the Library in search of Tristram. She found him pulling on his boots ready to go on his morning ride.

'Tristram,' said his wife in an unusual tone of voice that made him look up in concern. 'You must read this.'

'What is it, my dear?'

'It's a letter from MillyVic to her Mama. Oh my God, Tristram. Sir Geoffrey is back in the country, and trying to get hold of the Deeds.'

Chapter 19 – 1903

Mr Archibald Farquharson was not a happy man. He had served Henderson & Co. man and boy for his entire working career. He had been reliable and apposite, learning the business from the bottom up. Although he had never had the opportunity to qualify as a Solicitor as such, there was little he did not know, or if he didn't know it, knew where he could find out. He had built up a fine library of reference books over the years at his own expense, and was familiar with how to use them.

And now, in his advancing years, just as he was considering retirement, he had been asked to leave the London office and to take temporary charge at the Reading branch. Apparently the Messrs Henderson, Senior and Junior, had suffered a sudden bereavement and needed to be away for two weeks.

On seeing his dismay at this suggestion, Mr Harold Henderson Senior had been almost rude about it.

'Any man would consider it a promotion, Mr Farquharson! Are you not grateful to receive such recognition?'

'Does this promotion include any increment in salary, Mr Henderson?' asked Mr Farquharson. 'It will involve considerable outlay, and my living costs in London will still need to be paid at the same time. Where am I to stay?'

'It's only for two weeks, Mr Farquharson!' replied Mr Henderson Senior patronisingly. 'We can review the matter on our return. You will keep your receipts, of course.'

'And might there be any expenses to cover my initial outlay, Mr Henderson?'

'Yes, yes, of course. I had not forgotten that,' said Mr Henderson Senior, irritated because this unlooked for expense had not occurred to him.

Mr Farquharson had never married, and as Mr Harold Henderson Senior later remarked to Mr Horace Henderson Junior, 'Why would getting himself and a few effects from London to Reading cost very much at all? You would think the man ungrateful.'

Another thorn in Mr Farquharson's flesh was that he could very clearly remember his first interview with the Henderson brothers. They had been impressed with his school reports and his demeanour, and considered his name particularly suitable for a solicitor, should he ever be allowed to speak with the clients. They had most definitely implied that if he worked hard and applied himself, and stayed with the firm until his retirement, he would receive a small bonus as a reward at the end of it.

To the young Mr Farquharson, retirement at that time

was an event far off in the mists of time, and not knowing what this payment might be, he had clung to the thought of it, and allowed their promise to compensate for the woefully inadequate stipend he received each week, and which barely increased over the years.

However, when he had more recently mentioned this promise to Mr Harold, hoping to get a clearer idea of the reward to which he could look forward, and plan how to make it last throughout his declining years, he was horrified to hear his employer say, 'A promise, Mr Farqhuarson? I think not! We put nothing in writing, and as you know from your dealings with our clients all these years, if it's not in writing, there is no evidence, and without evidence, what can be done? Oh no, no, no, Mr Farquharson, I do not recall any promise. And I am sure my brother does not recall it either.'

Nursing his grievances, Mr Farquharson took himself off to Paddington railway station on the Monday morning of his first week in Reading – why should be travel on his only precious day off on the Sunday? – and was further aggrieved when he discovered the cost of a return ticket.

'How much?' he demanded of the bored young clerk at the window of the ticket office. When he repeated the figure, Mr Farquharson reminded himself that he could claim this iniquitous expense on the Henderson's return, and demanded a receipt.

'Your ticket is your receipt,' said the bored young man, impatient now as he noticed the queue increasing behind this awkward customer.

'But I have to surrender my ticket on leaving the station at my destination!' argued Mr Farquharson.

'Well we don't give no receipts,' said the ticket clerk, and peering round his customer, shouted, 'Next!'

Relieved to see the elderly man at the head of the queue so summarily dismissed, the next customer jostled him out of the way, and requested his own ticket.

Once on the train, Mr Farquharson became steadily more indignant and irate, and arrived in Reading in a very bad mood indeed. This did not go down well with the resident staff, and having got off to a rather poor start on their first day together, it left a bad taste and Mr Farquharson remained unpopular until the day he left.

It was on the following morning, and in this unfortunate frame of mind, that Mr Farquharson received a visit from Sir Geoffrey Turnbull, who insinuated himself into his office with a degree of oiliness that should have aroused his suspicions, but being preoccupied with his own affairs, unfortunately did not do so. He had dealt personally with Sir Geoffrey only once when he had visited the London office to collect the Deeds to Brightwell Manor many years ago, but he had known his father, the Earl, before him, and had held him in some affection. He knew nothing of Mr Tristram Sinclair's more recent visit to the Reading office because, of course, he himself had been in London.

'Good morning, Sir Geoffrey,' he said, rising from behind his desk as one of the office clerks announced him, and withdrew. 'What can I do for you?' he asked as they shook hands. 'I believe you have been abroad?'

'Yes, indeed, I have, Mr Farquharson, and I have only just returned. But I have been fortunate in America, indeed, more than fortunate, and I have come to arrange collection of the Deeds of my house to see what is to be done.'

Offering Sir Geoffrey a seat, Mr Farquharson in confusion said, 'Oh but they are no longer in your family safe box in London, Sir Geoffrey. You personally collected them from me yourself some years ago.'

'Yes, I am aware of that,' said Sir Geoffrey testily, hoping this old man was not going to be difficult. 'They have been lodged here in your Reading safe by someone who has no right to them. No conveyancing was done in any way, at any time, so the property is still legally mine.'

'But it has been some years since,' protested Mr Farquharson, 'and I suspect there is little you can do about it now.'

'Well, what would you . . .' Sir Geoffrey was about to say, 'What would you know?' but realising this man was his only hope of an ally, hastily re-phrased his question. 'Well, what would you . . . er . . . recommend, Sir? I need the return of my Deeds – and of my home, now that I have returned from America, without further delay.'

'I do not know what to say to you, Sir Geoffrey. Or where the Deeds might be. Mr Henderson Senior is the person you should be talking to, but he has suffered a bereavement and both he and his brother will not return for two weeks.'

Sir Geoffrey immediately perceived that he was more likely to persuade Mr Farqharson to assist him than the Messrs Henderson, and proceeded to charm and confuse him as much as he could.

'Well, you are aware that I myself collected the Deeds from your London office,' he agreed smoothly. 'And they were placed in safe-keeping at Brightwell Manor. As I was going abroad, it seemed appropriate to let my home to a stranger during my absence, and he has repaid me by stealing my Deeds, and lodging them with you in his own name.'

'That is indeed most shocking,' agreed Mr Farquharson. 'I can hardly believe that any man would behave in such a manner.'

'It is beyond comprehension, Sir,' replied Sir Geoffrey, perceiving that Mr Farquharson was beginning to sympathise with him. 'And after my success in America, I am more than willing to defray any expenses you might personally suffer as a result of returning my Deeds to me.'

The elderly clerk was at first shocked as Sir Geoffrey's

meaning was born in upon him, but then as light dawned, he began to feel that if the Messrs Henderson were refusing to defray his current expenses, or to fulfil their promise at his original interview of a small sum in gratitude on his retirement, then here might be a chance of the compensation that was assuredly his due.

'What had you in mind, Sir Geoffrey?' asked Mr Farquharson, willing to listen to his proposals, but still almost certain that he would reject any suggestion that was not entirely propitious. Yet when Sir Geoffrey named a sum far beyond his wildest imaginings, he was immediately persuaded that if there was anything in his power that he could do to assist this delightful gentleman to re-acquire his birthright, and justice served, he would do it with pleasure.

'I would be honoured to assist you, Sir Geoffrey,' he said, feeling quite shaken. 'I will ask the Clerk to bring them immediately.' He looked across his desk at his client, whom he could see was well dressed, and obviously very well fed. He had an air of success and even smug satisfaction about him.

In response to his summons, the Clerk put his head round the door and received his instructions. His eyes nearly popped out of his head but his was not to reason why. He went to Mr Tristram Sinclair's safe box in the massive safe, retrieved the Title Deeds to Brightwell Manor and took them back to Mr Farquharson, as instructed.

As he left the room, Mr Farquharson said, 'I have known your family for many years, and your dear father before you. My condolences on your sad loss, Sir Geoffrey.'

'Well never mind about that now,' said Sir Geoffrey impatiently, simply wanting to conclude his business and be gone. Mr Farqharson felt the same way; if Sir Geoffrey would only hand over the amount of money he had mentioned, he could retrieve his belongings from his Reading lodgings and his London home, and never have to work again. In all likelihood, his actions would not be discovered for some weeks, possibly even some years, and he would be long gone. He had nowhere particular in mind at that moment, but for many years he had fondly envisaged retirement beside the sea, with which England was well endowed. He was spoilt for choice.

Yes, it was the right offer at the right time, and despite years of condemning anyone who committed the least impropriety, Mr Farquharson had succumbed to temptation. It was all the fault of his employers, he realised that. If they had treated him fairly, stuck to their word and fulfilled their promises, he would have remained loyal. Now, he felt, they would simply get what they deserved. If indeed they ever found out!

But Mr Farquharson reckoned without the hapless Clerk who had had no alternative but to obey instructions and do his bidding, retrieving the Deeds from Mr Sinclair's safe box and apparently returning them to

Sir Geoffrey's care.

As soon as Sir Geoffrey had handed over the amount discussed, in cash, Mr Farquharson informed his colleagues he was going to lunch, and merely returned to his rented London home to give a week's notice. The following day he gathered up a meagre selection of his belongings that he felt necessary in his future life, and that he could conveniently carry. Thinking sadly of his wonderful collection of reference books that he would have to regretfully leave behind, he returned to Paddington railway station.

With nothing to fear, and no concerns about his perfidy being discovered, he stood at his leisure, reading through the list of destinations available to him and making his choice of where to spend the rest of his life beside the sea.

He did indeed get a few weeks' grace. On the return of Mr Harold and Mr Horace, the London office assumed Mr Farqhuarson was still working in Reading, and the Reading office assumed he had returned to London. And both thanked providence for that.

It wasn't until Mr Henderson Junior visited the London office himself, and discovered the absence of their longest-standing and, despite his unpopularity, possibly their most valuable employee.

'But where is he?' asked Mr Henderson Junior. 'When did you last see him?'

None of the other staff could remember. They were relieved he was no longer with them, and had not missed him in the least. 'But he may be ill?' queried their employer. 'He may have had an accident.'

The general consensus amongst the other office staff was that if he had, it was no great loss. But Mr Henderson obtained Mr Farquharson's address from the archives and conscientiously visited the lodgings, which he viewed with some distaste. A rather voluble landlady greeted Mr Henderson on the doorstep, where he was met with a barrage of complaints.

'Mr F. (as she called him) only gave a week's notice and he knows it should be a month. And he left a lot of clutter and rubbish behind for me to clear up. Who is going to pay for the disposal of his effects and the inconvenience caused?' ranted his outraged landlady. Mr Henderson retorted that he had no idea but it would not be him, and retreated in haste.

He returned to the Reading office and reported to Mr Henderson Senior.

'Well he can't have simply disappeared,' said the senior partner, but his confidence was misplaced. Mr F. had indeed disappeared. It was at this point that the hapless Clerk, by the name of Baines, had timidly knocked on the door of their inner sanctum and hesitantly reported that Sir Geoffrey Talbot had visited the offices the previous week, and that he, Baines, had been asked to retrieve from its safe box the Title Deeds to Brightwell Manor lodged with the firm for safe keeping in the name of their client, Mr Tristram Sinclair.

Mr Henderson Senior transferred his horrified gaze from Baines to his junior brother, and said, 'This cannot be happening.' On checking the safe box in question, and searching everywhere for the Title Deeds of Brightwell Manor, they gradually came to realise that it very much had happened, and that the offender was long gone.

'This is all your fault, Baines!' exclaimed Mr Henderson Senior. 'What on earth were you thinking?'

'But, Sir,' sputtered Baines, 'I could only do as I was bid. It was not my place to . . .' but Mr Henderson Senior was not listening.

'What are we to do now?' he asked of Junior, who had no response to offer. 'I think we need to consider our position here,' said Senior. 'Baines, you do not breathe one word of this to anyone, do you understand? We are not attempting to hush anything up, you understand . . .'

'No, Sir,' said Baines, uncomfortably aware of which side his bread was buttered, thinking of the four hungry mouths to feed at home. Five if you counted his saintly wife, who frequently went hungry in order to feed her young. 'Of course not, Sir.'

'We simply need time to consider our options, possibly to find Mr Farquharson, or indeed Sir Geoffrey Turnbull. I am sure there is a perfectly reasonable explanation, and it is all a silly misunderstanding. All will be resolved satisfactorily. In the meantime, you are instructed to keep your mouth shut.'

'Yes, Sir, of course, Sir,' said Baines again, and fled the room.

'I suppose we must let Mr Tristram Sinclair know, Harold?' asked Junior of Senior. 'He should be told, surely?'

'Well, of course, Horace,' replied Harold, in as matter of fact a voice as he could muster. 'It is only ethical. I am not suggesting otherwise. I simply feel we should investigate matters first. Imagine the bad publicity for Henderson & Co. if Mr Sinclair were to inform the constabulary.' He gave a theatrical shudder. 'It does not bear thinking about. We will of course inform him, but not immediately. We need time to gather our wits.'

Chapter 20 – 1903

If they could but have known it, Sir Geoffrey Turnbull was about to save them the bother. Since his return to England he had looked longingly at some of the new motor vehicles becoming available, but came to the conclusion that a horse was more practical for now. 'Perhaps in a few years time,' he thought, 'when they have developed a little more, and it is no longer necessary to have a man with a red flag preceding me along the road.'

So he had purchased a horse, remembering with a pang of sadness Grey Mist, whom he had abandoned so precipitately at Reading railway station all those years ago. She would be long gone by now, he supposed, but he hoped the beggar had given her a reasonable home and a good life.

Even as the Messrs Henderson were discussing the situation, Sir Geoffrey was riding up the drive to what he was already considering to be his home again, Brightwell Manor. Dismounting, he admired the old dolphin door knocker, now highly polished, banged on the door, and gave his name when the Butler, Nesbit, opened the door to him. Nesbit was now quite elderly himself, but he dimly remembered the name, and knew it was not good.

'If you would be good enough to wait here, Sir,' he said, leaving Sir Geoffrey in the outer hall, and resolutely closing the double doors to the inner hall while he went to find Mr Sinclair, and inform him of his visitor.

Tristram was with Grace in the drawing room when Nesbit entered, and after announcing his name, said, 'I have taken the liberty of leaving him in the outer hall, Sir.'

'Well done, Nesbit,' responded Tristram, aware that this was a mark of considerable discourtesy in modern society. 'Best place for him. I wish we could leave him there. Show him into the study, if you please.'

He stood up, heading for the study, when Grace, filled with foreboding, asked, 'Would you not like me to accompany you, Tristram?'

'Not on this occasion, thank you, my dear,' he replied. 'He is not a pleasant man and I cannot think his visit bodes well.'

'I feel I should be there though.'

Trusting his wife's judgement in all matters had become a habit with Tristram. 'Well, if you think so,' he said doubtfully. 'I'm really not sure . . .'

'Tristram, if you recall, I am the only person to have read the Title Deeds. We delayed lodging them with Henderson & Co. so that I could do so, do you not remember it?'

'Yes, indeed I do!' he exclaimed, now that he had been reminded. 'You are quite right, Grace, your excellent memory might prove useful.'

They entered the study together, and Nesbit ushered Sir Geoffrey inside, announcing his name in suitably stentorian tones. 'Sir Geoffrey!' said Tristram, carefully avoiding shaking hands with the man, and deliberately not offering him a seat. The three of them remained standing. Despite this calculated lack of courtesy, Tristram could not forget his manners towards his wife, and briefly introduced her. Turning back to Sir Geoffrey, he said, 'And what can I do for you?'

Sir Geoffrey had had a very brief opportunity to glance about him on his short walk from the outer hall to Tristram's study, but he could easily see the place had been repaired and restored to its former glory. It made him all the more determined to reclaim his birthright, so wrongly wrested from him all those years ago.

'I have come to inform you, Mr Sinclair, that I am now in possession of the Title Deeds to Brightwell Manor, and as with your good self after our card game, being in possession of the Deeds surely makes me the rightful owner?'

'I cannot see that that follows,' replied Tristram evenly, hoping his pounding heart was not visible in his chest. 'If you recall, having won the house fair and square, in front of many witnesses, I also paid you the value of the property. I feel it is wholly mine, and with a clear conscience.'

'Ah yes,' replied Sir Geoffrey, 'but in our enthusiasm, yours to move in to my home, and mine to leave the country, we omitted to complete the relevant paperwork for the conveyance of ownership. So the property has remained legally mine all this time, and I am almost tempted to ask you for rent for the entire length of your tenure.'

Having bitten her tongue as best she could, Grace interrupted. 'Have you read these Title Deeds yourself, Sir Geoffrey?' This flustered him for a moment, but he recovered quickly.

'No, of course not. Deeds are not for reading,' he said patronisingly, wondering why she was present at all. 'They are simply a legal document symbolising the ownership of a property.'

'I think if you read them you will find that is not quite the case.'

Tristram glanced at her, and wondered what she had learned from the Deeds that he had not.

'You will have noticed,' she continued, 'that they are written on vellum?'

'Calf skin? Yes, of course.' He was impatient with her now, wondering why she was addressing him, and not Sinclair himself.

'Did it not occur to you that might be a little unusual, given that this house was built in about 1680?'

'Unusual? No. Why?'

'Because vellum was used for indentures and title deeds from Medieval times until the early 1600s because of its excellent durability. Once fine parchments and good quality hand-made paper became available, they were significantly cheaper, and commonly used from the 1650s onwards.'

Sir Geoffrey stared at her. 'Well, what's that got to do with anything?' he said rudely.

Tristram considered remonstrating with him, but he could see his wonderful wife was entirely in control of the situation, and allowed it to pass.

'A great deal, I believe,' she said. 'When we first saw the property, we were confident that an older and finer house once stood here, built many years before this one. When I subsequently saw the Title Deeds, this was confirmed to me. And these Deeds refer to that property, not this one.'

Tristram was thunderstruck, not only by her knowledge and her memory, but as to why she had never told him any of this. She continued, 'All that remains of that original property is the chantry chapel . . .'

'A chantry chapel?' interrupted Sir Geoffrey. 'What is that? There is no chapel here.'

'No, it has been used as a barn for many years, and very useful it is too, but we have considerable evidence that is indeed what it was. So these Title Deeds, which you claim to have, and which I am sure you can have only obtained by nefarious and illegal means, only entitle the holder to the chantry chapel, or barn as it is now.'

'How come you know so much about everything?' demanded Sir Geoffrey belligerently, which was too much for Tristram. 'Excuse me, Sir!' he said in indignation. 'You will not address my wife in such a manner. Her knowledge of these matters far exceeds yours and mine added together.'

Grace smiled affectionately at her husband, and continued, having yet more shocks in store for this horrid and corpulent man. 'You may be aware, Sir Geoffrey, that possession is nine-tenths of the law, and we have been very much in possession for the last 20 years or so. And, if you wish to contest that in a court of law, not only would it be extremely expensive, but I think you might come up against the natural laws of squatters rights.'

'Well I've never heard of squatters rights,' muttered their guest, seeing that he was outwitted and becoming sulky now. 'But my family has been here for over 250 years, so I think that won't work for you either.'

'Ah, yes,' agreed Grace silkily, 'but our 20 years has been the most recent tenure, which is what will hold sway with the law.' She gave Tristram another look, almost triumphant this time.

'I should also add, Sir, that even if you did prove yourself to be the owner of the chantry chapel, or barn as it is now, you would have no means of accessing it because we would retain ownership of the remainder, and my husband is extremely unlikely to permit you to trespass on our land and property to reach what you consider might be yours.'

Tristram looked more thunderstruck than ever, but took this as his cue to end the visit.

'My wife is more than correct,' he said. 'I would never allow you anywhere near the place. It is legally mine, and you know it. This is bluff because you appear to have made good on your travels. I know not how or where, and I care less. I simply wish you to leave the premises.'

As he spoke, he gave a light tug on the bell pull, and Nesbit immediately entered the room. Grace wondered how he could have heard the bell jangling below stairs if he was outside the door, and realised the man must have been listening at the door, and was grateful for it.

'Nesbit,' said Tristram, 'Sir Geoffrey is leaving. Would you kindly escort him off the premises and ensure that he goes immediately. Thank you so much.'

Sir Geoffrey stood for a moment, considering his options, but quickly realised he had none. There was nothing he could do under the circumstances that would not make him appear even more foolish than he already felt. So for the second time in his life, he pulled the vellum Deeds from his pocket and threw them on the desk behind which Tristram had strategically retreated.

'Here!' he said, knowing he had been totally outwitted

by this woman, and resenting it more than if it had been by a man. 'Take them. And take the damned house too. You have stolen my birthright and may you rot in hell for it.'

Nesbit had opened the door and spoke imperturbably but authoritatively. 'This way, Sir, if you would.'

Defeated, and having no alternative, Sir Geoffrey walked through it, and they listened as his footsteps echoed the length of the inner hall, and then the outer hall. They breathed a sigh of relief as they heard the front door closing very firmly behind him. Nesbit went to one of the windows and discreetly watched as Sir Geoffrey mounted his horse and rode dejectedly down the drive of Brightwell Manor for the last time. It may have been his imagination, but it seemed to Nesbit that the horse was not the only one with his tail between his legs.

Tristram was ecstatic and turned to hug his wife and then kiss her very fondly. 'My dear!' he said, 'I had no idea of any of that! You never told me. Why did you never tell me?'

'I did not wish to cause you concern, dearest. You had so much else to worry about, and I don't think I ever really quite believed he would have the temerity to return here. Or to obtain the Deeds. I wonder how he came by them? They were lodged safely in our personal safe box in Henderson's massive safe.'

'I shall visit them tomorrow,' said Tristram, 'and demand to know what is going on. But you have saved the day, my darling. I could not have managed all that without you.'

Grace raised her eyes to heaven and laughed. 'I was on very thin ice, my dear,' she said. 'I didn't really know any of that legal stuff. It might be true, it may not, I am not perfectly certain.'

'My dear! You mean you were bluffing?'

'Well, only a little, Tristram. It was true about the vellum and the Deeds referring to the previous house on this land. But I am almost certain the Deeds would cover the ownership of the land too, so although I was accurate about the dates, the bit about trespassing and not being allowed access to the chantry chapel was perhaps just conjecture.'

Tristram smiled broadly and hugged her again. 'My dear! It all sounded highly convincing and I shall never be able to believe another word you say ever again.'

She laughed up at him, exhilarated by her success, but then another thought occurred to her.

'Well, we do seem to have got away with it, my darling, and we even have the Deeds in our possession, which I must say I did not expect. But what we should really be asking . . .'

'Ye-es?' said Tristram, with foreboding. 'What else should I know?'

'Well, if all that is so, where are the Deeds to this property? Won't we need them in the future for our own son? When the time comes?'

'Don't let's think about that now,' said Tristram. 'I will sort it out, I promise, but it will most certainly not be with Henderson & Co. In fact, I shall call and see them in the morning. For now I am merely relieved that Frederick is not our first born son. If he was to inherit Brightwell, he'd only lose it again in another game of cards somewhere else!'

Grace smiled fondly at the thought. 'Yes,' she said, 'you are probably right. Is he gambling a great deal these days?'

'It would seem so, yes. I have warned him against it, but he only points out that I won Brightwell at play, and look what it did for me.'

'That is our son! He always has to have the last word. For now, let's just be grateful things have worked out as well as they have.'

Chapter 21
1904 – 1915

Late one afternoon, when Frederick had not long turned 16, Tristram was greeted with the mesmerising site of his son walking up the drive leading his horse and pushing a bicycle. It seemed Frederick's career as a mechanic was about to begin.

'Where did you buy that?' asked Tristram, walking down the drive to meet him, and eyeing the bicycle with some foreboding.

'Reading, Papa. A new shop has opened there, but mine will be in Newbury, so no competition.'

A frown crossed Tristram's brow as he wondered how his son had paid for the machine.

'Was it expensive?' he asked.

'Well, yes, but I got the price down a bit, so it was a bargain, and, er, I have had a bit luck of play.'

'Well, that makes a change,' said Tristram, but Frederick only laughed. 'Have you led the horse and pushed the bicycle all the way from Reading? It doesn't look very comfortable.'

'Well, it's not,' replied Frederick candidly, 'but I could

hardly ride the horse and lead the bicycle, could I!'

'Where are you going to keep it?'

'There's heaps of room in my bedroom, I'm going to take it apart and put it back together again to see how it works.'

Tristram's heart sank. 'I'm not sure your Mama would appreciate a lot of oily bicycle parts inside the house. Why not use one of the outbuildings, and have it as your workshop? That way you would not need to put everything away each time you worked on it.'

'Could I, Papa?' said Frederick with great enthusiasm. 'That would be grand!'

'Let's go and see which one would suit you best.'

So together they walked through the now immaculate gardens at the side of the house, and found Boddington in conversation with Jeffreys and Stebbins in the stableyard. They were all immediately interested in the bicycle.

'It's a good one,' Frederick informed them proudly. 'It is a safety bicycle, chain driven, and it has steering, comfort and speed. Women are beginning to ride them too. The women's version has no bar, and a skirt guard.'

'You are right to get in at the very beginning of the craze,' said Stebbins. 'They are becoming quite popular.'

'Yes,' agreed Frederick. 'And I am going to be able to mend them for people if they are broken, and sell them at a profit too. It doesn't make sense to wait any longer, or other mechanics will get in ahead of me.'

'We need one of the outbuildings for a workshop,' added Tristram, delighted by his son's ambition and determination. 'Which do you gentlemen recommend?'

There was some discussion and they all went off to view the various merits of the two favourites. Frederick chose the second on the grounds that it had larger windows and was therefore lighter, which would help with his work. So he leaned the bicycle against the wall and extracted some specialised tools from the saddlebag on the back.

'If you're going to take it apart,' said Stebbins, 'you need a blanket to lay out all the pieces in order.' Frederick had thought pretty much the same thing himself, and was delighted when Stebbins produced an old horse blanket from the stables, no longer in use.

'That wasn't Sylvester's blanket, was it?' asked Tristram immediately.

'No, Mr Sinclair,' smiled Stebbins gently at the memory of the fine stallion. 'We buried Sylvester in his blanket in the lower field.'

'I still miss him,' said Tristram simply, and Stebbins nodded in agreement.

'He lived to be a good age, Sir.'

Dismantling the bicycle was soon accomplished, and Tristram and Grace were surprised – and relieved! – that Frederick was able to put it all back together easily. He did it again several times, achieving it more quickly each time. Once it had been dismantled and reassembled satisfactorily, Frederick took to riding it everywhere. He still exercised his horse regularly, but being seen out on the bicycle around the town was good advertising. Frederick was assessing the market.

Convinced he could now sell and repair these machines, he visited Tristram in his study one morning, and announced that he was ready to seek commercial premises in Newbury for the purpose of sales, with a workshop at the back for repairs.

To Tristram he seemed very young for such a venture but as he himself had once pointed out, other boys were earning their living at a much younger age.

'I shall only need help with the initial rent and the deposit,' announced Frederick. 'I anticipate that business will be brisk, and I should be able to pay my own rent after the first month or two.'

Tristram thought this a little optimistic, but he decided to go along with the venture, and asked Boddington to accompany them in their search. They weren't exactly spoilt for choice, but Frederick soon decided on a property with a lot more space than he currently needed.

'It has potential, Papa,' he said. 'Later on, when motor cars are improved and more affordable, I can use this space for them too. And look, it's beside the main road through the town, so I will be able to instal petrol pumps one day, and sell petrol. There's good profit in petrol.'

It all seemed very futuristic and speculative to Tristram, but he decided that if it didn't all work out as Frederick seemed to think it would, being rented they could give notice and cut their losses. But to his surprise and delight, over the years it did work out, just as Frederick had prophesied. He was selling bicycles on a regular basis, and was able to increase and replenish his stocks soon after setting up in business.

The repairs side flourished too, not because there was a lot wrong with the bicycles, but because people didn't yet know how to use them properly, and caused most of the problems themselves out of ignorance. Frederick was good at diagnosing what the problem was, and explaining how it had arisen, so that the grateful riders went happily on their way, convinced that Frederick knew his trade well, and to recommend his services, and the benefits of bicycling in general, to their friends.

The ladies took to bicycling with great gusto, and the larger proportion of his sales were to the fairer sex. It gave them a freedom and independence they had never had before, and when Harriet and MillyVic came down from University, they bought one each as well. They were thrilled with the idea of being able to go where they needed to go when they wanted, and took delight in cycling to the school at which they had both been appointed teachers.

Selling to the ladies also gave Frederick an opportunity to practice his charms, and led to an inexhaustible supply of new friendships and the chance to invite them out on bicycle rides after hours in summer and even on Sundays in the winter when the weather was fine.

At about the same time as Harriet and MillyVic finished University, and found jobs as teachers nearby, so Hugh finished his training at Cirencester Agricultural College. He had made a lot of new friends himself, and was saddened that his two best friends were returning home to New Zealand to become sheep farmers.

'You must come and visit us,' they had said, and Hugh promised them he would. He also invited them to Brightwell Manor before they left, to see a real English estate, and to talk of their exciting plans for the future with his father.

Although the estate had been more than paying for itself for many years, Hugh was keen to develop the farming side of things now. Tristram was pleased in his turn. 'I did think of it myself when I first came here,' he told Hugh. 'But there was so much else to do to get the place up together, I never got around to it. It would be good to see cows and sheep, chickens, ducks and geese in the fields and outbuildings. And the stream running through the lower fields is a great advantage too.'

Hugh had learned well at Cirencester, and was keen to get started with as many sheep as they could afford. 'Wool and young English lamb for the table,' he said wisely. 'Very profitable.' But he counselled against a dairy herd.

'It's too labour intensive, Papa,' he said. 'We'd need to build a milking parlour, employ a cowman, feed the cows in winter when they could not get enough grass. I think beef cattle would be the way to go.' So that was decided upon, and Hugh went off to market and chose his flock and herd wisely.

He also bit his tongue as far as Frederick was concerned. The old tensions between them seemed to have been left in the past, and he was pleased to see Frederick thinking in the same way as he did himself, about what was profitable, and what was cost effective, albeit in a different profession.

By early 1914, despite rumours of war, Frederick's new business continued to flourish, and he was very much in funds. It was unfortunate that this allowed him to pursue his fondness for gambling, and in addition to the card games he had enjoyed with his cronies for many years, he was able to go further afield and visited Ascot where he bet on the horses, and the very new greyhound racetrack, where he did well betting on the dogs. He usually invited one of his lady friends to accompany him, and was always welcomed by the turf accountants and touts who enjoyed his patronage.

Despite his gambling, with which he had mixed success, and even with brother Hugh under the same roof, all progressed harmoniously for some years, until one day in August Betsy sought out Grace in the Library and had bad news. 'I can hardly bear to tell you, Mrs Sinclair . . .'

'What is it, Betsy? Is Millicent Victoria unwell?'

'No, no,' said Betsy, 'it's not her. It's worse than that. It's the new chambermaid. She is increasing.'

Grace's heart sank. 'Oh no,' she said, suspicion immediately dawning. 'Does she say who . . .?'

'Yes, she does,' said Betsy, wishing she could say something, anything, to protect her dear mistress from the truth. 'She claims it was Frederick.'

'Oh no,' said Grace again. 'The stupid stupid boy.'

'Yes, ma'am,' agreed Betsy. 'Stupid girl too. I'm not sure how ignorant she really is. She says she didn't know what was happening, but she is a flighty piece . . . Not the usual sort of girl we have here, but chambermaids are becoming more difficult to find these days. And if this war takes off as everyone is saying . . .'

Grace had no alternative but to seek out Tristram and tell him what she had heard. She was extremely distressed, which in itself made Tristram angry. 'If the situation had been otherwise,' she said, 'this would have been our first grandchild. A time of happiness.' And she began to weep silently.

He took his wife in his arms and tried to comfort her. He had never felt such outrage in his life. Indeed, he had no idea he was capable of such wrath. A muscle flicked in his jaw, and he wondered what on earth his heart was doing, banging away and, it seemed to him, missing a beat now and then too. When Grace appeared to have her tears under control, he said, 'Where is he? Does he know this news himself? Why hasn't he said anything? He is of an age to take responsibility now.'

'He is at his workshop in Newbury,' Grace reminded him.

'I will see him the minute he returns home. He is old enough to know better. How dare he?'

Tristram turned on his heel and went to the door of his study. 'Excuse me, my dear,' he said, not wishing Grace to see how very angry he was. 'I will see Frederick the minute he returns home,' adding over his shoulder, 'but for now I am not fit company.'

Grace obviously passed this on, and noted Frederick did not need to ask why his father wished to see him. 'I should go quickly,' advised his mother. 'He is very angry, you would not wish to make matters worse by delaying.'

So it was that on his return, still somewhat grimy from his day's labours, Frederick knocked on his father's study door physically trembling. He took a moment to tell himself this was ridiculous, he was 26 years old, and an adult. Although the new chambermaid being pregnant was most unfortunate, she had been more than willing. That said, it was his mistake and he would take responsibility for it. He had no idea how, but he would come up with something, one way or another.

'Come in!' snapped Tristram, hearing the knock on his study door. His anger returned at the sight of his son.

As he stood there in silence, Tristram said, 'I see you have no need to ask why I wish to speak with you?'

'Well, I imagine it is about the new chambermaid, Papa, but I am an adult.'

'Why don't you behave like one then?' demanded Tristram. 'As far as I can see, you have behaved like a selfish, idiotic sixteen-year-old.'

Nothing could have irked Frederick more. He smarted at the insult and his determination to remain calm was severely tested. 'I am sorry, Papa. It is most unfortunate.'

'Unfortunate?' said Tristram, rather more loudly than he had intended. 'You call a major disaster, that will change our lives for ever, and the life of an innocent young girl . . .'

'She wasn't that innocent, Sir. Indeed, she was very willing.'

'How dare you! I am not interested in the details. You wronged her, whatever she might have said, just for two minutes of your own selfish pleasure.'

'Well, steady on, Papa,' protested Frederick, 'it took much longer than two . . . '

'Spare me your boasts of prowess!' snapped his father, physically trembling himself now. 'The consequences are far reaching, and despite your claims of being an adult, you have not considered that.'

'Well, I have, Sir . . .'

'Have you considered your mother? She is distraught.

If you were married, this would be her first grandchild! It should be a moment of joy, of happiness, instead of which she has been brought to tears.'

Frederick knew that nothing was ever permitted to upset Mama, and he was genuinely sorry to have caused her grief. 'I will talk to her,' he said.

'Yes, you should. But what are you going to tell her? What are you going to do about it? Have you discussed it with . . . What is the wretched girl's name, for God's sake?'

'Er, I'm not quite certain . . .' mumbled Frederick.

'What?' roared Tristram. 'You've made love to the girl and you don't know her name?'

'Well, it wasn't really love, Sir.'

Tristram stood stock still and shook his head. 'I do not understand you, Frederick. I really do not understand you. You don't want for female company, do you? You always seem to have some lady or another on your arm. They seem to find you charming, though God knows why. And yet you resort to the chambermaid . . .'

'Yes, but the nicer ladies are very proper, Sir. They keep their distance. Whereas this chambermaid, she was casting lures at me for weeks. It was hard to resist.'

'Well if that is the truth, and that is how it was, did it not occur to you that she wanted this to happen, so that you might marry her? Or give her money? Or to compromise you in some way?'

'No, Sir. I didn't think of that.'

'Well, what do you intend to do? What has she asked you to do?'

'Well, I've avoided her so far, Sir. She did seek me out to tell me what had befallen her, but I told her I would sort it out. She didn't actually ask for anything, Sir.'

'Will you stop calling me Sir!' shouted Tristram, goaded beyond endurance. 'I'm your father, for God's sake, not your school teacher or your commanding officer.'

'Sorry, Sir,' said Frederick, hiding a smile and then stopping in horror as he realised he had just done it again.

'Oh God,' said Tristram, sinking his head in his hands. 'What a damnable mess. What are we to do? If we send her away, she will likely starve, and she will take with her our grandchild, our flesh and blood. But if we keep her here, and give her one of the cottages to live in, that will be worse.'

He remembered Betsy and Millicent Victoria, all those many years ago, and reflected that the daughter had turned out to be a fine young woman, a talented teacher, and a valuable member of society. 'Do you wish to marry this chambermaid?' he asked.

Frederick looked revolted. 'Good God, no, Father. I most definitely do not.'

'Well what is to become of her then?'

'We could give her some money and send her away.'

'So you care nothing for her?'

'No, of course not.'

'Where would she go?'

'Would it matter?'

Tristram shuddered at his son's indifference. 'Well, it would to her,' he replied. 'What do you intend to do then?'

'About what?'

'The girl. The baby. The situation.'

'I thought I might volunteer for the cavalry, Father.'

'What? What cavalry?'

'If this war takes off. I could join the cavalry. I'm an experienced rider. I should think they would be glad to have me. And I'm older than most of the lads volunteering. They might make me an officer.'

'Well God help the men under your command,' groaned Tristram. 'I see,' he added. 'So you go off to war, ignore the whole mess you have created here, and it will all just disappear?'

'Something like that, Sir, yes. I mean Father.'

'I hardly think that is going to solve anything. Get out of my sight.'

Relieved, Frederick was delighted to do as he was told for once, and slipped quietly out of his father's study, and went down to the kitchens to charm Mrs Hatton, the cook, into feeding him early because he was so hungry.

As if all this was not enough to contend with, Hugh was waiting outside the study door to speak to his father in turn. Tristram looked up in surprise. 'Hugh?' he said.

'I cannot bear it, Papa!' said Hugh. 'The shame he has brought on this family.'

'Frederick?' said Tristram, surprised. 'How did you hear so quickly?'

'Mother told me. She is deeply distressed. We all are. What a brat he is.'

'Yes,' agreed Tristram. 'I am afraid you are right, Hugh.'

'Well, I cannot bear it. I am ashamed to be a member of this family. I shall take up the invitation from my friends in New Zealand and visit them for a few months.'

Tristram was shocked. 'Leave Brightwell?' he said. 'But what about the farm . . .?'

'We have plenty of staff, Papa. Stebbins is marvellous with all the animals. He does a great deal of it anyway.'

'Well what if there is a war, as everyone seems to think will happen? Hardly the time to go to sea, surely?'

'I'll be fine, it will only be a skirmish, and over by Christmas. If it happens at all.'

'Frederick is thinking of volunteering for the cavalry.'

'Running away, Papa. That's what Frederick is doing.'

'Yes,' agreed Tristram, considering the matter. 'But what is he running into? That is the question.'

'He'll survive,' replied Hugh in a voice tinged with regret. 'He always lands on his feet and comes up smelling of roses.'

Grace made it her business to seek out the new chambermaid, and to at least ask her name, which turned out to be Constance. On any other occasion, Grace would have found this somewhat amusing, but under the circumstances it was simply ironic. 'What do you want to do?' Grace asked her, and like Frederick, she seemed to have little idea.

Overwhelmed by an interview with her employer, she lost the coquettishness that had lured Frederick, and said, 'Do you want me to get rid of it, Ma'am?'

'Get rid . . .?' said Grace, puzzled and then shocked. 'No, no, of course not. You would risk harming yourself as well as the baby.' Her eyes filled with tears, and Constance noted it with some satisfaction.

'I could marry him if he will have me?' she said hopefully.

'Well, no,' said Grace, taking a fervent dislike to the girl, and beginning to suspect she had tempted Frederick deliberately, with a view to improving her lot in the world. 'I don't think that is the solution either. Let me give it some thought and discuss it with my husband. I will speak with you again in the morning.'

A night's disturbed repose did little to restore her spirits, and a conversation with Tristram over breakfast made her feel even worse.

'Volunteering to join the cavalry?' repeated Grace in horror. 'But he might never come home again.'

Tristram allowed himself the thought that that might be the best solution all round, but knew his wife would not agree with him. 'And even if he goes off to war, Constance and his baby will remain. They aren't going to disappear, are they now.'

'You are very right, my dear,' agreed Tristram. 'They most certainly are not.'

Chapter 22
1914 – 1918

How quickly the world can change, thought Tristram during his morning ride. Jack had made a fine naval career, but was apparently now on his way to Jutland in a battleship, preparing for a confrontation at sea the like of which had never been seen before.

Hugh had apparently reached New Zealand safely, but was planning to stay there longer than anticipated, because of the war. A good excuse, thought Tristram, but then, more sympathetically, who could blame him?

Frederick's idle threat to join the cavalry had become reality, and he had gone off putting on a brave face, leaving his father to wind down the bicycle shop and give notice to quit the premises. And leaving his mother to resolve the question of Constance and his unborn baby as best she could.

Although they did not care for the girl, Tristram and Grace had not the heart to turn her away, and gave her Mr & Mrs Dawkins's cottage to live in, as they were long gone, having died within a few months of each other some years ago. This meant Betsy had a new neighbour, and although she did not care for Constance either, she cared very much about babies, and knew she would not be able to resist helping Constance once it was born, just as Mrs Dawkins had once helped her. History repeats itself, thought Betsy grimly, only this time, being the Sinclair's own flesh and blood, it seemed even worse.

No sooner had these arrangements been put in place, than Constance suffered a painful miscarriage. The midwife was called, but said there was nothing to be done. Once recovered, the girl realised she had made herself extremely unpopular and, now that Frederick had done a disappearing act and there was no possibility of his marrying her, she decided to leave Brightwell too. Even Constance did not have the temerity to ask for a reference and, using a generous gift of money from Grace, which she ungratefully called conscience money, went off to try her luck in London, where the war was causing major staff shortages, people were desperate to find servants, and did not ask too many awkward questions of prospective employees.

'So Frederick was right,' Grace had said with a weak smile at breakfast next morning. She was saddened by the loss of the baby so late in its term, but she could see it was most definitely for the best.

'Oh?' said Tristram. 'That makes a change. About what?'

'Going off to war and everything here just going away.'

'Yes, Hugh said he always falls on his feet and comes up smelling of roses.'

'Well, let's hope that applies to this awful war and his time in the Cavalry as well,' said Grace.

It was yet another sad day when an official telegram arrived to say the government was commandeering any suitable horses for the war effort, shortly followed by a visit from a non-combatant officer in Captain's uniform. Following the tradition that began at Tattersall's when Tristram first bought a pair of matching chestnuts to pull his carriage and curricle, as they aged and were put out to grass he had replaced them over the years with as good a match as he could find.

The smart Captain chose this pair from Tristram's stables, realising they could pull gun carriages into battle, but left him Merry Feet, his main mode of transport, because she was too skittish and nervous. Tristram was surprised by this as Merry Feet was usually good tempered and quiet, but neither he nor the Captain noticed Stebbins innocently standing near her hind quarters, somehow causing her to shy sideways and at one point to rear up. The Captain didn't want a troublemaker in his ranks, even if it had four legs.

He was accompanied by the hay procurement officer who went off to satisfy himself that Tristram had no hay in his barn. There was some as feed, but too little to make it worthwhile commandeering and loading.

As they left, taking his pair of chestnuts with them, Tristram sighed and thanked his lucky stars this had not happened during Sylvester's days. If they had come then, thought Tristram, he could not have borne the heartache.

Tristram's current mount was a fine one, but he had never re-established the bond he had had with Sylvester. He was on his way to visit his old friends, Charles and Isabella. Their two children, James and Amelia, had grown up and done well for themselves. Amelia was training to be a nurse, loving her work in a grand London hospital.

James had fulfilled his early promise, become an engineer, married a lovely wife and was living in fine style at Tower Court, in separate accommodation to his parents and, thought Tristram, not unkindly, sitting pretty ready to inherit when the time came. They had two delightful boys and he was educating them at the best boarding school he could find. They did not seem to be enjoying it very much, but they were certainly getting a good education.

'Thank God they are too young to volunteer for this awful war,' said Charles over coffee in his study.

'And most of our loyal staff are too old,' agreed Tristram. 'You are more fortunate than I,' said Tristram moodily, thinking of Frederick. 'Or else done a better job at parenting.'

'You cannot blame yourself,' insisted Charles. 'I blame this war for half of it. Values are changing from when we were young.'

A month later news came that Jack had died a hero's death in the Battle of Jutland, and Tristram and Grace were devastated. 'I can't believe we will never see him again,' she said sadly, shedding more tears. Her husband felt inadequate in trying to comfort her. What was there to say?

Time passed and eventually brought a letter from Hugh in New Zealand. He had met the love of his life there, and was planning to marry and start a new career as a sheep farmer. This brought yet more sadness to his parents, but as Tristram bravely said, 'Who can blame him? He is safer over there. We might never see him again either, but at least we know he is safe. Alive. Which is more than we know about Frederick. I wonder if he simply hasn't written letters home, or whether he has and they have not arrived.'

And then one day, some months after news had filtered through about a terrible battle at Passchendaele, Frederick came home. He had walked up the drive, coughing badly, before anyone had noticed him coming, and he was glad of a moment's respite on the doorstep to get his breath back.

The war had begun with horses but ended with tanks and armoured cars. Yet to the end of the campaign, guns, ammunition and supplies were hauled up to the front line by horses and mules. He had suffered the trauma of having his horse shot from under him, and had resorted to the trenches some distance away.

The gas in that battle had almost done for him, as it had for most of the others, but he had been hauled out and propped up in a spot where the ambulances could reach him, and eventually took him away. He knew he was one of the lucky ones, despite the breathing problems and the cough.

After a short period in a field hospital, his eyesight mostly recovered but it was realised he was too ill to return to the Front, so he was sent back to England where he was given a rail pass to get home as best he could.

Nesbit answered the door and was surprised out of his usual pomposity.

'Mr Frederick!' he exclaimed. 'Come in, come in,' and immediately offered his arm for support.

'It's alright, thank you,' said Frederick breathlessly.

Nesbit grandly threw open the double doors to the inner hall and went in search of whichever parent he could find first. Tristram was out riding, but Grace came running as the news travelled through the house, and came to hug her son with all the pent up love and pain and longing for her three sons.

'Steady on, Mama,' said Frederick, trying to make light of the situation. 'You'll crush the breath out of me. What breath I have!'

She led him into the dining room, telling Nesbit to have the cook bring what ever food she had since it was not a meal time. She was shocked by how thin he was.

'You must be hungry!' she said.

'Mama,' said Frederick wearily, 'I have been hungry for the last two years.'

'You always were!' laughed Grace amid her tears, and held on to his arm, needing to feel the harshness of the cloth of his uniform, and the solidity of her son beneath it, even though it impeded his eating slightly, but he did not seem to mind.

At length his father entered the room too. He had walked his horse back to the stables and been greeted by the news that Mr Frederick was home. He hurried round the side of the house, through the front door and Nesbit, awaiting him, said, 'In the dining room, Sir.'

Frederick looked up doubtfully as his father entered the room, remembering their painful last interview before he left, and rose to his feet.

'Lo, the conquering hero comes,' he said, but his father ignored his bravado, and shook his hand fervently. 'My son!' he beamed, 'you're home.'

Surprised and relieved at this welcome, Frederick said, 'Yes, Father, not in the best shape, I'm afraid, but I shall soon recover.'

'We can talk when you have eaten,' said Tristram, and left the boy to his mother, who wanted to hear all about everything, and to tell him all that had been happening at Brightwell during his absence. He was sad to hear about the loss of his brother Jack, unconcerned by Hugh's departure for New Zealand, and relieved that Constance and his love child had disappeared so conveniently. He felt life had given him a second chance, vowing that he would be a better man because of it.

This resolution lasted longer than anticipated. The hacking cough from his exposure to gas did improve, but was to remain with him for the rest of his life. It didn't stop him smoking, however, a habit he had learned in the trenches where there had been little else of comfort.

After some months of good food and fine country air, Frederick improved considerably. He retrieved his beloved bicycle from the depths of the outbuilding where his father had stored it, and virtually cycled himself back to health. He liked to go into Newbury to buy a newspaper and glean what news he could of the on-going war. He looked into acquiring a radio, and tried to make some sort of crystal set but it wasn't very successful and reception was appalling.

When news finally came through that the war had ended, on 11th November 1918, no one was more jubilant than Frederick. He went into Newbury in uniform on his bicycle, and joined in the street celebrations. There was dancing until late into the night, and he slept in the arms of a pretty young lady who was only marginally happier than he was. But he truly slept and in the morning he remembered his manners, politely doffed his cap, went in search of his bicycle and rode home.

Chapter 23
1919 – 1930

After more sleep, a shave and a wonderful hot bath, Frederick went in search of his father. After their initial awkwardness, they had become easier with each other and harmony restored, even if the past could not be entirely forgotten.

'I'm thinking about the future now, Father,' he said.

'Yes, indeed. At last we can all do that.'

'Do you remember years ago, we talked about my setting up a garage?'

'I do, my son, indeed I do.' This was encouraging.

'Well, now the war is over, I think the motor car is going to develop quickly. There will be mass production and lower prices. One day everyone will want one. And I think I should get in at the start of it. I could set up with bicycles initially, and then as the cars become available, move on to them. Those premises I had previously were ideal. I wonder if they might be available again.'

'Why not look into it then,' said Tristram. 'I said I would set you up in a business, and I will.'

Frederick beamed. 'Well, as long as you are willing,' he said, 'I would like to make it happen.'

The next day he cycled back into Newbury and visited his old premises. It had fallen into some disrepair during the four years of war, but to his delight there was a For Sale sign nailed to the door. It looked as if it had been there for sometime. The fact that the town was plastered with For Sale signs was no deterrent.

He immediately contacted the owner who certainly remembered him and his bicycle shop, and heartily agreed that it would be the perfect site for a garage. So they struck a deal at considerably less than the asking price, and Frederick went home to tell his father the good news, and arrange payment of the money.

Tristram insisted on using a solicitor to do the conveyancing properly, but it all went through speedily, and Frederick was thrilled to find himself the proud owner of new premises.

He had judged the market well. After the war, it seemed everybody wanted a bicycle. Business soared, and later the mass produced motor car was on its way. The Model T Ford was the first car Frederick stocked, built at Trafford Park in Manchester with parts imported from Detroit in America. He had one on his forecourt, and people came to view but not to buy. Then one day it sold, so he ordered two more. And so it went on, with the bicycle his main bread and butter, but car sales the jam, soon to become the cherry on the cake.

Frederick made a point of learning how they worked,

although he did stop short of taking one apart and putting it together again. He could see how simple and basic they were though, and was the first to offer any sort of service or help when they went wrong. This led to a loyal band of customers, and increased sales of both bicycles and motor cars.

Word went round about this handsome young soldier, injured in the war, who had come home and was doing well. Which was how the young lady he had danced with the night the war ended discovered him. She came into the garage one day, and he recognised her immediately. Her name was Megan, and she was mainly interested in meeting the handsome young soldier again, but being Frederick, he sold her a bicycle at the same time.

They went off on bike rides together when ever they had a free moment and the weather was kind. They took picnics, and talked for hours. She even made herself useful at the garage, making him cups of tea and sometimes bringing a brown paper bag full of broken biscuits.

The burgeoning car sales helped Frederick decide it was time to instal tanks and pumps for petrol, the first in Newbury, and he looked into the costings of it. He had been putting some money by, although he continued to visit Ascot and the greyhound race track, which had inevitably depleted his funds somewhat. So he went to see his Papa, in the stables this time, and talked about what an excellent investment petrol pumps would be.

'It doesn't make sense to wait, Father,' he said, 'It's all about getting in at the start of these things.'

Tristram raised an eyebrow and said he would think about it. The truth was his inheritance had had something of a battering over the years. He had invested it wisely, and interest rates had been worthwhile, but the house, his family, educating Hugh and the girls, and paying the staff, had been a huge drain on his resources. He still had enough to be comfortable, and did not need to worry Grace in the matter, but he knew he needed to be a little more circumspect in the future.

However, he could see the business opportunity for Frederick, and after much thought he eventually agreed to fund the installation of pumps and tanks. He did consider making it a loan, so that Frederick would appreciate the value of it the more, but in the end he paid up and said nothing. 'My main role in life,' he observed to Grace with a wry smile.

Once installed, petrol sales started slowly, partly because it was sometimes difficult to get petrol at all. This was of course reflected in the price at Frederick's pumps, but as word spread that it was available in Newbury, there was more traffic and increased car sales. Frederick was jubilant, and Megan even offered to serve on the new forecourt, pumping petrol and taking the money. Bicycle repairs continued apace too, so Frederick hired a young lad with aptitude, Robert, as an apprentice, and taught him to do the work instead.

He was delighted one day when his father brought his friend Charles to visit, interested in looking at the cars for sale. He was now stocking the Morris Oxford and the Morris Cowley as well as the Ford. Tristram was interested but not tempted, and after a couple of visits, Charles went ahead and bought a Bullnose Morris. Frederick encouraged the decision with a small discount because he was a friend of the family, and Tristram was amazed at his son's business acumen and salesmanship.

In turn Charles was of course proud to show off his new acquisition to his son, James, and it was not long before James visited Newbury and bought one too. Not having seen each other since childhood, Frederick and James were pleased to meet up again after so many years, and chatted amiably on the forecourt while Megan dashed about serving petrol, taking money, making tea and bossing the new apprentice.

The two childhood friends chatted again each time James came for petrol, service or repairs. Both being engineers now, they had a lot in common, and a good friendship was gradually forged. James invited Frederick to visit him at Tower Court, and realising James would inherit the family home from Charles when the time came, and had no need to purchase a house, it occurred to Frederick that perhaps he should acquire some property himself.

He realised he could not afford anything as grand as Tower Court, but he was more practical and after a run of unaccustomed luck at the race track, he went into Reading and bought a shop, which he then rented out. Later he bought a couple more, with no intention of using them himself, but certain his tenants would keep paying the rent. He also suspected the value of property would increase over the years, and was confident he was making a good investment.

With money from the business cascading in, regular rents from the shops, and an occasional win at the racetrack, both horses and dogs, Frederick began to see himself as comfortably well off. Megan was still making herself useful, but had by now negotiated a small wage for her labours. She was a good girl and worked hard, and Frederick decided it was time he got married.

He knew Megan liked a cuddle, but having been well brought up, she would never let him go too far. Despite his memories of Constance the chambermaid and the miscarriage, this state of affairs did not suit Frederick, so the following Sunday they went for the customary bike ride, and after they had eaten the picnic she had brought in the basket on the front of her bicycle, he surprised her by proposing.

They were stretched out on the blanket with the remains of the picnic yet to be tidied away, and Frederick had made his usual attempts to get past the kissing stage without success.

'Come on,' he said, 'you know you want to.'

'Of course I do, Frederick,' she said, 'but what if I get pregnant? Mater would kill me.'

'You won't get pregnant,' he assured her, but neither of them believed that. He pushed thoughts of Constance to the very back of his mind, but at such times as this the fear of a second unwanted pregnancy deterred his advances almost as much as Megan did.

'Well, let's get married then,' he said.

Megan abruptly sat up and turned to look at him.

'Really?' she said. 'You mean it?'

'Yes,' he said, almost as surprised as she was. 'Might as well.'

'Might as well! That's not very romantic.'

'Well, you know I'm not the lovey-dovey sort,' said Frederick lamely. 'But I do love you.'

'Do you?' she said with increasing excitement. 'Oh Frederick, I love you too.'

'So shall we?'

'Yes,' she said, 'I'd love to.'

So Frederick was taken home to meet mater and pater, and was suitably impressed to find them living in a beautiful house on the banks of the River Thames at Maidenhead. Having worked his charm on her mater, and casually mentioning Brightwell Manor on a couple of occasions, he obviously met with approval. Megan's pater took a little more convincing, but realising Frederick had a successful business in the town, he was reassured that his daughter would be well provided for.

After that things took off rather more quickly than Frederick had anticipated. A date was set for the wedding and arrangements were made by the bride's family without very much reference to him. It seemed Megan had Irish blood in her veins, and there were a lot of cousins in America, offspring of the family that had left Ireland during the potato famine in the 1850s. They were all invited too, but of course had no hope of reaching England very speedily, and could not afford the cost of the crossing anyway. It was enough for Megan's mother that they knew her daughter had made a good match.

Grace and Tristram were introduced to Megan shortly before the wedding. Although she was not what they would have chosen for their son, she was pleasant enough, and Grace admired her for taking him on at all.

Being a Saturday, Harriet and MillyVic were able to attend the nuptials, as the school at which they taught and lived was not too far distant. Afterwards at the Reception in the big house on the banks of the Thames, Grace allowed herself to say, much against her better judgement, 'Maybe you two girls will be next? Are there any nice young men in teaching these days?'

Harriet looked at her Mama steadily. 'MillyVic is all I need, Mama,' she said. 'And I am all she needs too.'

Frederick smirked, but he could see their Mama had no idea as to her meaning.

Not really in love but hoping to make a go of things, Frederick had prepared the very nice flat over the garage in anticipation, and after a brief honeymoon spent at Clevedon, to which they drove in one of the cars Frederick had been displaying for sale on his forecourt, they moved in.

They were both surprised when Megan did not conceive for sometime. 'I kept telling you there was no need to worry!' he joked, but he silently wondered if he was to blame, and that the gas in the trenches, and the deprivations of war, had affected more than his breathing. Eventually though, after three years when Megan had virtually given up hope, she gave birth to a little girl whom they called Irene Grace.

Megan continued to serve petrol at the pumps for some months beforehand, Frederick having assured her that no one was as good at it as she was. She had to stop while Irene was young, so Frederick cheerfully hired another young lady, Daphne, for the job. Daphne was quite glamorous, which caused Megan some disquiet. Once Irene went to school, however, Megan took her job back, and the glamorous Daphne was sent on her way.

By the late-1920s most of Frederick's business acquaintances were noticing a slowing down in trade and a drop in profits. Petrol sales remained fairly steady;

although bicycle repairs remained in high demand, sales were down, but Frederick convinced himself this was because anyone in the Newbury area who wanted a bicycle had already bought one. Cars didn't seem to be shifting at all. When the display model on his forecourt did sell – at somewhat less than the asking price – Frederick did not replace it. They were still available, of course, but now you had to order it. The trouble was, nobody did.

Almost all of Frederick's money was tied up in property in Reading, and he devoutly hoped the rents would continue to be paid.

Chapter 24 – 1930

News kept coming in of serious economic problems in America. In October 1929 their Stock Market crashed, and the resulting Depression shook the world's economy, rich countries and poor alike, and Brightwell Manor felt the reverberations too. Tristram's investments had done reasonably well for many years, but now interest rates plummeted, and some of the companies in which he had money disappeared completely.

He consoled himself with the thought that it was worse for the Americans. As the dole queues increased, the unemployed had no option but to default on their loans, and even the banks were failing by the dozen. There were rumours of men booking into high-rise hotels simply in order to throw themselves from the windows on the higher floors; Tristram hoped it was not true.

In Halifax his brother Hugh was making economies where he could, but exports were down, sales in Britain were disappearing, unemployment was going through the roof. Hugh was devastated to add to their numbers, but he was laying off loyal staff that had been with him all their working lives.

One by one the tenants in Frederick's shops in Reading gave notice to quit, even when the Lease was not due for renewal. The ladies' hairdressers was the last to go, which showed their priorities, even in a Depression, but go it did. Even when the shops were empty, the government was still demanding the business taxes and rates on each property, and there was little hope of selling them.

Petrol sales at the garage in Newbury also became virtually non-existent. Owners could hardly afford to drive anywhere, those who had any horses left to them after the war thanked God grass was free, and reduced the amount of oats fed to their animals. Consequently, Megan's days serving at the pumps were long and empty. Robert the apprentice had been let go long since, so she had no one to talk to, and time dragged.

This was unfortunate as it gave her time think, and her thoughts were not optimistic. This is no life, she told herself yet again. Being married was no life.

Disappointment had set in soon after her wedding day. When a man said, 'Will you marry me?', what he really meant, decided Megan, was 'Will you cook and clean for me, and let me have sex as often as I like whether you want to or not, and will you bring up my kid so that I can ignore her most of the time, and go off and do what I like when I like. And will you run the business for me while

I'm gone, free labour, so that I have no worries, and don't even have to pay you a wage.' That was what a man really meant when he proposed. Or at least, it was what Frederick had meant, and she didn't suppose he was the first; he certainly wouldn't be the last.

'Should have left him years ago,' she had told her mother on several occasions. 'But where would I go?'

She instinctively knew she would not be welcome to return to the family home. 'What would I do? How could I earn enough money to support myself and little Irene? Especially now with this Depression. We'd starve.'

So Megan had stayed put, but had grown steadily more resentful by the day. 'You can't leave him,' advised her mother, thinking of what the neighbours would think, and the cousins in America. 'Divorce isn't respectable. You'd be on your own for the rest of your life.' Megan thought that sounded wonderful. If she ever got rid of Frederick, she wouldn't make the same mistake twice.

Late one afternoon, as she was serving her third customer of the day, two men walked across the forecourt towards her. Their brimmed hats were pulled low over their faces, and she instinctively felt they were a little sinister.

'Is Mr Sinclair about, darlin'?' asked the taller of the two, coming closer than she cared for.

'No,' she said sulkily. 'He's gone off to Ascot. Enjoying himself. Come back tomorrow.'

She concentrated on the needle on the petrol pump dial until it reached two gallons; no one filled the tank any more. She took the money and watched as the driver pulled out onto the road, leaving her alone with the two men, now looking around the premises with a proprietary air and stepping into the office where she had just put the meagre takings in the till.

'Only we're the new owners,' said the taller one chattily, who seemed to have appointed himself spokesman. She looked at them. What was he talking about?

'New owners?'

'Yes, but don't worry,' he said with an ostentatious wink. 'You'll keep your job, darlin'. Gorgeous girl like you.'

'I'm Mrs Sinclair,' she said, drawing herself up to her full height, which wasn't very much compared to him. 'The proprietor's wife. You don't understand. He has gone to Ascot for the day. If you wish to speak to him, you'll have to come back tomorrow.'

'It's you that don't understand, Mrs Sinclair,' said the tall one. 'He bet this garage on a horse, dead cert it was – aren't they all? And he lost. So now the garage is ours.'

Megan stared at them, uncomprehending. 'Bet the garage?' she repeated. 'There must be some mistake.'

'Well yes,' he agreed, 'but it was your hubby's mistake. Could we have a look at the accommodation upstairs? After all, it is ours now.'

'No, you can't,' she said rudely, surprised by her own courage. 'It's our home. And I have a young daughter. It's my husband you need to see, and I keep telling you, he won't be home until late. Come back tomorrow.'

Then she added as an afterthought, 'You're welcome to the whole lot of it then. I'm closing the garage now, and I'm going upstairs to pack a suit case. Should have done it years ago.'

The two men sniggered, and to her surprise and relief, slunk away into the gathering dusk.

'Won't be any trouble getting her out then,' said the tall one to the shorter one. 'It's usually the wives that are the difficult ones, but she looked quite grateful.'

By the time Frederick arrived home, he was feeling very foolish, and was wondering how to break the news to his wife. Megan was waiting for him. She had packed a bag, as she had threatened, two bags, in fact. She had also been back down to the office and taken what money there was in the till and the safe. She regretted having been to the bank with the takings just a few days previously. But it was all she was ever likely to get, and that, as far as she was concerned, made it hers.

She had packed for Irene too. Irene was almost a teenager, and not inclined to do anything she was told. 'We've got no option,' Megan had argued back at her when she refused to do it herself. 'You father's lost the garage at Ascot, and we are being turfed out by the new owners.'

'I'm not coming,' said Irene sulkily. And then contradicting herself, asked, 'Where are we going?'

'Back to grandmama's for now,' said Megan, totally at a loss to think where else they might go at such short notice.

Into the midst of this argument, Frederick entered, wondering how to tell his wife the news, unaware that she already knew. All the way home he had been wondering whether to grovel apologetically or act it out with bravado. He glanced across at his wife to see how the land lay, and she spoke first.

'What have you done?' she demanded angrily. 'What have you bloody done?'

'You know?' he said. 'How do you know?'

'Two men came. Said they were the new owners.'

'Oh. Yes.' He didn't know what else to say. Then he noticed the luggage.

'You're leaving?'

'We've all got to leave, Frederick,' she said, as if speaking to a five year old. 'They have given us notice to quit. It's just that I'm leaving you at the same time.'

'You've been wanting to do that for a long time.'

She stared at him. 'You knew?'

'Of course I knew,' he said. 'Known for a long time. It was obvious.'

'Well why didn't you do something about it then?' She felt more hurt than ever.

He shrugged. 'Didn't know what to do,' he said. 'You were happy enough when times were good. Liked the money coming in. Now it's gone . . .'

'It's not just the money,' she said defensively. 'Our home has gone too. And the business. It's all gone. On a horse. On a bleeding horse.'

'Well the business hasn't been making any money for a while. But we still had to pay rates and stuff. So it was a drain on what we had left. Better off without it, Megan.'

'Well you probably think you'll be better off without me and Irene as well,' she said, and picking up the two bags, she walked to the door. 'Come on,' she said over her shoulder to Irene. 'Say goodbye to your father. We're going.'

'I'll miss you,' he said.

'Of course you will,' she said, turning at the door. 'No one to skivvy for you any more. No free labour. No more sex on demand.'

He raised his eyebrows. 'I meant Irene.'

Once they had gone, rattling down the wooden stairs with the bags banging against the bannisters, Frederick sat for sometime, mulling over his options. He knew the new owners would be returning in the morning, so he did not have much time.

He soon realised his best – his only – option was to open up one of the currently empty shops in Reading, and live in the flat above that. Not an ideal arrangement, and what on earth could he sell that would be in demand during a Depression?

He soon had the answer to that too. In a time of make-do-and-mend, surely an ironmongers would be the most practical? People would need screws and nails and seeds for the garden, slug pellets and fertiliser, any amount of things. There was no other ironmongery in Reading as far as he knew, and he could choose between the shop in Broad Street or the one in Station Road, both good sites.

Eventually he stirred himself, and went to pack the very few things he wished to take with him. He checked the till and the safe downstairs, and realised Megan had been there before him. He could not blame her, it was all she was likely to get.

He would rise early and leave before the new owners arrived. He realised he had given little thought to losing the garage. Good riddance, was his immediate reaction. It had not been making money for some months now, yet there had still been crippling business rates to pay, electricity bills, petrol to pay for. It had been a drain on what finances he had left for long enough.

He knew though, that Papa would not see it like that. He also knew he had to go and tell his father what had happened, but he would get the Reading shop up and running first, so that he could give him the good news as well as the bad.

He knew where he could get some stock pretty quickly, and would sort that out in the morning. For now he was tired and went to bed, where he slept right through as though he had not a care in the world.

Chapter 25
1931 – 1932

The next few weeks went well for Frederick. The flat above the shop in Broad Street was spacious, but had been left pretty dirty. He soon found someone to come and clean it for a pittance, placed his few belongings in the cupboards, and quickly felt at home.

He went to see a couple of his contacts, and soon acquired some stock for the shop.

'Take the lot, lad,' said the disenchanted ironmonger in Newbury. 'I hope you do better with it than I have.' So they agreed a deal and Frederick was pleased with his bargain.

He did wish he had purchased a car for himself during the good years at the garage, it would have been handy now. He borrowed one from an old customer instead, who might have refused had he known Frederick was planning to fill it with garden forks and spades, buckets and watering cans, gas mantles and light bulbs, chicken feed and bulging boxes.

He conveyed it all to Broad Street and returned the car, not too much the worse for wear but smelling of paraffin, and looked around with some satisfaction. Once it was all neatly stacked on the shelves, he opened his doors to the public. Trade was slow at first, but soon gathered momentum as word spread of the new ironmonger in town, and his amazingly reasonable prices.

Keeping enough stock became an imperative, and he set out to find other ironmongers who were down on their luck, bought their stock at knock down prices, and they were grateful to be rid of it. But he found it tiring serving in the shop all day and going out and about collecting stock outside shop hours. He soon convinced himself it would be an investment to hire some help, so that he could devote more time to getting out and about and stocking up.

A notice on the door soon produced a small queue of applicants since unemployment was high and getting higher. Despite several qualified and experienced young men, Frederick hired an inexperienced but attractive female, Mrs Hall, and life was looking good again.

With everything in place and going so well, he had no more excuses to avoid visiting his parents. He rode his bicycle up the drive of Brightwell Manor in some trepidation, knowing his news would not please them. He hoped his mother would be at the interview too, she had a knack of calming Papa when all else failed.

Unfortunately Mama was busy elsewhere, unaware that he had come to visit, and his father was not in a good mood. More bad news of his investments had arrived that morning, and things were looking serious.

'You've done *what?*' said Tristram incredulously, and somewhat loudly. Frederick winced.

'Lost the garage, Papa. At Ascot.'

'Oh my God. On a horse.' His heart started tightening in his chest again, and he felt rather unwell.

'Since then, though,' continued Frederick hastily, 'I have set up an ironmongery in one of my empty shops in Reading, and it is doing very well.'

'How long ago did you lose the garage then?' asked Tristram, becoming suspicious.

'Oh, just a few weeks.' It had in fact been six months.

'And you didn't think to come and tell us before now?' His words sounded ominous.

'Well, I've been busy,' said Frederick, which was actually true.

'But that garage was bought with my money!' said Tristram, becoming angry. 'And the pumps and tanks were installed with my money. Granted, it was in your name, but surely to God, I had an interest in it too? At least enough to be told!'

'Well, yes, Papa, I can see that now, but at the time it was just about survival.'

'Whose minding the shop now?' demanded his father.

'I hired some help. She's very conscientious and reliable.'

'She?' said Tristram, picking out the one word Frederick did not wish him to seize upon. 'Where's Megan? And Irene?'

'They've left me,' he said airily. 'But that's fine. I couldn't afford to support them anyway on what the garage was making.'

Tristram looked genuinely baffled. 'So you've lost your garage, your wife and your daughter, and you didn't think to come and tell us until now?'

'Well, to be honest, Papa,' said Frederick, 'I've been putting it off. I didn't think you would be best pleased.'

'I think that is a pretty fair assessment of the situation, Frederick. What has become of them?'

'Who?'

'Your wife and child, man!'

'Oh. I'm not really sure. I think they went back to her mother.'

'You're not sure? You haven't been in touch with them since they went? To see if they are alright?'

'Well, they left me, Father,' said Frederick defensively. 'They haven't come to see if I'm alright either.'

At last Grace heard via the house grapevine that Frederick had come to visit, and hastened to Tristram's study where they had to go through it all again. It hadn't seemed too bad to Frederick before they made so much fuss, but now he was beginning to realise the enormity of it all. They could not be diverted by how well he had managed for himself since, and did not seem particularly pleased by the good news about how well the ironmongery shop was doing.

It was difficult to say who was the most disappointed in the other, and Frederick left as soon as he decently could. He slipped round to the back of the house and noticed the side gardens on the way were not as immaculate as they had been. He went to see what the kitchens had to offer, but Mrs Hatton had retired and the new cook did not know him from Adam. Once introduced, she managed a frosty smile, but she had not been there long, and was very busy. Things took longer when you were new, and didn't know the ropes yet, she told Frederick, hustling him out of her way.

Prudence was still there, quite elderly now, but content with her lot. She was fond of Frederick, and noticing his disappointment that Mrs Hatton had left, told him she had retired and gone to live with her sister by the sea in Broadstairs, Kent. 'I collected a letter from her at the post office only last week,' said Prudence. 'She wrote to say she has met a very nice gentleman called Archibald who seems to be very well off financially. He used to live in Reading himself, so they have a lot in common. She is hoping he is going to propose.'

Frederick listened to her prattle but thought little of it, and asked after Betsy, knowing she at least would be pleased to see him, but it seemed MillyVic had a free period at school that afternoon, and they were going to meet up in Newbury for a cup of tea. At least their jobs were safe, thought Frederick. Even in the Depression, with war clouds gathering, there would always be a need for teachers.

So he took himself off to the stables to see Stebbins, at least he was pleased to see him, but seemed to know immediately that he must be in trouble or he wouldn't be there. Both Mr Boddington and Jeffreys, the groom, had retired but not been replaced, and Stebbins was doing both their jobs, plus a little gamekeeping, as best he could. 'Most of the younger gardeners went off to the war,' he said, 'and none of them came back. Those that did survive wanted other work when they returned. Chedworth, the young lad, is driving one of the new trams. I don't know what has become of him since this Depression began. And there's talk of another war looming.'

'Another war?' said Frederick concerned. 'I hadn't heard that.'

He had been too busy to pay attention to the newspapers, but another war, that was bad news indeed.

'A war would get us out of this Depression,' prophesied Stebbins gloomily. 'People can make a lot of money during a war.'

'Is that so?' asked Frederick, brightening at the prospect.

Things seemed to be in decline at Brightwell as well as everywhere else, and he returned to Reading in a very subdued frame of mind. He couldn't understand why his parents had allowed things to get so bad, it was unlike them. He had not noticed his father's pallor, or that he seemed to have aged since he last saw him.

A few weeks later, soon enough to convince Grace that it was Frederick's fault, and long enough to allow Frederick to convince himself it wasn't, Tristram suffered a major heart attack. The doctor was called, and did what little he could, but it didn't seem to make a lot of difference.

Afterwards Tristram was so tired, he stayed in bed resting most of the day, getting up for a little tea and a walk round the gardens in the afternoons. That did not cheer him, since the gardens were falling into disrepair, the weeds were asserting themselves, and the shrubs were in sad need of pruning. Grace was concerned about him, and more protective than ever. She carefully avoided the subject of Frederick.

One day Tristram said to her, 'I wonder if Hugh might like to pay us a visit sometime soon?'

'I could write and ask him, dearest,' she replied. 'It's a long way to come from New Zealand.'

'I should very much like to see him again,' said Frederick quietly. 'I would like to be reassured that when the time comes, he will return home and claim his birthright. He is the only one capable of running the place as it should be run.'

Grace realised from this that Tristram felt his time was coming, sooner than he would have liked. So she wrote immediately to Hugh, but knew the letter would take some weeks to reach him.

'What ever he decides,' said Tristram, 'don't let Frederick inherit Brightwell.'

Grace smiled at him lovingly. 'I won't, my dear. You have told me that before. Although I can't think Harriet would want it either.'

'Just so long as Frederick doesn't get it. He will only lose it at cards. Or Ascot.'

He fell into a reverie, and Grace could tell from the sadness in his eyes that he was anxious and concerned.

'It would be better to sell the place and let the three of them share the money than allow Frederick to inherit.'

Not long after this conversation, Tristram suffered another massive heart attack and died in her arms. There was no time to call the doctor, and Grace decided there and then they should have one of the new telephones installed.

This time she sent a telegram to Hugh, which was rather expensive, but needs must. 'Papa died yesterday STOP Funeral in one week STOP Do you have a telephone? STOP'

There was no hope of Hugh getting home in time for his father's funeral, and it had to go ahead without him.

He had no telephone either, so Grace, utterly grief stricken, didn't pursue the idea, but continued to function with dignity. She sent word to Frederick's shop in Broad Street, and made it clear she expected him to attend. Harriet and MillyVic were there, Charles and Isabella, very shocked; Grace's brothers, all the staff, and so many neighbours who had thought well of Tristram.

Afterwards there was a funeral tea at Brightwell Manor, and the question on everyone's lips was what would happen to the house now? Grace, elegant in her widow's weeds, managed a smile and said she did not know, they were waiting to hear from Hugh in New Zealand.

In the meantime, Grace contacted their solicitor and discovered the true state of Tristram's financial affairs. It came as a severe shock because he had said nothing to her about it, but his original fortune had become much eroded, partly because of the house and family, but also because several of his investments had disappeared with the Wall Street crash.

There had also been some rather hefty bequests for his brother's children, and for Charles's two, all of whom were now grown up and far better off than she was. Grace was visibly shaken and, knowing how much the upkeep of Brightwell cost, she began to wonder how she would manage. Or more accurately, how Hugh would manage.

Prudence was almost as devastated at Tristram's sudden passing as Grace herself.

'He always told me I would go far!' said Prudence, remembering the first day Mr Sinclair had arrived with Sir Charles Worth in her kitchen, and she had made them tea and served them two slices each of her best fruit cake. That was the day he had given her a golden sovereign. 'But I haven't, have I?'

'No, Prudence,' said Grace with a sad smile. 'You have stayed here and been loyal to the family and served us well. And I hope you will continue to do so.'

Prudence smiled her gratitude at these kind words, and stay she did, but Brightwell never felt quite the same after the master had departed.

Chapter 26 – 1938

The death of his Papa had a more profound effect on Frederick than he had anticipated. It made him realise for the first time that we are all mortal, and that he himself was going to die one day.

This thought hit him quite hard, and he began to think, at the age of 50, that perhaps it was time to settle down and make something constructive of his life. But what?

The Depression continued, but his Ironmongery shop kept busy. He had judged the market well, and people were in need of the most basic things in order to make do and mend. It became more difficult to obtain stock at the right prices, but Frederick had his ways and means.

One of his other shops remained empty, and the third had been let to a bakery. They had installed a bread oven, and told him about it afterwards, but he did not mind. People would always need bread, and as long as the owners continued to pay their rent, that was fine by him.

Mrs Hall had turned out to be one of his better decisions. She went industriously about his business, kept the shop swept and dusted, was popular with the customers, made him cups of tea on a regular basis, and was meticulously honest with the money she handled. She was also surprisingly good company, and he found that he wanted to go out buying stock for the shop less and less, and started asking his suppliers to deliver.

The only thing she complained about was serving paraffin. She did not like going out to the tank in the cold backyard, unscrewing the lid of what ever unsuitable container the customer provided, filling the metal jug up to the correct measure, and pouring it into the receptacle using the freezing metal funnel.

That accomplished she would then remove the funnel, replace the screw top, and carry the now heavy container back into the shop. 'It makes my hands stink,' she said, 'but the customers don't want to wait while I wash them, so I take their money and that ends up stinking of paraffin as well.'

Frederick could see her point of view, and most certainly did not want to upset her, so he produced a pair of heavy duty rubber gloves from stock, and gave them to her.

'There you are,' he said magnanimously. 'They are your personal pair. No one else is allowed to use them. It's a pity you are married.'

She looked up at him in surprise, flustered and blushing.

'In name only,' she said darkly, picked up the rubber gloves and took them out to the paraffin tank to find a suitable hiding place.

Frederick hadn't really meant to say that, but he had been thinking it for sometime, and had not the grace to feel embarrassed in his turn. He fell to wondering what she meant by, 'In name only', and came to the conclusion that hers was a loveless marriage, as his had been.

He had given her the job at the outset, partly because she was attractive, which he knew would go down well with the mostly male customers. But now, more and more, he was noticing just how very attractive she was, and he was finding it distracting.

He watched her as she bent down to find something on a lower shelf. He couldn't help noticing the soft curve of her breast as she reached up for something hanging from one of the hooks in the ceiling.

She must be quite a bit younger than he was, he thought, still fit and supple. She dressed well too. Not in an obvious, common way, but her clothes certainly flattered her shape.

When she returned from hiding her new rubber gloves near the oil tank, she said, 'Would you like a cup of tea, Mr Sinclair?'

'Why don't you call me Frederick?'

So she did, and made him a nice cup of tea into the bargain.

'What's your first name?' he asked as they sipped the brew and ate Rich Tea biscuits that she had put out on a plate. She wasn't the sort to buy broken biscuits or to eat them straight from the bag.

'Winifred,' she smiled shyly. 'But everyone calls me Wyn.'

'Does that mean I can too?'

'I suppose so,' she said.

He decided that was far enough for one day, and to leave it there for now. He didn't want to spook the woman.

Over the next few days, if he was passing behind her standing at the counter, he would accidentally brush against her, and she did not seem to mind. Later he innocently put his hands on her shoulders, just to move her gently out of the way. She giggled.

Next time he took her by the waist, ostensibly to move her along a bit so that he could reach the drawers behind her. She blushed and smiled, but did not object.

On the Wednesday morning they were very busy, but in the afternoon it went quiet, with very few customers coming in at all.

'Everyone seems to have done all their shopping this morning,' he said conversationally. 'Early closing for a lot of them around here.'

'Chance for a bit of a tidy up on those top shelves,' she said, and fetching the wooden step ladder she mounted it and started rearranging the piles of navy overalls and working caps that were kept up there.

Frederick's eyes were on a level with her hips, which swayed gently as she turned one way and then the other.

'Very nice, Winifred,' he said, looking up at her admiringly. 'Very nice indeed.'

He looked lingeringly at her breasts above him, and allowed his gaze to run the length of her, down to her calves, with an occasional glimpse of the back of her bare knees as she reached upwards, and her hemline rose accordingly.

When she had finished the job to her own satisfaction, she began to descend the ladder, one step at a time.

'Don't you fall now,' he said, stepping forward. 'Let me help you.'

They both knew she did not need his help, but she let him take her hand anyway, and on reaching the floor, turned to face him so that his free arm slipped easily around her waist. When she did not seem to mind that either, Frederick realised she was as ready for a cuddle as he was.

Nonchalantly adjusting the straps of her brassiere, she said, 'Can I make you another cup of tea, Frederick?'

'That would be very nice, Wyn. Thank you. It's very quiet in here this afternoon, we might as well shut up shop and have it upstairs in my flat. What do you think?'

'An excellent suggestion, Frederick,' she said, and waiting while he shot the bolts on the front door, turned the Open sign around to read Closed, and switched off the shop lights, she made sure she walked upstairs in front of him.

He followed very closely and checked his clothing, smoothing his trousers as best he could but to no avail. As they entered the flat, and he closed the landing door behind him, she made no attempt to move on to the kitchen, or to put the kettle on.

She stood quietly, waiting to see what he would do next, and smiled a coy smile right into his eyes. Frederick needed no further invitation and, drawing her into his arms, kissed her on the lips. She leaned against him and responded hungrily, slipping her arms inside his jacket and around his waist.

Frederick could not believe his good fortune. She seemed so proper when she was in the shop, but now . . . He pulled back from her a little and said politely, 'Would you like to see my bedroom, Wyn?'

'Frederick,' she replied, 'I have been wanting to see your bedroom for some time.'

After that occasion, when ever it was quiet in the afternoons, they would shoot the bolt on the front door, turn the Open sign to Closed, and slip upstairs together. Frederick was in heaven. If only Megan had been as interested in him as this, he would never have let her go. He even feared he was falling in love with Wyn, so accommodating and adventurous was she. All his dreams and fantasies were being realised at once. He had no idea a woman could enjoy it all as much as he did, and as frequently too. They were the perfect match.

Afterwards she would put on her clothes and hurry away to get home and cook her husband's tea. Frederick found himself wishing she would stay and cook his tea. And his breakfast.

Then, one day, she came in to the shop and seemed different. She was quiet and thoughtful for most of the morning, and he asked her several times – between customers – if anything was the matter. More customers kept coming in and interrupting their conversation, but by lunchtime he could stand it no longer. He shot the bolt, turned the sign, and announced, 'Winifred, we are closing for lunch. Come upstairs and talk to me for God's sake.'

Upstairs he put the kettle on and made her a cup of tea, which was a first. He sat down on the other side of the kitchen table and possessed himself of her hand. 'Right,' he said, 'What's happened?'

'You're not going to like it,' she said.

'No, it doesn't look as if I will,' he agreed. 'Has your husband found out about us?'

'Not yet, but he will shortly.'

'How?' said Frederick, slowly and with growing suspicion. Without further preamble she said,

'I think I must be pregnant.'

'Oh. Great.'

'You don't mean that.'

'Well, no. Not exactly. But it could be great.' She raised her eyebrows. 'You're sure it's mine?'

'Yes, definitely.'

'You don't think he might just assume it's his?'

'I very much doubt it,' she said. 'We haven't been together like that for years. He hasn't been up to it lately.'

Then Frederick heard himself saying, 'Why not leave him and come and live with me?' There was more. 'We could have the baby here. Look after it between us. It would be fine.'

Winifred was surprised and touched by his response. She had been braced for anger, outrage, blame. And here he was, pleased.

'I've got four other kids,' she confessed.

Frederick blinked. 'Four? How old?'

'Fifteen. Sixteen. Thirteen. Eleven.'

'Old enough to leave then.'

'Not really. Not the eleven-year-old.'

He realised then how little he knew about her. She had a whole life away from the shop and it had not occurred to him. But he didn't want to lose her now. Or the baby.

'If it's definitely mine . . .' he started.

'It is. No doubt.'

'Well, if I'm the father, then don't I get a say? I don't want you to do anything rash.'

'Get rid of it?' she said sharply. 'No, I won't do that. I promise.'

Relieved, he took her other hand as well. 'If you were a free woman, Wyn,' he said, 'I'd ask you to marry me. Here and now.'

'If I was a free woman,' she smiled, 'I'd say yes.'

He sighed. 'What do you want to do then?' he asked. 'What's the answer?'

'I don't know at the moment. I won't get rid of it, that's for sure.'

He nodded, reassured.

'It won't show for a while,' she continued. 'He won't notice for ages. So we have a bit of time.'

Frederick nodded again. 'No pressure.'

He sensed that was what she needed. Time to think it through without pressure. She obviously wasn't in a hurry to leave her husband. Or more accurately her children.

'Is it still safe to . . .' he glanced in the direction of the bedroom door and she smiled.

'Oh yes,' she said. 'Perfectly safe,' and they rose from their chairs with one accord, and headed for the bedroom.

Afterwards she dressed quickly, ready to go home and cook the family tea. 'I can carry on working,' she said, buttoning up her coat. 'For ages yet.'

'Thank God for that,' he said. 'But no heavy lifting.'

'No, OK,' she said. 'No more paraffin!' and he laughed, happy not to have the last word for once.

Chapter 27 – 1939

The next few months were happy ones for Frederick and Wyn. He watched her little bump grow bigger, and caressed it lovingly after they had made love, and were lying naked together on his bed. He felt like a different person, contented and free, allowed to be himself at last. He had never felt like that with Megan.

Then one day she said, 'He's noticed.'

Frederick looked at her anxiously. She continued.

'He said, 'Are you putting on weight, Wyn?' and I said, 'No, Harry, I'm pregnant."'

Harry. He hadn't known that was his name. It made him seem real for the first time.

'What did he say to that?'

'Not much. He realises it can't be his. We haven't been together like that for years. He's thinking about it.'

A few days later, as they again lay on the bed together, happy and spent, she said, 'We've made a deal.' Frederick was listening.

'He says I can stay,' she said. 'And I can have the baby in hospital, but I can't bring it home.'

'Well I don't want you to take it back there either,' said Frederick. 'I want you to stay here with me, and we'll look after the baby together.'

'I'd like that too, Frederick,' she said, 'but I can't leave my other kids.'

He knew she couldn't bring them with her.

'He knows it's my boss,' she continued. 'The Dad.'

'He's not going to come round and beat me up, is he?' asked Frederick, only half joking.

She smiled. 'No. He isn't up to beating anyone up these days. He understands. He knows he's not capable any more. Hasn't been for a while. Years. He accepts what's happened, but he doesn't want me to leave him. Or the kids. But at the same time, we can't expect him to bring up someone else's baby.'

Frederick did not know how they were going to manage, and had nothing to suggest.

'Hell of a time to come into this world,' he said, speaking to the bump rather than to her. 'They are saying there's going to be another war soon.'

'Yes,' she said. 'I heard that. Probably won't happen.'

A thought occurred to him. 'Surely you'll have to have the baby with you for the first few months?' he mused. 'So that you can feed it yourself?'

'I told him that,' she replied. 'And he said, just for a while then. People will assume it's his, and think nothing of it. But he doesn't see why he should bring it up full time.'

'I don't want him to,' said Frederick. 'I want to do that. If it's money . . .? I can pay its way. No problem with that.'

'Alright,' she said. 'That might help. I'll tell him.'

She carried on working as long as she could. Despite no longer having to serve paraffin, when it became difficult for her to bend over, and too uncomfortable to stand all day, she had to give in gracefully and stayed at home. He missed her a great deal, and wondered constantly how she was getting on without him to look after her. She came to see him when she could, but it was quite a walk, and she promised to get word to him when she went into labour.

The baby slipped quietly into the world on 2nd April 1939. He was born in the hospital because the doctor said Winifred was an older mother. 'I told him I'm a natural,' she said to Frederick indignantly. 'Like shelling peas, I said. But he wouldn't have it. Said he knew best. I ask you.'

One afternoon a young lad came panting into the shop. 'Ma said to tell you,' he puffed. 'Baby's on its way. She's just gone to the hospital now.'

'Thank you!' said Frederick, and gave him a sixpence. It occurred to him later, the lad was obviously one of her sons. He hoped the sixpence would not cause offence, but the young lad was not in the least offended, and refrained from telling his Pa just in case he took it off him.

She had warned him these things could take a while,

so not to come straight away. He waited impatiently until closing time, which fortunately coincided with visiting hours. Grabbing his hat, Frederick turned the Open sign round to read Closed, switched off the lights and slammed the shop door shut behind him. He had checked in advance, and could take a tram that dropped him off right outside the hospital.

'Mrs Hall,' he said to the young nurse manning the desk at the entrance to the Maternity Ward.

'Are you Mr Hall?' she said.

'No, but I am the father.'

'Sorry,' said the nurse, losing interest. 'Husbands only,' and she turned away. Frederick was incensed. 'But it's my baby she's having!' he called after her departing back. Then he realised that left no one on the desk, and entered the ward anyway. He looked the length of the rows of beds on each side, and saw her half way down. She was asleep, but there was no one with her except the baby beside her bed in a little crib. He walked the length of the ward and stopped at the foot of her bed, holding the brim of his hat in his hands, regretting not having thought to bring her something. Flowers, perhaps.

She opened her eyes and smiled. 'How are you?' he said.

'Fine,' she said, heaving herself into a sitting position. 'Told you. Like shelling peas. Come and see your son.'

Frederick walked to the crib and beamed down at the little face. His son. 'We haven't thought of a name yet,' he said. All that time together, all that talking, and they hadn't thought of a name.

'We'll get to know him a bit first,' she said. 'No hurry.'

'You choose his first name,' he said, 'and I'll choose his middle name. Frederick. After me.'

She smiled but said, 'You can call him what you like,' and slipping out of bed, picked up the unnamed baby in her arms and handed him to his father. Frederick was surprised and received him gingerly, but could not hide his delight. He hadn't been allowed to hold Irene at all, and here he was, cradling his son who was not yet two hours old.

He assumed the little chap was asleep, and was surprised the movement had not disturbed him. But then the baby opened his eyes and appeared to be looking accusingly into his father's face, as if he knew something Frederick didn't.

'You're probably a bit of a blur to him,' said Wyn. 'They don't focus for a few days. Or is it weeks? I'm not sure,' she ended vaguely, and slipped back into bed. Frederick didn't care. He was mesmerised. Then the baby gave a gusty little sigh, closed his eyes and went back to sleep. Frederick sat stock still and held him safe, not speaking, until the bell rang and visiting time was over. Reluctantly he put his son back in the hospital crib.

'When will you be coming out?' asked Frederick diffidently.

'Maybe tomorrow,' she answered. 'No reason to stay. I'm fine.'

'Only it's easier to visit you in here. I don't suppose I'd be welcome at your house?'

'No,' she said. 'Probably not. I'll send you word, and I'll bring him to see you in the shop as soon as I can. I can't come back to work yet . . .'

'No, indeed,' he said hastily. 'Of course not. I'll just hope to see you as soon as you can come.'

Next day the same young lad appeared in the shop. 'Ma said to tell you she's home. But not to visit her there. She'll come as soon as she can.' Then he waited.

Frederick nodded and thanked him, and realised he was waiting for another sixpence. He fished in his pocket and paid up.

Now that the baby was actually here, Frederick realised they had made no real plans as to how to cope with him. He was grateful that Harry was prepared to allow the baby to stay while Wyn was breast feeding, but had thought little further than that. He didn't even know how long that was likely to continue, or how soon they would need to make some decisions. He smiled to himself. Decisions implied you had choices.

After an endless week, one day as the door opened and the bell went ding, he looked up to see Wyn coming in the door with his son in an elderly and battered perambulator. It had obviously seen good service and had

had a hard life, but she had cleaned it as best she could, and the bed linen inside was freshly washed and ironed.

'Here's your Daddy!' she said to the pram, and big blue eyes turned as Frederick took his little hand, and the fingers clasped around his thumb. Frederick beamed.

'He doesn't cry much, does he?'

'No, fortunately, he doesn't. They commented on that in the hospital. Quiet little fellow, but nothing wrong at all.'

'Oh he's laid back like me,' said Frederick, wondering if he might be allowed to pick him up. But she did not offer, and soon took her leave. 'Come again when you can,' he said. 'I miss you.'

'In case you need to know,' she said, 'I'll probably be able to come back to work in a month or so.'

'It'll be good to have you back, but you'll have to take it gently to start with. I can help you.'

'I was wondering . . .' she began, but hesitated.

'What were you wondering?' he said tenderly, surprised at the amount of love he felt inside for the pair of them.

'Would it be alright to bring him in the pram and keep him here during the day? I can feed him then . . .'

'Of course!' said Frederick, horrified that she might have even considered leaving him at home with her husband. 'I always assumed you would. We can take it in turns to look after him. I'd love that.'

Once she had gone, the shop seemed lonely. Customers drifted in and out, sales continued to be more than satisfactory. But she was as good as her word and was back in the shop after just over three weeks. He was amazed by how strong she was, tough even, and nothing seemed to faze her. She fed the baby in the sitting room behind the shop, changed his nappy (that was decidedly not Frederick's department) and life continued pretty much as it had previously. For a while she didn't particularly want to come upstairs after closing time, saying she didn't have the energy while she was feeding, but he understood and was more interested in watching his son develop and begin to take notice.

Later that year, on the 3rd September, war was declared. Having been preoccupied with the shop and the baby, now named Aubrey Frederick, this caught Frederick by surprise. He had not been keeping up to date with the news, and when the sombre announcement was made that day, Wyn immediately decided their son should not remain in Reading any longer than was strictly necessary.

Nothing seemed to happen for sometime, but even so, Wyn told him again how she felt. 'He'll have to go soon anyway,' she said in a matter of fact voice. 'Harry keeps asking how much longer I'm going to have to feed him. He's getting a bit fed up. But where will he go?'

Even though he had no idea, Frederick was reassuring. 'We'll think of something,' he said. 'Don't worry.'

Wyn was in the back sitting room feeding Aubrey one morning when the door opened, the bell went ding, and Frederick had the surprise of his life when Megan walked in carrying a large envelope.

'Don't panic!' she called, 'I haven't come back to you.'

'It's been a while,' he said.

'Yes. I haven't missed you though,' she said sweetly. 'Have you missed me?'

He ignored that and merely said, 'How's Irene?'

'Oh well done,' she said, without the sweetness this time. 'You remembered you have a daughter. She's fine. Doesn't miss you either.'

'That's alright then. So to what do I owe the pleasure of this visit?'

'I've brought you some divorce papers to sign,' she said. 'That's all. With this war gearing up, I thought we ought to get things sorted.'

'Oh, I don't know about that,' he said, pretending to sound wary and worried. He was merely taking refuge in humour, but as usual it fell wide of its mark with Megan, who thought he was being serious. It seemed she had gone ahead arranging the divorce in much the same way as she had arranged the wedding, with very little reference to him.

'I'm divorcing you on the grounds of cruelty,' she explained kindly.

'Cruelty?' he repeated. 'I wasn't cruel to you. Or Irene.'

'No, I know,' she said chattily. 'But there's nothing else

to describe it really. Losing our home and business at the racetrack wasn't exactly kind, was it? Plus the fact that you haven't paid me a penny towards Irene's keep. We could have starved for all you cared.'

'Well when you left,' said Frederick, quite stung, 'you said you were going back to your parents, and that you'd be better off with them than you were with me.'

'That is true,' she admitted, 'but Pater doesn't see why he should pay to bring up your daughter.'

'Nor do I,' said Frederick, which caused his wife some surprise. 'But you didn't make contact, and you didn't ask for a contribution. How much would you like?'

'Blimey,' said Megan. 'You've changed.'

'Yes,' said Frederick. 'I have. But I was always fair and decent to you. What else do these Divorce papers claim?'

She handed over the large envelope, and said, 'I've been told I have to leave it with you for 21 days so that you can read it through and think about it. Money is very tight, Frederick. I have taken a job.'

'What are you doing?'

'Only looking after someone's children. Evacuees from London. Two little boys. But it doesn't pay much.'

'Well, I've already said how much would you like.'

She looked around. 'Business good is it?'

'Can't grumble.'

It was unfortunate that Winifred chose that moment to come back into the shop with Aubrey, and wheeled the perambulator in from the sitting room beyond. He couldn't decide which of them was the most surprised, and was left no option but to introduce them.

'This is my shop assistant, Winifred,' he said to Megan, adding unnecessarily, 'She's just had a baby.' Then he turned to Winifred and said, 'This is my, er, ex-wife-to-be, Megan. She's come round with the divorce papers.'

Both women looked suspiciously at each other, but Megan couldn't resist walking over to the perambulator and taking a peep. 'He's lovely,' she cooed, which mollified Winifred. But when Megan stood up she looked across at Frederick and said accusingly, 'He's obviously yours. He's just like you.'

'Is he?' said Frederick, absolutely amazed, and certainly pleased, and looked into the perambulator. He couldn't see the likeness himself, but Wyn assured him men never could. And it was then that Frederick suddenly had a brilliant idea.

Turning back to Megan, he said, 'Winifred and I . . . that is, we, are looking for somewhere for Aubrey to be evacuated.' Winifred looked at him with raised eyebrows and dawning respect. 'We don't want him to stay here in Reading. The bombing hasn't reached here yet, but London has had it bad, and I read that they've had it in Liverpool. And Portsmouth.'

'Yes, but they're ports,' said Megan, ever practical. 'Big ports. The Germans would want them out of action.'

'That's true,' countered Frederick, 'but Reading has its railways, and an aerodrome over near Woodley too. They are worried that Reading is probably on their list.'

'He's a bit young to be an evacuee,' she objected.

'Yes,' agreed Winifred, with some spirit. 'And he's too young to die as well.'

It was Frederick's turn to look at her with approval.

'Maidenhead is too small to have to worry about bombing,' said Frederick, warming to his theme. 'Plus the fact that you are well out in the countryside, on the banks of the Thames.'

Wyn liked the idea of her son going to live on the banks of the Thames in a grand house.

'And it's not as if it's for that long,' he added. 'It's not permanent. He can't come until Wyn's finished breast feeding, and we'd want him back as soon as the war is over, and it's safe again.'

Megan looked from one to the other of them. And then back at the perambulator.

'He'd be no trouble,' said Wyn. 'He hardly ever cries. They commented on that in the hospital.'

Megan was weakening. She was tied with the evacuees she had already. What difference would an extra one make? It would help with the money too.

'Well, it is quite expensive,' she said.

'You just said it didn't pay much,' said Frederick.

'Not in wages, no, it doesn't. But you have to pay for

his food on top. Electricity. Other staff. Things like that.'

'Well, he doesn't eat a lot, that's for sure,' said Frederick. 'How much?' he added, thinking he would pay anything to solve the problem, and keep his son safe but not too far away. Megan named a figure. 'Plus you have to sign the divorce papers.'

Frederick had not even considered refusing to sign. 'Alright,' he said, 'I'll do that, and I can afford the fees, as long as it doesn't go up any more. Are we allowed to come and visit him sometimes?'

'Well, yes,' agreed Megan doubtfully. 'But apparently it unsettles them a bit.'

Wyn nodded at Frederick to show she was happy with the arrangement, nay, relieved.

'Shall I let you know when he's ready to come? When Wyn finishes breast feeding?'

'Alright,' said Megan. 'I could come and collect him.'

'No, we'll bring him over. That way Wyn can see where her baby is going to be looked after.' As a further incentive, he added, 'And I'll bring the Divorce papers. Signed.'

Megan nodded and left, hoping mater and pater wouldn't mind another child to deal with. Plus nappies to wash. She hadn't thought of that.

Chapter 28
1938 – 1940

Hugh read the telegram with dismay, devastated to think he would not see his Papa again. His wife, Olivia, had of course not met her parents-in-law, but she felt his grief and tried to comfort him.

'Brightwell is mine now,' he tried to explain to her. 'In England, property goes to the eldest son. I should go back and help Mama. She will be beyond comforting, I know it. They were so close, and loved each other very much.'

After a few more days of thought, when Olivia felt he was far away and she could not reach him, he said, 'How would you feel about going to live in England? With the children, obviously.'

By this time they had three children; two boys, William and George, and a girl in between, Emily.

Olivia looked at him in dismay, and Hugh realised it would be a piece of work to persuade her.

'Our lives are here, surely?' she replied.

'Yes, indeed,' he agreed, 'but before I came to New Zealand, I had a whole life in England. Brightwell is a lovely old manor house, and the fields – nothing on the scale we have here, of course – but green fields, where we could have not only sheep, but cattle too. And ponies for the children. And servants. Well, not servants nowadays. Staff. There are staff to take care of things, a cook, and maids, and a housekeeper. We could hire a Nanny too, if you would like that?'

'The children are getting a little too big for a Nanny,' said Olivia, who could not comprehend allowing someone else to bring up her children. But she liked the idea of a cook and maids and a housekeeper. That sounded very good indeed!

'The thing is,' he continued, trying to make her understand a system totally alien to her. 'The thing is, as the eldest son, I inherit all of it. Papa called it my birthright. My inheritance. My brother, Jack, died in the war, and my other brother, Frederick, is too ramshackle to have any part of it. Mama says it was Papa's dying wish that Frederick should not inherit, he would only lose it at cards, or on the horses. Or dogs.'

After a lot of thought and discussion to the exclusion of all else, Olivia came to see that Hugh wanted to return home more than he realised it himself. His descriptions of home became more appealing, and he grew steadily more homesick. In the end, she agreed they should go, and Hugh was touched and grateful for her understanding.

'Are you sure?' he said.

'No,' she laughed. 'How can I be sure when I have

never been there? But we will see. I am sure everything will be alright. It is right for our children to see their birthright too.'

Hugh took his wife's agreement to mean they should sell up their land and flocks in New Zealand, and return to England permanently. She was shocked by this initially, but when she saw his surprise that she might think otherwise, she went along with his wishes.

By the time he had found a buyer, and put his affairs in order, another year had passed. He booked tickets on the next ship departing for England, and wrote to his Mama to let her know they were on their way. It meant some weeks at sea, and of course there were risks; Olivia began to regret leaving her homeland as soon as they embarked. The seas were rougher than anticipated for the time of year, and she dare not let the children out of her sight for a moment lest they disappear overboard.

It was a bad introduction to a new life despite Hugh's efforts to keep everyone cheerful, including himself. Olivia was quite traumatised, and the children took their example from her. Eventually, however, after too long at sea, which was rough and inhospitable, they docked in Southampton. Hugh booked the best nearby hotel he could find for a few days in order to allow his family to recover, but the weather had turned inclement. It was colder than they were accustomed to, and the leaden skies did nothing to lift their spirits.

He let his Mama know they had at last reached England, and were recovering for a few days before coming on to Brightwell. Grace went into a flurry of preparation, glad to have something to think about other than the loss of her beloved husband and, with the housekeeper, a now elderly Mrs Nesbit, prepared bedchambers for the new arrivals, stocked up on the best foods she could find, and had the house cleaned from top to bottom in anticipation.

The family took a train from Southampton to London, then Paddington to Reading, and hired a taxi for the rest of the journey. They had a few bags for their immediate needs, and the rest of their luggage was to follow, no one knew quite when. As they came up the drive, Nesbit saw them approach, and sent word to Mrs Sinclair, so that she was there to welcome them.

It was a momentous occasion for Grace, and for Hugh, who hugged his mother in both joy and consolation for their loss, but Olivia and the children were considerably daunted by how very old everyone seemed, and how large and dominating the house appeared to be. The enormous rooms were distinctly chilly, and the now darkened wainscoting and windows obscured by fine tapestries to shut out the drafts, were utterly overwhelming.

Grace was thrilled to meet her daughter-in-law and her only grandchildren, and was solemnly introduced first to Olivia, and then to William, Emily and George.

'How was your journey?' asked Grace. 'Was it exciting to travel on a big ship?'

'Not really,' said Emily, honest to a fault. 'The sea was quite rough and we were all very seasick.'

At last, when the exclamations were over and their hand luggage had been taken away by an elderly footman, Grace said, 'You must be hungry! What about some tea?'

So they went into the dining room and, over the business of tea being served, and the children trying foods they have never seen before, Olivia watched in dismay. The house was cold; there was no sun to warm them, and it had not occurred to Grace that, even though it was summer, they might have liked a fire, so the grate glared back at them, black and empty.

'We will need to go shopping for more clothes,' said Olivia, smiling sweetly at her Mama-in-law, making an effort to be friendly and polite. 'Even when ours arrive, they will probably not be warm enough.'

Grace was dismayed that she had not thought of the difference in temperatures, indeed, had not known, and immediately asked Mrs Nesbit to put more blankets on the beds. The bathroom that had so impressed her as a young bride was now very dated, and hardly up to the task of producing hot water for a family of five.

'We had to wash in cold water!' announced Emily scathingly as they came down to breakfast one morning. Grace glanced guiltily at Hugh, who looked in exasperation at his daughter, and tried to change the subject.

Everyone was very careful to avoid mentioning the possibility of a second war. Hugh contacted a few friends from college days who could scarcely remember him. Olivia took pleasure in riding one of the few horses that remained in the stables, and the children discovered one of Frederick's old bicycles stored there. It was too big for them and they tried to ride it with painful results. Hugh attempted to teach them, but as he had never ridden a bicycle himself either, his efforts were not a success.

On market day, Hugh went off to see what was for sale, but was not tempted to buy stock this early in their tenure. Olivia was happy with the availability of staff, and enjoyed having meals served without any effort on her part. It was wonderful that their clothes were washed for them too, as that would have been a Herculean task for her, waiting for the old copper to heat the water, and the antiquated equipment available. But with everything done for them, she quickly became bored with too much time on her hands.

As the long summer holidays ended and a new term began, the children were taken to the village school, but it was all very different to the way they had been taught at home, and their knowledge and abilities were somewhat in advance of the local children. This led to the boys feeling bored too, so that they no longer enjoyed their lessons. Emily adjusted better than they did, and once she had made a couple of new friends, even began to enjoy it. Most of the other children saw the newcomers as being different, particularly the boys, and were not very friendly towards them.

Despite these early warnings, Hugh soon went ahead and bought a good-sized flock of sheep, rather too large for the land available to them, and a herd of fine beef cattle. He tried to get the children interested in hens and ducks and geese, but they had not had them in New Zealand, and they were rather nervous of their noise and inclination to peck if they went too close.

'Give them time,' advised Grace, when Hugh expressed concern about his family not settling. 'This is such a wonderful home for a growing family, I am sure they will grow to love it soon enough.'

But her optimism was misplaced, and it became evident that this was becoming more and more unlikely every day. Olivia felt exasperated with her husband for bringing them to such a place, and he was hurt and surprised because their sheep farm in New Zealand had been far bigger, and far more remote. 'But that was normal there,' argued Olivia. 'And warm! It's so wretchedly cold here. And damp. And this is in the summer! What is it going to be like in the winter? We will all expire of hypothermia.'

Grace began to despair.

'It's never going to work out,' she confided to Betsy, who missed Tristram almost as much as she did herself, and had been trying desperately to help make things work. 'They just aren't happy here.'

Then came the news that everyone had been dreading, and war was declared. It was 1939 and the family had been there almost a year. Olivia was horrified to think that it would be even more unsafe to return home by sea with a major war breaking out over her head, and relapsed into depression. Hugh was anxious and desperate and sought refuge with the animals, which took up much of his time during the day.

'Will there be bombs, Grandmama?' asked William and George with relish. 'Someone at school said the Germans have aeroplanes in this war, and that they would be dropping bombs on us.'

'Not out here in the countryside,' said Grace stoically. 'Only in the big cities and towns, where there are lots of buildings. And people. Those Germans had better watch out,' she added. 'England has aeroplanes and bombs too.' Even to her own ears, this did not sound in the least reassuring.

For this second war, instead of asking for volunteers as they had in the first war, men were being called up, and it was compulsory to go. Fortunately Hugh was well above the age that they were currently recruiting, but there was the worry that if the war dragged on, they would call on older men too. Even women were signing up, and going off to war. Those that stayed at home did war work, which Olivia refused to join in on the grounds that it was not her responsibility since she was a New Zealander, and not English.

Then, in 1940 there came a telegram from the War Office to say that Brightwell Manor was to be requisitioned, shortly followed by two officers who came to inspect the property, and to see if it would lend itself to additional security. It was not large enough to be used as a hospital, but because it was relatively remote from any village or town, it was seen to be ideal in other ways. Being relatively convenient to London, some of the war's leaders could gather there and hold their Councils of War in private.

The officers also visited the outbuildings including the wonderful barn, the cellars and attics, and decided that some of the more precious artefacts from the country's museums, galleries and cathedrals could be stored there. England had many valuable artworks to be protected, and some very fine stained glass windows, carefully dismantled and numbered, to be reinstated when the war was over.

All this meant a need for the highest security, and the family was at first told they would have to vacate the premises entirely. When Grace protested, forcefully and vociferously, that she had lived there all her married life, and that furthermore, her son and his family had only recently come all the way from New Zealand in order to inherit on the recent loss of her husband, the army officers tried to be accommodating and said they could remain but would have to live in the cottages on the estate. Even this was only permitted because they fronted onto the lane, and could therefore be accessed independently, without the residents having to intrude on the rest of the property.

In theory, this was not as unreasonable as it sounded, since Betsy lived in one of the cottages, Nesbit and his wife in another; Stebbins, Lilly and their children occupied a third; and Prudence had the fourth. The other two were currently empty. Grace could readily understand Hugh's outrage, and Olivia's bewilderment, at being demoted from the grand house to what was little more than servants' accommodation, and very outdated at that.

She mustered her courage and such staff as were left to her, and set about preparing the remaining two cottages for human habitation. How ever hard they dusted and scrubbed and polished, they could not make them any larger, and Olivia was determined not to have her children sleeping in the same room as Hugh and herself. Despite Grace's efforts, and shining example of dignity in defeat, in practice it was untenable.

After one particularly sleepless night, when Grace could hear her son and his wife arguing, which had never happened in all their years together in New Zealand,

Hugh came to her and said, 'I am sorry, Mama, but we are going to return home. To New Zealand.'

'But how can you?' said Grace aghast. 'Travel by ship is hardly safe at the moment. Apart from rough seas and poor weather at this time of year, there is the danger of aircraft overhead, or being torpedoed from below. They apparently have ships that sail under the water – submarines! You cannot possibly take to the high seas in the midst of a war.'

'Well nothing much has happened yet,' he replied. 'It's been months and they are calling it the Phoney War. I think it's all going to fizzle out and come to nothing.'

'But what if it doesn't?' asked Grace quietly, and knew that what ever she said it would not change his mind.

Hugh was adamant, and took comfort from the claims of the cruise lines that passenger ships were safe, and that only battleships and warships would be legitimate prey; cruise ships with civilians on board would never be a target. Grace did not believe this, and was beside herself with worry that passenger ships would be as vulnerable as any other.

Hugh remained intransigent. 'I am sorry, Mama,' he said, 'but the first war was looming when I went to New Zealand, and I survived. You must understand, I simply have to do what is best for my wife and children.'

'But how can taking them to sea in the middle of a war be for the best?' asked Grace distraught, remembering

Jack dying a hero's death in the Battle of Jutland.

'That is the cruise line's responsibility, and I have to put my trust in them. You are welcome to come with us if you would like to,' he added as an afterthought. 'Olivia is more relaxed at home, and will be far easier to get along with. I have never seen her like this. And that probably goes for the children too. I should never have brought them.'

'How can I leave Brightwell?' countered Grace sadly.

'What is there to stay for?' he demanded. 'You've already left Brightwell! The Army has seen to that. If you get it back at the end of the war, and that is a big If, it will not be in the condition it is now. And you are living in what is little more than a hovel!' he added, as if that decided everything. 'How can you live in such conditions after what you have been accustomed to?'

'But your Papa is buried in the churchyard nearby. And what of all the animals you've just bought? And the staff? How can I leave them?'

'Mama, I'm sorry if this is harsh, but Papa is dead. The animals can be sold, or the Army can take care of them, they will be glad of fresh cows' milk at least. Eggs too. And the staff are all in the process of leaving you! The younger ones are being called up, and the older ones are nearing retirement. And well beyond it in some cases!'

Part of her dilemma lay in the fact that if she left for New Zealand she would never see her other children or friends, but if she remained in England, she would never see her only grandchildren again. So there was joy and sadness in equal measure which ever side of the world she chose.

'You forget, Hugh, your sister Harriet is working at the school not far from here. And then there is Frederick . . .' Her voice faltered at the mention of Frederick, and Hugh looked at her witheringly.

'I would have thought leaving Frederick behind would be an incentive to sail for New Zealand on the first possible vessel!'

Despite herself, she laughed, but she was torn by indecision.

'Whether I stay or come with you,' she said, 'what will become of Brightwell Manor when I die?'

'If the Army returns Brightwell to you at the end of the war,' replied Hugh, 'whenever that might be, it will need a great deal of repair and restoration. It won't be your home as you know it. But then it can be sold, and the money divided between the three of us.'

'You, Harriet and Frederick?'

'Yes, Mama.'

'That is what your Papa suggested. Would you do that? Make sure they each had a third share of the proceeds?'

'Yes, Mama,' said Hugh again. 'Even Frederick.'

Chapter 29 – 1940

Grace agonised for days over whether to accompany them or not. She realised Hugh's invitation had been an afterthought, and her pride suggested she should not go. On the other hand, she was worried about what would happen to her if she remained. She was now 80 years old, and although she was healthy and strong, she knew she would not live for ever. If she began to need help in the future, she could not rely on Frederick, God forbid, and Harriet had a very responsible job. She could not be expected to spend her valuable time caring for an ailing Mama.

She asked Betsy if she would consider coming to New Zealand with her, even though she knew what the answer would be. 'Oh, Mrs Sinclair, you are so lucky, I would love to come with you, but I cannot leave Millicent Victoria. She is all I have in the world. I cannot leave.'

'But will you be alright here on your own?' argued Grace, thinking the same considerations applied to her too.

'Well, I won't really be on my own, will I?' countered Betsy. 'We're all friends in these cottages, and have known each other since for ever. Plus with the Army here, and all this security to protect us, we are even safer than before.'

Grace did not try to persuade her further. It was different for Betsy; she had lived in her cottage for a long time, whereas it was a massive change for Grace who had been accustomed to the spaciousness of the big house and staff to do her bidding.

Grace even sought Frederick's opinion. She wrote him a letter which he finally picked up when he remembered to check at the post office, asking him to come and visit as there was something she wished to discuss with him. He was horrified to find the Army ensconced in the house and his mother living in one of the servants' cottages.

Fortunately Hugh was out in the fields checking the sheep when he arrived, but Frederick was introduced to Olivia, and to the children when they returned home from school. Although Emily was a little shy of him, William and George thought Frederick great fun, and liked him on the spot. He soon taught them to ride the bicycle, much to Hugh's chagrin when he found out. He even showed them how to ride it towards the hissing geese, sending them squawking in all directions, which delighted Emily and she thawed towards her big handsome uncle.

Before his visit, Frederick was worried that Mama had somehow found out about his new baby, so he was relieved to discover that all she wanted to discuss was whether she should stay in England, or accompany Hugh and his family back to New Zealand. As it happened, it would suit Frederick very well to have his Mama on the other side of the world, thus running no risk of her finding out about his son. Admittedly Aubrey was now safely out of the way in Maidenhead as an evacuee, but what would happen when the war ended, all the evacuees returned home again, and one of them popped up calling her Grandmama?

To be honest, Frederick was quite amazed that anyone should ask his opinion, and he wasn't quite sure what to say. 'Well, what do you feel is best for you, Mama? If you get there at all, New Zealand would be safer. They aren't in this war, are they?'

'Not yet,' said Grace doubtfully, and did not find his words in the least comforting. But his visit did have one good outcome, in that it reminded Grace of the Title Deeds to the house. When Frederick had left and Hugh returned from the fields, she said, 'You must make sure you take the Title Deeds to the house with you when you go, Hugh.'

'Wouldn't they be safer here?' he said in surprise. 'What if they go down with the ship?'

'My dear Hugh!' she said in remonstration. 'I wish you would not joke about such things. Frederick said something similar. It is not in the least funny.'

'Sorry, Mama,' said Hugh, grinning at his wife and children, who had found it amusing. 'But why should I have the Deeds with me? Surely they should stay here in the house, and remain handy for when the property is sold.'

'Well, ordinarily, yes,' said Grace, prevaricating as she and Tristram had never told their children about Sir Geoffrey Turnbull's visit to re-claim the Deeds some years ago. 'But with the Army here, and the possibility of my leaving with you . . .'

'Oh, you're coming now, are you?' teased Hugh.

'I don't know, I still haven't quite decided. But trust me, the Deeds should be with you at all times.'

So Hugh had sought permission from the Army to enter his father's study and retrieve some old papers. An officer remained with him for the duration of his visit, and watched carefully to ensure that Hugh did not touch any of their precious administrative papers.

'I'm not in the least bit interested in any of your stuff, old chap,' said Hugh, trying to appear friendly. 'I shan't touch anything that didn't belong to my father, I promise you.'

The officer grinned. 'Orders is orders, Sir,' he said, and maintained his position at Hugh's elbow.

'That's another good reason to leave this country,' confided Hugh to his wife on his return to the cottage. 'I couldn't submit to that mindlessness, doing what you are told even though you can see it doesn't make any sense whatsoever.'

'There are many reasons to leave this country,' said Olivia darkly. 'I cannot think of a single reason to stay. Has your Mama decided whether she is coming with us?'

'Not yet, no,' replied Hugh. 'At least, not when I spoke to her last. But it has been almost all afternoon since I saw her, and she may well have changed her mind again. How do you feel about her coming with us, my dear?'

Olivia shrugged. 'I get on with her well enough under the circumstances. Things will probably be easier back home, but I don't know what she will do with herself all day. She is used to being busy.'

Hugh had his doubts too, but having invited her, he had to now let his mother make her choice. The trouble was, she could not be expected to have any idea which country she might prefer since she knew nothing about New Zealand at all. She was also terrified of the dangers of going to sea during a war.

In the end Hugh went off to Reading to buy tickets for their passage, and bought one for his Mama to show willing. That way she could decide at the very last minute. He was somewhat disconcerted when the shipping clerk revealed that the sailing the following week would be the last for sometime. 'We haven't been officially told yet. In fact,' he added, leaning forward confidentially, 'it's top secret, but a lot of the ships are to be requisitioned by the Navy for troop movements. So they are taking out a lot of the good stuff the Navy won't need. I think it's mad, if you ask me. The cruise line can't afford to lose any of its ships.'

'Nor any of its passengers, I hope!' responded Hugh, and went home with a troubled heart. He liked to think if the ships were safe enough for moving troops, they were safe enough for his family. But by the time he reached home, he had convinced himself it probably wasn't very safe for any of them.

He also knew though that if he did not take his wife and children back to New Zealand, Olivia was quite capable of taking them herself. He deeply regretted not having come to visit his Mama on his own, done what he could for her, and then returned to their sheep farm to resume life as normal. Instead of which he had sold up everything they possessed, and now they had to go back and start again from nothing. Well, he thought, he had done it once. He could do it again.

The fact that he had bought her a ticket seemed to reassure Grace, and eventually she said she would go. It broke her heart to leave Brightwell Manor, Harriet, Frederick and Betsy too, who had become a true friend. When Hugh told her they would be sailing early next week, she went into a frenzy of packing and unpacking, unable to decide what to take with her, and invited her other son and daughter to visit Brightwell to say goodbye.

She then arranged with the Army that her staff, Mr & Mrs Nesbit, Prudence, Stebbins's family and Betsy, were to be allowed to remain in the cottages at all costs. The other few remaining staff, such as was left of them, were despatched, and the new cook was most disgruntled, having just arrived and settled down, to have to up sticks again. She blamed Mrs Sinclair, rather than the Army or even the war, and packed up and left in a very bad humour.

Frederick and Harriet arrived at Brightwell at the same time, and were quite pleased to see each other again after so long. 'Sorry the marriage didn't work out,' she said to him with some sympathy.

'Nice wedding though!' he said, making her laugh.

Grace soon found them and even insisted Hugh should come to say goodbye to his brother and sister. Hugh was more than happy to say a final farewell to Frederick, and felt he hardly knew Harriet anyway. Much against her better judgement, Grace allowed herself a few tears. It did not seem to occur to them that they would never see her again. It grieved her to think she would be buried in foreign soil, so far away from her beloved Tristram, but she refrained from saying so to any of her offspring.

With Hugh there, after some fifteen minutes Frederick decided it was time for him to leave. 'Goodbye, Mama,' he said, giving her an unaccustomed hug. 'Have a safe journey and enjoy your new life. If the ship is called *The Titanic*, don't get on it!'

Harriet hid a smile and Frederick went blithely on his way. Hugh shook his head at such inappropriate humour, and Grace allowed herself more tears.

Chapter 30

To everyone's surprise and to Grace's huge relief, their ship eventually reached New Zealand safely. It took so long, with so many hold ups at various ports along the way, Grace – and even the Captain of the vessel – began to think they would never get there.

The children missed their freedom and independence; Hugh was patently worried about what he would do on their return, and Olivia was feeling guilty for having persuaded him to come back against his will.

Grace knew quite soon into the voyage that she had done the wrong thing, and was filled with regret. She constantly reminded herself that if she had remained at Brightwell, living in the little cottage, she would have been equally certain she had done the wrong thing, and that she should have gone. There was no right or wrong answer.

So it was an unhappy little band that trooped off the ship in the port of Auckland on North Island. Initially Hugh found them a hotel in which to recover, but after so long at sea, as soon as they set foot on terra firma, post-voyage vertigo hit Grace particularly hard. She felt seasick all over again. The children were not so badly effected, but Grace took to her bed and it was several weeks before she recovered completely.

After only a brief respite, Hugh spent his days touring the area to see if there were any suitable farms for sale in his price range. Prices had not increased significantly during the time he had been away, but they had not fallen as much as he had hoped either. He soon realised it was going to take time to find somewhere suitable, and should not be rushed, so he rented a house on the outskirts of the city, where they had less space than they needed.

In order to make amends to the staff she had left behind, and for Betsy in particular, Grace soon decided that the cottages should be divided from the Brightwell Manor estate, and given to each present incumbent.

'Given, Mama?' remonstrated Hugh, who had more important things to think about.

'Yes, given,' she repeated. 'They have served us for so long, and been so loyal. The cottages front onto the lane, as you know, so access is not a problem. It is the least I can do for them.'

After further discussion, Hugh agreed; it would make little difference to the value of the estate, or to the Army, currently resident there, so he agreed to instruct a solicitor. 'Not Henderson & Co. in Reading!' said Grace with conviction. 'Anyone but them. They are not to be used under any circumstances.'

Hugh was surprised by her vehemence, but went along with that too. Anything for a quiet life. He merely instructed his own solicitor to make contact with an English one in Reading – anyone but Henderson & Co.! – and to sort it all out.

The solicitor immediately wrote back asking what he should do about the two empty cottages. Grace had no hesitation, and said one should go to Frederick and the other to Harriet. Even if they did not wish to live in them, they could sell them one day, and perhaps put the proceeds towards buying a house of their choosing.

Grace then felt able to write to her son, her daughter and each of her friends – they were no longer her staff, and they had become friends over the years – and tell them what was being done on their behalf. Harriet and Betsy replied to her letters, telling her how grateful they were, and saying how much she was missed. This further increased Grace's homesickness, and her distress at being made to feel in the way by her daughter-in-law. If she had not come, the boys could have had a bedroom each in the rented house, instead of having to share, which led to squabbles and even fights between them.

As the conveyancing process was grinding through the labyrinthine legal system, Hugh's solicitor wrote to ask if he had considered offering the Army the opportunity to purchase Brightwell Manor at the same time. It had not occurred to Hugh to sell before the end of the war, but as his Mama had come with them, and no longer lived there, he could see little reason to hold on to it. He discussed it with Grace, who could see the logic but could not bear yet another wrench so soon after leaving. The solicitor was told no, Brightwell Manor was not yet for sale.

Meanwhile, back in England, Wyn had weaned Aubrey off the breast and onto a bottle, with some solids too. They were hardly solid, as everything had to be laboriously mashed with a fork to within an inch of its life, and most of it seemed to end up smeared all over his little face and clothes.

Frederick laughed and took a turn at feeding his son when he was available. He seemed to be better at it than Wyn; he was certainly more patient. This progress was a two-edged sword, however, because it meant the time had come for Aubrey to be evacuated to Maidenhead.

'Are you sure you want him to go?' asked Frederick for the umpteenth time. 'Maidenhead is actually nearer to London than Reading! I think he would be pretty safe here.' He longed for her to move in with him, bringing their son, he knew they could cope with him together. But she was adamant.

'Oh, Frederick,' she said. 'Not this again. I've explained a dozen times, I can't leave my other children. Nor Harry, he's not well, we don't know how long he's got, and I can't abandon him now. You know that. My kids are too old to be evacuated by the government, but there are a lot going from Reading. He'll be safer out in the countryside near Maidenhead. You did agree.'

So Frederick gave in and accepted that mother knew best. He wrote to Megan saying they would bring the little boy the following week, together with the signed Divorce papers, and he really thought his heart would break when they handed him over and walked away.

Wyn didn't seem to be upset at all. It was a huge wrench, and Frederick wished his mother was still at Brightwell. He would have been proud to introduce them to each other, and knew she would not have cared a jot about the little lad's doubtful lineage.

He consoled himself with the thought that Megan had been a good mother to Irene, and that Aubrey would flourish. He had hoped he might see Irene during their visit, but she was not at home.

'She's growing up,' said Megan defensively at sight of his disappointment. 'She's always off and out. Talking about going to America to see her cousins when the war is over.'

'And God knows when that will be,' said Frederick, longing for the day because it meant his son could return home. He was a bit confused by Wyn's logic, but he had to accept that he couldn't look after Aubrey on his own. If her husband was as ill as she said he was, perhaps he wouldn't last much longer, thought Frederick hopefully, and she would come and live with him at last. He would have to be patient.

At least the war had driven off the Depression. Those tough years had left their mark though, and people were still being more than careful with the little money they had. The ironmongery thrived, and he was just considering starting up some other sort of business in his empty shop, when that too was rented. Some brave soul was going to try starting up a clothing shop, on the assumption that, war or no war, people would always need clothes. He wished them well, and looked forward to receiving the rent on a regular basis.

With a new chemist opening on one side of his own shop, and a sweet shop on the other, more and more people were visiting the area, and business was booming. Wyn continued to work behind the counter, and their habit of closing the shop early if things were quiet had reasserted itself. She was as loving as ever, but rarely mentioned Aubrey. Frederick thought perhaps talking about him made her sad. Even though the shop was busier than ever, he hesitated to take on another assistant because their early closing times might have to cease. It would have been embarrassing to continue if there was anyone else on the premises.

To celebrate Aubrey's birth, Frederick bought a light van for the business. It was not a new one, but it was a Bedford and he trusted the name. As part of the deal he persuaded the garage to have their coach painter put his name on the side, Frederick Sinclair & Son. He had a matching sign painted over the shop front too, and felt very proud of himself. Wyn teased him about the '& Son' part of it, and said she thought it would be a while before Aubrey was driving.

Despite his contentment with Wyn, and pride in his new van, Frederick missed his son, and always seemed to feel unsettled, as if a part of him was missing. He even admitted to himself that he felt lonely in the evenings, once Wyn had left for the day.

Because so much had been going on, Frederick had not been to the races for sometime. Ascot was over for that year, but greyhound racing was becoming increasingly popular and Frederick went along to the new track off the Oxford Road, which was very handy. It gave him something to do in the evenings while Wyn was at home with her husband and children. It was a strange situation, he knew that.

Chapter 31
1941 – 1945

A year later, on a Saturday afternoon when the shop had finally quietened down, and Wyn was counting out the money in the till, she said absently, 'Are you doing anything exciting tomorrow?'

Frederick looked at her in surprise. 'It's the 2nd April,' he said. 'Aubrey's birthday. He'll be a year old.'

'Oh, so it is,' she said, carrying on counting. 'I forgot.'

Frederick looked at her perplexed. 'I can't wait to visit the little lad. I assumed we'd go together?'

'Well I can't on a Sunday, can I?' she said, still counting, which was beginning to annoy Frederick.

'Not usually, no,' he said, having accepted the situation for some time. 'But tomorrow is special. Surely you can make an exception?'

'Well, it's special to you,' she said. 'And to me, too,' she added hastily. 'But to Harry and my kids, it's the one day of the week when they get to see me.'

Frederick shook his head, and waited for her to finish balancing the till. He didn't suggest going upstairs for a cuddle at closing time, and for the first time since he'd known her, was glad to see her go. She never seemed to mention their son, or seem particularly excited when he did.

He had been sending Megan a regular monthly cheque for Aubrey's fees, and she always sent him a receipt. He thought she might have included a brief covering letter, reporting on the lad's progress, but she never did. A letter from the solicitor had arrived sometime ago, to say they were now legally divorced. He hadn't contacted Megan at the time, and had not heard from her, so he assumed she had what she wanted, and was happy. He hoped she wouldn't mention it tomorrow.

Next day he drove the van to Maidenhead and right up the drive to the house where he hoped Megan would see it. She was expecting him, and had dressed Aubrey in a new outfit for which she was planning to claim reimbursement from his father.

'Hello, Aubrey!' beamed Frederick, unable to stop smiling at the sight of him. 'I'm your Pa.'

Holding on tightly to Megan's hand, Aubrey walked unsteadily towards his father across the gravelled drive, who picked him up and held him close. 'He's walking then!' he said to Megan, and planted a kiss on the little boy's cheek.

'Yes,' she said, with some pride. 'He's not saying a lot yet, but he's walking early.'

'Who's a smart boy then?' he said to his son. 'He looks good in that outfit, Megan.'

'I'm glad you like it,' she said, and told him how much

he owed her. He laughed and paid up.

This improved her mood considerably, and she said, 'Nice van.' Then she read the coach-painted writing on the side and laughed. 'I think it'll be a while before Aubrey can see over the counter in your shop!'

It was the same every year after that. Frederick would have gone to visit his son every Sunday, but was worried Megan might not like it. He lived for his annual visit, and every year, Wyn made him go on his own. The following year it fell on the Monday. 'You go,' she said, 'I'll stay here and mind the shop.'

'We can close the damned shop for one day of the year!' remonstrated Frederick.

'No, no, it's alright,' she insisted, as if she was doing him a favour. 'We can't start messing customers about.'

So off he went, and was amazed by his son's progress every time. The war dragged on interminably, but Frederick had to admit it hadn't effected him a great deal. Wyn's concerns about Reading being bombed seemed to have been unfounded, and he began to wonder if evacuating their son had been strictly necessary. Indeed, there were evacuees from London who had been brought to Reading! He wondered yet again why Wyn had been so determined Aubrey should be elsewhere.

And then on Wednesday 10th February 1943, a single German aircraft strafed the town with bombs and machine gun fire in a straight line from Minster Street, through Wellsteads department store, ending at the Town Hall. Frederick was shocked because Wellsteads was at the lower end of Broad Street, and he was not far away. Wyn felt vindicated by her decision to have their son evacuated after all, and Frederick felt relief until someone came running into the shop to tell him the clothing shop had been hit and was in ruins.

Being one of the three shops he owned and rented, Frederick left Wyn in charge and hurried round there to see if there was anything he could do. There was nothing to see but a pile of rubble, and they kept telling him to get back and just wanted everyone out of the way. It was obvious the lady must have been killed, and any customers that might have been in there too. Later he discovered she was safe and sound; being a Wednesday it was early closing day and the shop was closed, something he had never bothered with himself. Next day the newspapers said 41 had been killed and over a 100 injured.

The following year on 2nd April, when Frederick visited for his son's fifth birthday, the talk was all about starting school.

'Where will he go?' he asked Megan.

'There's a little private school down the road,' she said reassuringly. 'It's run by a lady who used to be a teacher.' She told him what the fees would be, and again Frederick paid up cheerfully. Nothing was too good for his son.

The following year Frederick asked him if he was enjoying school, but Aubrey was non-committal.

'What have they been teaching you?' asked his Pa fondly, expecting him to say reading, writing and sums.

'French,' admitted Aubrey, but he was no linguist, and was not doing very well.

'French?' repeated Frederick incredulously. 'Why would he want to learn French? He can't speak English yet!'

'Well, they teach him singing as well,' supplied Megan.

'Singing?' said Frederick, horrified. 'I'm not bringing him up to be a bloody opera singer! Surely to God they teach him more than that, don't they?'

'I expect so,' said Megan to reassure him. The school was a convenient walk from her front door, and she had no desire for the boy to be moved to a school further afield. 'I'm sure they do.'

But by the time the war ended on 2nd September, 1945 and Aubrey was six years old, Frederick's first thought was that they could finally bring their son home. Surely Wyn would come and live with him now? Wyn was doubtful. 'Perhaps we should leave it a bit longer?' she said. 'Just to be sure.'

'Sure about what?' demanded Frederick, becoming more disillusioned with her than ever. 'No,' he said. 'It's been long enough. Too long! Let's fetch him today.'

Yet again she said she'd stay in the shop, but Frederick insisted this time.

'Wyn,' he said firmly, 'this is one of the best days of our lives. We'll go and fetch him together.'

So they left the shop closed, and set off in the van for Maidenhead. She was quiet and thoughtful, and little was said. Her other children were now grown up and supporting themselves, so she had run out of excuses about staying on at home to look after them. Harry hadn't grown any more exciting during the war. And she wasn't getting any younger. It was time she started living the life she wanted to live. But did that include looking after a six-year-old boy who had never really felt like her son in the first place? And come to that, did it include looking after Frederick too? They had good times, true, and she enjoyed working in the shop, earning her own money. But he was years older than she was, and he wasn't likely to get any more exciting either. She had huge doubts about all of it.

They arrived at the house and Megan had Aubrey dressed smartly in new trousers and jacket, with a brand new suitcase too, that Frederick knew he was going to have to pay for.

'Hello Aubrey!' said Frederick in an excited voice. 'Here's your Mother come to see you, and bring you home.'

He looked at her seriously for a moment or two, and then gave her a shy smile. She softened.

'Hello Aubrey,' she said. He put out his hand to shake hers, and said, 'Hello, Miss.' Then he turned to Megan and said goodbye very politely. 'Thank you for having me,' he said, as if he had just been for afternoon tea. She had obviously briefed him carefully about being on his best behaviour, whereas Frederick had been hoping he would be excited about going in the van, and moving to a new home.

He did thaw a little on the drive back, asking about a few of the landmarks he had not seen before. At last Wyn spoke. 'Alright then,' she said. 'No promises, but we'll give it a go.'

He knew immediately what she was referring to, and was overjoyed. All of them coming home to start a new life together.

And then Aubrey spoke. 'Pa?' he said, from the box of paint tins on which he sat in the back of the van. Frederick beamed with pride.

'Yes, son?'

'What's a Mother?'

Chapter 32
1945 – 1948

Frederick had never been so happy in his life. After the drive home together, Wyn went back to tell Harry the news and to pack her things. She said she would return in the morning. Frederick could hardly wait. She never revealed what Harry had to say when she told him, and Frederick did wonder if he would survive such a blow, given the apparently perilous state of his health.

She did return in the morning, as she had promised; Aubrey had forgotten about being on his best behaviour by then and was becoming curious about his new surroundings. The flat seemed small and gloomy after the grand house in which he had been living. The brown paint below the dado rail, and the dull cream paint above it were in strong contrast to the light and airy rooms looking out onto the river.

Frederick had arranged for him to go to a private school a short tram ride away, and when the new term began he briefed his son carefully as to where he should get on the tram, gave him the correct fare, and enough for the return journey too. Frederick watched him go, bursting with pride, but thinking he looked such a little chap to be going off into the world on his own.

Unfortunately, in his excitement, Frederick had forgotten to tell Aubrey where he was to get off the tram, and although he had explained which school he was going to, he hadn't really given him detailed directions. So Aubrey sat on the tram until they reached the terminus, and the conductor told him that was as far as they went.

'Where are you going, lad?' he asked.

'School,' said Aubrey uncertainly.

'Yes, I guessed that much,' said the conductor, who was a father himself. 'Which one?'

'I'm not sure,' said Aubrey.

So the conductor put him off anyway, and went off for his cup of tea. Aubrey was still there when he came back ready for the return journey. 'You'd better go home and start again, lad,' said the conductor, not unkindly. 'Hop on!'

So not much more than an hour after departing, Aubrey returned to the shop and confessed what had happened. 'It's not your fault, son,' said Frederick. 'I should have written it down for you. Stay here with us for today, and I'll take you myself on the tram tomorrow.'

So Aubrey started his new school a day late, and arrived with his Pa pointing out all the landmarks on the way. They alighted from the tram at the right stop, and Frederick showed him where to cross the road and how to find the school gate, where he stood and watched him cross the playground and find the right door.

He was eventually directed to the right classroom, and after calling the register, the teacher announced they would have some Dictation. Bewildered, Aubrey sat and listened and watched, and his new teacher began to discover just how little he had learned at his previous school. Once Frederick was informed, he knew it wasn't the boy's fault, and arranged for him to have extra lessons on Saturdays until he caught up.

'I'll give that Megan bloody French and singing!' he said angrily, and vowed to make it up to his son.

The other children soon asked why his grandfather had brought him to school. Aubrey was puzzled and said, 'He didn't. I haven't got a grandfather. That was my Pa.' When Aubrey reported that they had been seen arriving together and asked if it was his grandfather, and now other pupils were teasing him about having an old Dad, Wyn said, 'Fancy schools are like that. Teasing can turn to bullying, and we're not having any of that. He can go to the state school round the corner like God intended.' Frederick agreed; she was right.

That was walking distance, and Aubrey found it without difficulty. He arrived home after his first day to report that Miss had to see his birth certificate. Frederick looked at Wyn in some dismay, and said, 'What does she want to see that for?'

'I dunno,' said Aubrey. 'Somefink to do wiv my date of birf, I fink.' Frederick stared at him.

'What are you talking like that for?'

'That's how they talk at school,' said Aubrey in his usual voice.

'Well, you don't need to talk like that, son,' said Frederick. 'They should try to talk like you, not the other way round.'

But the new way of speaking continued. It grated on both Frederick and Wyn, but they realised Aubrey stood out from the crowd by being well spoken, and he was just trying to fit in.

'Miss told me off today,' he reported on his return one afternoon.

'Why?' demanded Frederick. 'What did you do?'

'I didn't do nuffink,' said Aubrey, mildly indignant. 'She says I 'aven't brought my birf certificate and she's got to 'ave it.'

'I'll try to find it,' said Frederick, and hoped Miss would forget about it as the term wore on.

The new accent continued, however, and Pa was not happy.

'I'll tell you what, son,' said Frederick after a week or so. 'If that's how you need to talk at school, that's fine. But why don't you speak normally when you're at home? That way, you'll fit in with the other kids during the day, and you'll fit in with us when you're here.'

So Aubrey said he would try, and remembered for the most part, but occasionally he forgot, and got things the wrong way round. This was greeted at school with mocking jeers and exaggerated impersonation, and mild reproval at home. Miss reminded him about the birf certificate on several occasions, and Aubrey simply said, 'My Pa's lost it miss. He's searched and searched, but it ain't nowhere.'

It wasn't long after that on a Saturday afternoon when Frederick looked up as the doorbell went ding, and had the surprise of his life when his sister walked in. 'Harriet!' he exclaimed. 'Come in. Good to see you.'

She smiled and looked about her. 'Nice shop,' she said approvingly. 'Doing well?'

'Yes, very well,' he said. 'What about you?'

'Much the same,' she said. 'Little changes in the halls of academe. But I have exciting news.'

'From New Zealand?' he asked.

'Yes, but it effects us. It's taken so long, but Mama has finally arranged for the cottages at Brightwell to be given to the staff living in them. And the two empty cottages are to come to us. You and me. One each.'

That was indeed a surprise. 'They've been divided off from the main estate,' she continued, 'and you know they front onto the road, so there's good access. Apparently the Nesbits died some time ago, they were pretty ancient, and their cottage has been sold to a young couple who fit in well. Betsy is still there, but she says when she goes, MillyVic will inherit hers. So I'm having the one next to hers, we might even knock them into one cottage eventually, to make a bigger home.'

'Well,' said Frederick, absolutely delighted with the news but ready to share news of his own. 'With Mama safely over there in New Zealand, your secret and mine are safe now. She'll never know.'

'My secret?' said Harriet, all innocence, but with a glance over her shoulder, making sure the shop was empty.

'What you told Mama at my wedding?' he prompted. 'When she asked if you might ever get married, and you said MillyVic was all you needed, and you were all she needed.'

Harriet blushed. 'Clever boy, aren't you?' she said sheepishly. Then, changing the subject, 'So what's your secret?' she said. 'I think we are all aware you prefer the ladies . . .'

Frederick laughed. 'Yes indeed,' he agreed. 'Very much so. My secret, Harriet, is that I have a son. Would you like to meet him?'

Harriet looked more than surprised and beamed her delight. 'A son? Here? How old is he?'

Frederick went through the door at the back of the shop and called up the stairs.

'Aubrey!' he shouted. 'Are you there?'

Aubrey came to the top of the stairs. 'Come down, son,' said his Pa. 'There's someone here I'd like you to meet.'

Aubrey came down the stairs and into the shop, and Frederick introduced him to his Aunt. Before he could ask, 'What's an aunt?' he explained. 'Harriet's my sister,' he said. 'That makes her your aunt. My brother, who you've never meet, would be your uncle.'

'Hello, Aubrey!' said Harriet heartily, as if he was one of her pupils. 'How old are you?'

'I'm seven now,' said Aubrey.

'Well, I'm very pleased to meet you,' she said. 'Where do you go to school?'

Aubrey launched into a list of the schools he had attended so far, and Harriet raised an eyebrow at her brother. 'How come so many?'

'He was away in Maidenhead as an evacuee for the first six years of his life,' said Frederick defensively. 'But they only taught him bad French and singing, which he can't do for the life of him, bless him.' Aubrey grinned self-consciously.

'He only came back to us last year,' continued Frederick. 'We sent him to the private school over yonder, but then Wyn decided the local school was good enough, if not better.'

'Do you like it there?' asked Harriet. School was very important to her.

'It's alright,' replied Aubrey without enthusiasm. 'I'm having extra lessons on Saturdays to catch up.'

It wasn't long before Frederick bought his son a bicycle, and he soon learnt to ride it. 'He's a bright kid,' said Frederick proudly to Wyn. 'It's not his fault no one taught him to read or write.' Like his father, Aubrey turned out to be good at sums, and he liked the woodwork teacher, and did well at that.

Wyn often received letters from her daughter, Molly, so he didn't think anything of it when yet another arrived. But this one was different. A year had soon passed, and not long after Aubrey's eighth birthday, she said to Frederick, 'It's time I went.'

'Where are you going?' he asked casually, assuming she meant shopping.

'Away. I can't stay here any longer.'

'Away? Why? What's wrong?'

'Nothing's wrong. It's just that the boy will be better with you.'

'Just with me? He needs a father and a mother. He needs us both.'

'No, you're better with him than I am. You'll be fine.'

Aubrey sobbed when she told him. 'Don't go, Ma,' he begged. 'I'll be a good boy.'

She looked down at him, but seemed untouched by his tears. 'You're always a good boy, Aubrey. I'm not going because of you.'

'Well is it because of me then?' asked Frederick, near to tears himself.

'No, Frederick. You've been kind and generous. Don't worry.'

'Don't worry? How can I not worry? Are you going back to Harry?' he asked suspiciously.

'God no. I got away from him once. I'm not going back to him.'

'Where are you going then?'

'I'm going to see my other kids,' she said.

'Well, that's fine. Can't you just visit them and then come back, like other people do? This is your home now.'

'I can't come back, Frederick. I'm sorry, but I can't.'

And she packed her bags and went. Frederick was devastated. And baffled. He couldn't understand it. He had thought they were happy. They rarely had a cross word. They had made love the night before. Aubrey thought the world of her, and he was a good kid, never any trouble. It didn't make sense.

The door closed behind her, and Frederick reached out to his son, putting his arms around him and holding him close. 'Don't cry, son,' he said, a catch in his voice and tears in his own eyes. 'She'll be back. We'll be alright. We'll have fun together, you and me. We'll have some adventures. She's not your real Ma anyway.'

Next day he let Aubrey stay home from school. 'You ought to go really,' he said, 'but it's Friday, so we'll have the weekend off. But you'll have to go back on Monday, mind.' He needed the company really.

Aubrey nodded bravely and dried his tears, looking expectantly at his father.

'We'll close the shop for today,' he said, not feeling like serving customers himself. 'We'll put a notice on the door and we'll take ourselves off somewhere nice. And I'll find someone to keep it open tomorrow. There's plenty of people looking for work.'

So he put two notices on the door, one saying, 'Shop closed due to staff shortage. Sorry for any inconvenience.' And he wrote a second one to go below it saying, 'Staff wanted. Immediate start. Male applicants only.'

And with that he turned the Open sign round to read Closed, switched off the lights, and slammed the door shut behind them. They climbed into the van, and Frederick drove them out to the countryside. He found a nice field with a stream running through it. 'Come on,' he said to Aubrey. 'Let's go and get some trout for our tea.' And he taught his son how to lie on the bank and tickle trout, as he had done when he was a kid.

Next morning, as Frederick went downstairs to the shop, switched on the lights and turned the Closed sign round to read Open, there was a queue of young men, most of them recently demobbed, unemployed and keen to work. 'You're in charge of the shop,' said Frederick to Aubrey, and went outside to walk the length of the queue and pick out three of the hopefuls to invite them inside for interview. The rest he sent away disappointed.

He invited the chosen few inside and introduced himself. 'I'm Frederick Sinclair, the owner,' he said. 'And this is my son, Aubrey.'

Aubrey looked up and shyly said Hello to all three at the same time.

'Now if you would introduce yourselves, one at time, please.'

They all had a similar story to tell. None of them had any experience in shop work, they were all of a similar age. The shortest of them spoke well, and said he was good at adding up. The painfully thin one said his leg had been injured during the war, and although he could cheerfully do a good day's work, he might need to sit down from time to time.

The third applicant called him Mr Sinclair, looked him in the eye, said his name was Charlie Stokes, and that he was keen to learn. He added that he had worked in Stores during his time in the Army, so he knew about handling stock and he liked dealing with people. He also said he was very honest, his mother had brought him up to tell the truth and not to steal, so Frederick offered him the job, thanked the other two and said, 'Sorry to disappoint, lads.'

Turning back to Charlie, he told him what the wages would be, and Charlie closed his eyes in relief.

'I won't let you down, Mr Sinclair,' he said, and shook his new boss by the hand, gratefully clinching the deal. Then he shook hands with Aubrey too, and Frederick said, 'I forgot the most important thing.'

Charlie looked alarmed. 'What's that, Sir?' he asked.

'Are you any good at making tea?'

Charlie laughed. 'With six brothers and sisters, Sir, I'm well qualified.'

'Well let's start with that,' said Frederick, and showed his new shop assistant where to find everything. The tea soon appeared, with a packet of biscuits he'd found, and Frederick nodded in approval.

'Welcome aboard, Charlie,' he said satisfied, and spent the day showing him everything in the shop, as well as the paraffin tank outside in the backyard, and the rubber gloves in their hiding place. 'They're just for you to use,' said Frederick with some relish. 'No one else will use them.'

By the afternoon Charlie was allowed to serve his first customer, who only wanted glue.

'What sort of glue do you need, Sir?' asked Charlie. 'There's several different kinds, you see.'

When the customer described his project, and said he was making some shelves for the wife, Charlie sold him the right sort of glue, plus some screws and a new screwdriver as well, and went on to suggest some nice stain for the wood.

'That'll do for now,' said the customer. 'I might come back for the stain. Thanks very much for your help.'

Frederick was well pleased, and knew he had made the right choice. At the end of the day, he paid the lad, and said he'd see him bright and early on Monday morning. Sunday was everyone's precious day off, and when Frederick asked his son what he would like to do for the day, Aubrey was keen to go fishing again.

'Well, we had fish for supper last night,' said Frederick. 'And the night before. Do you like rabbit? Why don't we go and catch a rabbit for today?'

Aubrey had never had rabbit, and he was surprised when his Pa went to the cupboard and pulled out the fishing nets again. 'I thought you said we weren't going fishing?' he said.

'We're not, son,' said his Pa. 'These are to put across the mouth of the rabbit burrow. We'll jump up and down on top and catch them as they come out.'

'We could get a gun?' suggested Aubrey hopefully. 'And shoot them.'

'Too noisy, son,' said Frederick. 'Don't want to go making a lot of noise about it.'

He was true to his word and caught several rabbits, which his neighbours and friends were only too happy to accept without asking any questions. School and keeping the shop open intervened during the week, but on the following Friday evening, Frederick surprised his son by asking him if he was tired.

After a week at school during the day, and helping Pa

make supper and not getting to bed very early in the evenings, Aubrey most certainly was tired, but he sensed the correct answer was No.

'Not really, Pa,' he said manfully.

'Good for you,' said Pa. 'Sleep when you're tired and eat when you're hungry, that's what I say. We'll go to the cinema and see that new film,' and off they went.

It was pretty much a full house, with just a few seats available at the back, but Frederick walked boldly forward, and by persuading a few people to move into a couple of single empty seats further along the row, he made room for them, and ushered Aubrey along in front of him.

Unfortunately everyone was taller than Aubrey, and all he could see was the back of somebody's head. So Pa got his pipe out, which surprised his son.

'Pa?' he said. 'I didn't know you smoked a pipe as well as cigarettes?'

'Watch and learn, son,' replied Frederick, tamping tobacco into the bowl. 'Watch and learn.'

Lighting up, he soon started puffing away on it, but when this provoked no reaction, he inhaled the smoke and blew it gently over the couple in front. After a few minutes of this, being non-smokers, they got up in disgust and moved to the only other seats available much further back.

The film was *Road to Rio*, with Bing Crosby, Bob Hope and Dorothy Lamour, and although everyone else seemed to be enjoying it hugely, Aubrey's eyelids began to droop, and he slept through most of it.

On the Saturday evening, anxious not to stay home in the empty flat and impatient to be off doing something, Pa said, 'Come on, son, we'll go and watch the dog racing.'

Having by now caught up with his sleep, and spent the day with not much to do, Aubrey enjoyed the dog racing hugely. Pa went off a few times to give a man some money, and even on a couple of occasions went to see him and got some money back, but Aubrey's attention was riveted. He watched as the greyhounds were placed in the traps, then the hare whisked into action and the dogs released. It was all over in minutes, but it was exciting while it lasted.

'Those dogs are beautiful,' he said to Pa. 'And fast. Can we have a dog?'

'Not at the moment, son,' said Frederick. 'We'll have one when we don't have to live over the shop any more.'

And so Aubrey was indoctrinated into the arts of poaching, dog racing and even getting people to move out of his way in the cinema, and felt more hopeful. Pa wasn't just saying it, they really were going to have a nice lot of adventures together. And Pa thought so too.

Chapter 33
1941 – 1948

Having arrived back in New Zealand in 1941, well into the war, Hugh was becoming increasingly concerned. They had been there over a month already, and there really didn't seem to be any property for sale that suited his purpose. He had contacted his two New Zealand friends, Chester and Lucas, met during their time together at Cirencester Agricultural College. They were pleased to see him and his family back in the country, but knew of nothing suitable either.

Then, a week or so later, Lucas drove over to the despised rented house to have a word with him.

'It may not be of interest,' he said, not wanting Hugh to get too excited. 'It depends on how desperate you are!'

'Pretty desperate,' replied Hugh with a grimace, pouring coffee for his old friend.

'A nephew of mine owns a large spread with a massive flock of sheep. And the idiot wants to go off to war. Everyone he knows has tried to dissuade him, including his wife and kids, but he says it's something to do with never having left home. He was born on the place and inherited it, and this seemed like an opportunity. So he's signed up with the ANZAC Corps and is awaiting joining instructions. They are fighting in Greece at the moment, but I should think it will be all over by the time he gets there.'

Hugh placed Lucas's coffee in front of him and sat down on the opposite side of the kitchen table, wondering how this applied to him.

'His father has said he'll lend a hand with the sheep, but they need someone to manage the place overall. Someone with your sort of training and experience.'

'Go on,' said Hugh.

'He's determined to go. We've all tried to stop him, but he's made up his mind and, here's the rub. It's only temporary. The place isn't for sale, they just want a Manager for the duration of the war. How ever long that may be. Assuming he comes back, he'll want his spread back.'

'And if he doesn't come back . . .?' asked Hugh.

'Yes, he's thought it all through,' continued Lucas, taking a sip from his mug. 'The place will be for sale and his Manager will get first refusal. There are conditions though.'

Hugh knew it sounded too good to be true.

'His wife and kids will be in the Homestead, and if he doesn't come back, they are to be allowed to remain there if they want to. Personally I can't see why they would want to stay in such a remote place for the rest of their lives, but that's not for me to say. They'll cross that bridge when they come to it.'

'Yes, but where would the Manager live?' asked Hugh, thinking of Olivia and wondering what she would have to say about it. And the children, for that matter. And even, as an afterthought, his Mama. She might be getting on in years, but she was as spry and energetic as ever.

'Oh yes, I forgot. There is a second house you can live in. Plenty big enough. Six bedrooms, I believe.' Hugh grinned. Olivia would approve of that.

'Income would be derived in the usual way,' continued Lucas, 'from the flock – wool, meat – no rent to pay.'

'Can I meet your nephew?' asked Hugh. 'What's his name?'

'Jordan. Jordan Crewe. You can but you'll have to be quick. He's expecting to leave early next week.'

'I'm definitely interested in what you've told me so far,' said Hugh, and a meeting was quickly arranged. In view of the time constraints, he decided to take the family along too, so that they could all view it together.

Hugh and Jordan immediately got on well together. They talked details and income and fleece per acre, and they ended up shaking hands on the deal. Meanwhile, Olivia and the children had met Jordan's wife and family, and they all got along famously. Grace seemed happy enough, especially when Jordan showed them the second house he had available, and she saw all those bedrooms.

Having Jordan's family nearby made it all feel slightly less remote.

Olivia would soon make the place a home, and she was thrilled to be back. Secretly Hugh was relieved, not just because they were at last starting a new life, at least for a while, but also that there was no initial outlay and no commitment. Everyone was able to keep their options open, and it allowed Hugh some breathing space. He knew his Mama was still homesick, and on the rare occasions he could bring himself to admit so disloyal a thought, so was he.

So they moved in and Jordan went off to war. No one could quite fathom out why he was so determined, and even he had his doubts when it came time to say goodbye to his wife and children.

Hugh moved his family in to their new home, and life became normal again. They had only been there about six months when Hugh discovered the lump in his wife's breast. They were making love at the time and, not wanting to spoil a beautiful moment, he waited until the following morning before mentioning it. She was not surprised, or overly concerned, so he wasn't either.

'It's been there ages,' she said nonchalantly. 'I don't think it's anything important.'

William and George took to the life immediately, and were very useful about the place. Hugh thought vaguely that maybe he should look into some sort of training for them, such as he had had at Cirencester. There might be something similar in New Zealand by now. In the meantime, there was work on the new spread for them if they wanted it. 'No pressure,' said Hugh. 'If you want something else, that's fine too.' But both boys elected to stay.

Emily was happy for the time being, but she had decided she wanted to be a teacher, like her Aunt Harriet. Although she had not taken to England, and found it cold and damp and everyone very elderly, she had quite enjoyed the school there, once she had settled. She thought it was a far better system than having to be taught at home, and she began to write to Colleges in New Zealand, asking for their prospectus.

Gradually Olivia began to feel unwell, and remembered the mysterious lump. She became tired easily, and Grace helped with the running of the home as best she could. She was more concerned about the lump than Olivia was, and suggested a visit to the hospital in Auckland. Olivia brushed the idea aside, and carried on as normal, not realising quite how much Grace was helping and supporting her.

By the time she eventually agreed to see a doctor, it was too late and nothing could be done. They kept her in the hospital and a week later she died. Hugh was shocked and devastated and simply could not believe it. 'It's just not possible,' he said to his mother. Having lost her beloved Tristram just as suddenly, she understood better than anyone else how he felt, but Hugh did not know that.

After the funeral, he threw himself into the work again, and the boys did the same. Emily turned to Grace for a while, glad to have another female to talk to. The family next door were supportive too, but the College year was starting, and Emily went off to begin her new life, training to be a teacher.

With Olivia and Emily gone, Grace became more homesick than ever, and so did Hugh. Gradually they allowed themselves to reminisce about Brightwell, and Grace's longing increased. Her heart missed a beat one day when he suddenly said, 'Thank goodness we decided not to offer Brightwell to the Army for sale. At least we still have our options open.' Was it possible that he was thinking of returning home too, wondered Grace?

Hugh missed his wife and daughter deeply, and began to feel there was little point in soldiering on, except that he had a gentleman's agreement with Jordan that he would remain until his return at the end of the war.

A decision was forced upon them when he did indeed return, very much alive and uninjured. He had changed, having seen things he could not talk about, but he was demobbed with thousands of others as the war ended in 1945, and he just wanted his life to get back to normal.

'You're welcome to carry on living in the second house,' he told Hugh, having offered his sincere condolences on the loss of Olivia.

'Take as long as it takes,' he said generously, assuming Hugh would soon find a farm of his own to buy. 'If it helps,' added Jordan, 'I'd like to offer both your boys jobs here, if they would like to stay. You've all done a fine job, and I could do with some extra labour now.'

But Grace could see Hugh was in a torment of indecision. She understood that too, having been similarly tormented when she was trying to decide whether to accompany the family when they returned to New Zealand. Now that Olivia had passed away, there was little reason to remain, except, of course, for the children. The boys were already taken care of, but Emily was too young to leave behind. She came home for the holidays, and was thrilled to see everyone, but she obviously missed College and her new friends.

Hugh sat her down one day and tried to talk to her. 'Now that your mother has passed away,' he said, 'Grandmama and I are thinking of going back to England.' Emily's eyes widened.

'*Are* you, Papa?' she said, surprised. '*Why?*'

Hugh explained as best he could, but faltered rather, and knew he had not presented his case very well. 'The thing is,' he went on, 'I feel you are too young to remain here on your own, and I wonder if you would like to come with us?'

Emily was horrified. 'Of course not, Papa!' she said, visibly upset at the very thought. 'We've already been once and come back again. It's cold and damp and not in the least like New Zealand. And I'm enjoying my course at College,' she defended herself. 'And my new friends.'

'I can see that,' said Hugh, feeling sympathetic towards her. 'But have you considered that in England they have some wonderful Universities. You could go to one of those, and get even better qualifications than you will here. And new friends too.'

Emily paused, and gave the matter a few moments consideration. 'But I like the course I'm doing!' she said. 'It will more than qualify me to teach here, which is what I want.'

Their interview ended without conclusion, but Hugh hoped she might at least mull over the idea. Then out of the blue Grace received a letter from Harriet, who wrote to say that she and MillyVic were considering leaving their present school, and starting up a private school of their own. Retirement was still some years away, but this was something they had been wanting to do for some time, and if they didn't do it soon, it would be too late.

They were looking for suitable premises, and Harriet was writing to ask if Mama could persuade Hugh on their behalf, that Brightwell Manor would make a wonderful school. Harriet was also wondering what Hugh was planning to do now that the war had ended and his dear wife had passed away. She knew the arrangement on the sheep farm was due to end when the owner returned from the war, and she went on to point out that if he decided to come home and work the estate, that would be entirely compatible with the main house being used as a school.

Harriet and MillyVic had obviously thought it all through very carefully. 'Of course,' Harriet had written, 'we cannot forget that a third share of Brightwell belongs to Frederick too. If he does not have need of it, Hugh and I could buy him out between us. He owns one of the cottages, thanks to you, although his shop is still open in Reading.' She carefully avoided any mention of Aubrey, and ended, 'Betsy is very excited about it all.'

Grace was immediately excited too, and longed to see Betsy and all her friends again. She spoke to Hugh at the first possible opportunity. He too could see the potential, but remained concerned about leaving Emily behind.

'Well,' said Grace, trying to be subtle. 'If Harriet and MillyVic are starting up a new school, they will soon be in need of qualified teachers, will they not?'

Hugh was delighted by this suggestion, and immediately went to seek out Emily. Unsurprisingly he found her reading in her room, and explained there was news from home. She listened attentively, and she too could see the potential. And the appeal.

'Would they need me to have been to an English university?' she asked tentatively.

'They haven't said so,' replied Hugh, 'but common sense suggests it would be better. Mind you, this part is

Grandmama's idea, Aunt Harriet hasn't thought that far ahead yet, obviously. But it does seem it would work for all of us.'

Strongly tempted, Emily said, 'I just wish we didn't have to go on that horrible ship,' remembering the seasickness and the boredom. Hugh perceived that she was seriously considering it.

'Well at least there's not a war on this time!' said Hugh, feeling a slight glimpse of happiness and relief at the thought of going home. 'So there's no danger of being torpedoed out of the water, and less red tape at the ports along the way. It shouldn't take as long this time.'

Seeing that she was weakening, and very tempted by the thought of an English university and the possibility of a new job at her Aunt's school, Hugh left her to think things over.

Grace was keen to know how his conversation with Emily had been, and he gave her what news he could. She too began to feel a glimmer of excitement at the thought of returning to Brightwell. She would live in one of the cottages quite happily. Harriet had said in the past that the new owners were building on at the back, adding a scullery downstairs, and even a flush lavatory. With her daughter, Betsy and other friends including MillyVic as neighbours, Grace knew she would be fine.

Hugh must have read her mind. 'What would you do, Mama? If we went back?'

She reassured him on that head, and then he said, 'What about the passage on board ship? You took a while to recover last time.'

Even that did not deter Grace. 'I'll be alright,' she said. 'It'll be summertime over there when we arrive, so hopefully the seas will not be quite so rough. And no war to worry about!'

A minor consideration such as rough seas would not deter Grace. And once Emily admitted she too could see the benefits of an English university, and the possibility of a new job as a teacher at the end of it, Hugh booked their tickets, and Grace wrote home to Harriet saying yes, yes, yes, to all her suggestions. They were on their way.

Chapter 34 – 1948

Despite all the adventures, the poaching and watching his son become more cheerful, and even settling down at his third new school, Frederick could not help but dwell on the absent Wyn. Why had she gone like that? Without explanation? They'd been happy. At least, he had been. He thought she was too.

He was desperate to find out what had happened, and where she had gone, and he could only think of one person who knew that. Harry. At first he was afraid to go round there, he didn't know what he might find. Harry was in poor health; the shock of Wyn leaving, followed by him turning up on the doorstep, might kill the old chap.

Eventually, however, with his thoughts tormenting him, he left Charlie in charge of the shop as usual, and plucking up courage one morning when Aubrey had left for school, he found the house. His knock was soon answered by a man somewhat younger than he was.

'Is Harry at home?' asked Frederick diffidently.

'I'm Harry,' he said, seeming cheerful enough.

'I hope you don't mind my calling on you,' began Frederick, so taken aback by the sight of Harry he had forgotten his prepared speech. 'Only I'm Frederick Sinclair . . .'

'Oh, you are, are you,' said Harry in a voice of resignation. 'I thought you might visit one day. Come in, Mr Sinclair.' And he opened the door wider for Frederick to enter.

Frederick took off his hat and thought all this very strange. He had been expecting an elderly invalid, anger, accusations, resentment. And here was Harry, younger than anticipated, apparently healthy, and being quite cordial.

'How are you?' he asked.

'I'm fine,' said Harry, surprised at his genuinely solicitous enquiry. 'How are you?'

'Well, I'm fine,' said Frederick, 'but Wyn said you were very poorly. That she couldn't leave you.'

'Oh you don't want to believe a word she says,' replied Harry, leading the way into a pleasant sitting room. 'Not one word. Take a seat. Cup of tea?'

Frederick was more perplexed than ever. 'Er, no. No thanks. I can't stop, I just wanted to know if you'd heard from her?'

'Not a word,' said Harry.

'Do you know where she is?' pursued Frederick.

'Oh,' said Harry, realisation dawning. 'She's left you as well now, has she?'

'Yes. Couple of weeks ago.'

'What about the boy? I bet she didn't take him with her, did she? Left him with you?'

'Yes.'

'Thought as much.'

'Aubrey. He's at school.'

'School age, is he?'

'Eight now.'

'Useless as a mother,' said Harry conversationally. 'Useless as a wife.'

'Well, you don't seem to have had a very good deal.'

'Nor you,' grinned Harry, and put the kettle on. 'Go on, have a cup of tea. I'm having one.'

So Frederick sat down and drank tea with Harry, which struck him as incredibly bizarre, almost as bizarre as the story that unfolded.

'She said you were ill. Dying.'

'Well, as you can see, I'm perfectly alright and very much alive.' He laughed. 'Did she also tell you she couldn't leave the kids?'

'Yes,' said Frederick. 'She did. She loved her kids.'

'Did she hell,' said Harry. 'Loves no one but herself, that woman.'

Frederick remained speechless and waited for more.

'Don't tell me she's been bringing up your Aubrey?'

'No, he went as an evacuee when the war started. To Maidenhead. Friend of mine.'

Harry nodded, unsurprised. 'Once she'd finished breast feeding, yes?'

'That's right.'

'Got rid of him quick as she could. And now he's back home, she's scarpered?'

'Well, with the war on . . .'

'She doesn't like them until they're grown up a bit,' said Harry. 'She got shot of all ours as soon as she could, even though there wasn't a war on. Molly and Peggy were both pitched off to a Convent at the age of five. And we're not even Catholic!' The disgust in his voice matched Frederick's. 'And I don't think they were very kind to them half the time. Funny lot, nuns.'

Frederick braced himself for more revelations. He knew there had been four children. At least, that's what he'd been told.

'When they left the Convent, she gave Peggy away. Went to live with another family and we haven't seen her since. Molly remembers her going, sobbed her little heart out. She turfed Molly out when she was ten, she went to live with some woman running a pub, an alcoholic. Molly worked in the bar, and was running the place at 14.'

'Running a pub?' repeated Frederick. 'At 14?'

Harry nodded. 'Sheila followed. Three girls in a row. I don't know why she kept having them. She said they were messy and got in the way. Her own kids! We finally had a boy, Bill. Molly took him on, in the pub.'

'So where are they all now?'

'Well, Bill's in Malaya, Prisoner of War. We've had a letter to say he'll come back as soon as he's well enough to travel.'

'Oh, they're grown up then?'

'Yes, big age difference to your little Aubrey. I can't think why she had him.'

'Well, it's difficult to stop it . . .' grinned Frederick.

Harry nodded in heartfelt agreement. 'You don't have to tell me,' he said. 'She likes the fun part, but not the children, and unfortunately one usually leads to the other.'

Frederick finished his tea and put the cup down.

'So where are they all now?' he asked.

'That's the bit I don't understand!' exclaimed Harry. Frederick thought he didn't understand any of it. 'She likes them when their older, off her hands. Loves them then! I think what's triggered her leaving is that our Molly got married. Her husband's well off, like, you know. Old enough to be her father, but rich,' he added. 'History repeating itself. All she wants is a big house, and to get the family back together. She told him that. She just wants to get the family back together.'

'Including her mother?'

'Yes, even her. God knows why.'

'They were in touch. Molly did write to her quite often.'

'Yes, and she got her rich husband to buy the house next door, so Peggy and Sheila could go and live in that.'

'Where though? Where are they all?'

'High Wycombe. Apparently Molly's new husband runs a business there. So yes, High Wycombe, if you please. Bit posh, aye?'

Frederick didn't know. Harry probably thought he was a bit posh himself.

'Do you have the address?'

'You're not going after her, are you?' said Harry disapprovingly. 'Waste of time.'

'I've got to find out,' said Frederick.

'Well, I've just told you.'

'Yes, I know, and I'm very grateful. But for Aubrey's sake . . . He misses her too.'

'She's a hard piece,' said Harry. 'She won't care.'

Frederick walked home in shock. It began to make sense. He remembered some of the things she had said. When Aubrey was born: 'You can call him what you like.' Never wanting to visit him on his birthday. Or even go along and collect him the day the war ended. And then, as she was leaving, 'He's better off with you.'

He wouldn't tell Aubrey. If he found it incomprehensible himself, how could a lad of eight be expected to understand? He didn't do anything for a few days, but mulled it all over. Then, on the Friday morning, as soon as Aubrey had left for school once more, he got in the van and drove to the address in High Wycombe.

Molly opened the front door. 'We're full,' she said.

'It says on the sign. No Vacancies.'

Frederick hadn't noticed. 'Full?' he echoed.

'You want B&B?' she said. 'Sorry, we're full.'

'No, no,' said Frederick, turning back to see the B&B sign behind him. 'I'm looking for Wyn. Is she home?'

'Oh dear,' said Molly. 'Are you Frederick? You'd better come in.'

Frederick entered and followed her through a door marked Residents Lounge. She left him standing there, turning the brim of his hat in his hands, and he heard Molly calling, 'Mum. Frederick's here. He wants to see you.'

Wyn came in then, carrying a tin of polish and a duster. 'Hello, Frederick,' she said quietly. 'How did you find me. Harry?'

'Yes,' he replied.

'Had a nice chat, did you? All about what a terrible mother I am?'

'Something like that,' he agreed. 'I had to come and see for myself. That you're alright. Aubrey misses you.'

'All my kids miss me,' she said. 'Strange when I'm such a terrible mother, but they do.'

She didn't ask him to sit down.

'I came to see if you wanted to come home?'

'I can't,' she said quickly. 'Molly needs me. She's running a B&B for long distance lorry drivers. Doing very nicely, thank you. And we've got Peggy and Sheila next door, in case of overspill. Between the two houses we've got eight bedrooms.'

'And you prefer that to the life we had together?'

She looked at him levelly. 'Yes, Frederick, I suppose I do.'

'You haven't even asked after Aubrey.'

'Well, no,' she said. 'He's more yours than mine. Don't you think?'

He knew then there was no hope, and he left. He sat in the van for a while, uncomprehending. Eventually he put the key in the ignition and drove home, hurt and bewildered. Aubrey came home from school, hungry as usual, and Frederick began cooking his tea.

A few months later, Harry appeared in the shop.

'Hello!' said Frederick. 'Fancy seeing you here.'

'D'you want a laugh?' said Harry. Frederick raised an eyebrow.

'You remember our Molly?' Frederick nodded. 'With the rich husband and the B&B? She's left him already. Gone off with one of the long distance lorry drivers.'

'What's he going to do?'

'He's already done it. Our Winifred is staying on to help with the B&B. And look after him. And we both know how well Wyn looks after her men.'

Chapter 35
1947 – 1948

The trouble with having a shop, decided Frederick, was that everyone knew where to find you. Just when he wanted to be left to lick his wounds in peace, Harriet bounced into the ironmongers one morning, big with news.

'Guess what!' she announced, sounding excited.

'What?' said Frederick, trying to sound interested.

'Hugh and Mama and Emily are on their way home!'

'Really?' said Frederick. Now that was a surprise.

Harriet had become a regular visitor of late, and had kept him informed as things in New Zealand unfolded. He knew she had written to ask if she and MillyVic could start their own school in Brightwell Manor, and that she had been awaiting a reply for weeks. Now it seemed her patience had been rewarded.

'Mama's letter has taken ages to arrive, so they might even be half way here by now.'

Frederick had a sudden vision of introducing his mother and brother to his son, of whom they had never heard. Unless Harriet had mentioned it?

'Do they know about Aubrey?' he asked.

'No,' she said. 'Unless you've told them yourself? I certainly haven't. I thought we agreed to keep each other's secrets.'

'We did,' said Frederick. 'But my secret is rather more visible than yours.'

She laughed. 'Hugh coming home too. I can't believe it. I told you Olivia passed away, didn't I?'

'Did you?' asked Frederick. 'I don't remember. Poor old Hugh. She was nice.'

'Yes, Mama says he's devastated. They have both been homesick for ages, and now that Olivia has died, he feels there is no point in staying over there. The boys are to carry on working on the sheep farm he's been looking after all through the war, but he's persuaded Emily to do her teacher training in this country. Mama has confessed she even suggested Emily might have a job at our school when she is qualified. I remember her. Bright kid.'

'What's Hugh going to do?' asked Frederick.

'He's going to run the estate, and get it so that it's self-supporting again. MillyVic and I have been inside the house since the Army left. There's quite a lot to be done to bring it up to standard. Mama says she can help with that. She's dying to use her expertise as an architect again.'

Frederick nodded wisely, and decided it was time to let go of his sadness over Wyn. She had moved on, so must he. So he joined in with Harriet's excitement, and looked forward to seeing his Mama again. She would understand about Aubrey.

His next visitor was a policeman. This coincided with the very Monday Charlie had not turned up for work. He had been so reliable ever since he had started working in the shop, that Frederick was concerned, and thought he should go round to his lodgings to see if he was alright. It was so unlike him.

'Good morning,' said Frederick to the policeman. 'Can I help?'

'We are looking into the possibility of stolen goods on these premises, Sir,' said the policeman politely. He was in uniform and had three stripes on his arm. Frederick looked genuinely puzzled.

'Not here, Sergeant. I'd never get involved with anything like that.'

'We were wondering if we might have a word with your employee,' said the sergeant. He consulted his notebook. 'Charlie Stokes, is it?'

'Well, as it happens,' said Frederick, 'he hasn't turned up this morning, for the first time ever. He is usually most reliable. I was planning to go round to see him later on.'

'I think we can save you the bother, Sir,' said the Sergeant. 'We've already been round, and he is not there.'

Frederick looked dumbfounded. 'Oh.' Realisation dawned. 'I see.'

'Yes, Sir,' said the Sergeant. 'We thought there might be a connection too. Do you mind if we take a look round?' Frederick wondered who the royal 'we' might be, as the Sergeant was patently on his own. He disappeared into the sitting room beyond the shop.

Frederick had been so preoccupied with his own concerns, he hadn't really kept a very good check on what Charlie had been doing. He was just grateful that he was reliable and very good at sales. Most of his customers went home having bought more than they intended. He had thought him honest too, but now that seemed to be in question.

Ever since Wyn had stopped feeding Aubrey in the back sitting room, it had been used for storing stock. In fact, it had been her suggestion, and a very good one it was too. The sergeant emerged back into the shop.

'Would you come and take a look at this, Sir?' he invited, holding the door open so that Frederick knew he had no choice.

Frederick was genuinely shocked to see several boxes of whiskey, gin and vodka secreted behind the other boxes of stock. 'Oh God,' he said quietly. 'I had no idea. We don't sell alcohol.'

This seemed a rather inadequate response to the Sergeant, and Frederick was invited to accompany him down to the police station.

'I've got to be here for 3 o'clock,' he protested.

'My boy will be home from school about then.'

'I'm sure you will be back by then, Sir,' said the sergeant smoothly, but Frederick was not sure. The man seemed to have decided he was involved in some way.

'I've had no part in any of this,' he protested. 'I don't even drink! Doesn't it occur to you that it's odd for Charlie Stokes to have disappeared, and not me?'

'We can talk about that down at the station, Sir,' said the Sergeant. 'We'll turn the lights off for you, and lock the door.'

To his relief, Frederick was back at the shop in good time for Aubrey. Once at the police station, he had thought to offer them sight of his bank account, to prove that he had not been receiving any extra income from such contraband. So they went off to the bank and he received a nasty shock himself when there appeared to be a rather large deficit. Charlie Stokes had been faithfully banking the takings for some months, and it seemed he had been cultivating the banking staff at the same time. Last Friday he had requested a large withdrawal, on behalf of Mr Sinclair, of course and, recognising Mr Stokes as a regular customer, the young bank teller had given it to him.

Mixed in with the shock and horror of that, however, was the relief that it at least proved his innocence, and that Charlie Stokes was the sole suspect. 'Sorry for any inconvenience, Sir,' said the sergeant as he opened the door of the police station for Frederick to depart.

'We will find him,' he added, 'but we cannot be certain that we will recover your money too.'

Frederick came home and made himself a cup of tea, deep in thought. He left the sign on the shop door to read Closed, and was only wakened from his reverie when he heard Aubrey knocking.

'What's up?' asked Aubrey. 'Why are we closed?'

Frederick explained as best he could without upsetting his son. He and Charlie had been good mates, Aubrey had trusted him too. First his mother walks out on them, now Charlie.

'I'm getting too old for this sort of life, son,' said Frederick, feeling his age. He felt he couldn't face the inconvenience of finding and training yet another employee. He obviously wasn't very good at it. Consequently he had made a few decisions since coming home from the police station.

'What do you say to you and me selling up the shop, and retiring? You'd still have to go to school, of course, but we could go and live in that cottage at Brightwell while we decide what to do. You'd like the village school. I went there when I was a boy.'

'Did you like it there, Pa?' asked Aubrey looking anxious.

'Well, yes,' replied Frederick, unwilling to lie to his own son. 'Most of the time. It was alright.'

So Frederick put the shop up for sale, and soon had a buyer. The place had a good reputation and, being between the chemist and a sweet shop, was in a good location, had excellent upstairs accommodation, and provided a good living. He was relieved that the new owner intended to keep it as an ironmongers, and wanted to buy the stock too. That saved a lot of complications.

With the sale of the shop sorted so easily, Frederick took Aubrey to see the cottage. It was very small, but they could see where the other residents had built on to the backs of their homes, and Frederick promised they would do the same. A scullery downstairs and a second bedroom upstairs, just for Aubrey. 'We'll have a bathroom too, shall we?' suggested Frederick, remembering the grand but dated bathroom at Brightwell.

Betsy and Prudence found them looking around and making plans, and were so excited to see them, they both burst into tears. 'Betsy!' said Frederick, guilty that he had neglected her for so long, and surprised to see how much she had aged. 'How are you?' he asked, and gave her a big hug. He did the same for Prudence, noticing how plump she had become.

'We're fine,' said Betsy, mopping her eyes. 'Who's this?'

'This is Aubrey,' said Frederick with pride. 'My son.'

Betsy made a great fuss of the boy, and insisted they come into her cosy little cottage for a cup of tea and a large slice of her homemade cake, and wanted to hear all their news. Aubrey looked around and decided it was even smaller than theirs.

'Of course, with the girls opening a new school in Brightwell, it's going to be a lot more exciting around here,' she said.

'The girls?' said Frederick, puzzled, and then realised she meant his sister and her daughter, both now in their fifties.

'Millicent Victoria says Hugh and your Mama are on their way home, and with his daughter too. Emily. It will be wonderful to see them again. Simply wonderful.'

Once the conveyancing for the shop had gone through, Frederick was a free man. He and Aubrey moved their bits and pieces in the van, and they unloaded it between them.

'Does this mean we can have a dog now?' asked Aubrey.

Frederick laughed. 'You've got a good memory,' he said. 'Yes, I'd love a dog myself. This is a perfect spot for one, with all the fields and space. We'll have a look round for one.'

Even though they were no longer living in Reading, they weren't far away, and Saturday nights were now regularly spent at the dog track. One evening a friend of Frederick's, Dominic, came along for a chat, and said he was thinking it was time he got out of the game.

'There's not the money in it like there used to be,' he mourned. 'My dogs are ready for retirement, and I can't afford to replace them.'

'What are you planning to do with them?' asked Frederick, unaware that Aubrey was listening.

'Knacker's yard,' said Dominic. 'Can't be doing with them if they're not earning their keep. Costs a fortune.'

'Pa,' said Aubrey, 'we could have them.'

Pa wasn't listening. 'Not now, son,' he said, listening to Dominic.

Unusually for Aubrey, he persisted. 'Pa,' he said. 'We could look after them. You said we could have a dog when we've got space.'

'Oh, I did,' said Pa, paying attention at last. 'Yes, alright. Dom, I'll take them off you.'

'Cheeky beggar,' said Dom. 'They're still worth something. Thoroughbred, they are. Take them off me indeed,' and he named his price.

Assuming it was two dogs, Frederick said, 'Now who's being a cheeky beggar? I'll give you half that.'

'They're worth it!' said Dom, but he knew he wouldn't get the better of Frederick. 'Oh alright,' he said, taking the money. 'Come round and collect them from the kennels when you're ready.'

Following directions, Frederick and Aubrey found the kennels, and Frederick was horrified when he discovered he had bought four dogs, not two. Aubrey was overjoyed, and plunged in amongst them up to his waist. They seemed to take delight in him too, licked his hands and face, and Aubrey laughed out loud and even kissed a couple of them.

'We can't manage four, Aubrey,' said Pa, knowing he was beaten already.

'We can build them a pen in the back garden,' said Aubrey, almost knocked off his feet as one jumped up. 'We can't let them go to the knacker's yard, Pa,' he insisted. 'What are their names, Mr Dominic?'

'Step Neatly; Step Lightly; Queenie, and the brindle is called Smokey,' recited Dom.

Queenie had gone to Frederick and was making a fuss of him now. He couldn't resist her either.

'Hello, Queenie!' he said, rubbing her back in just the right spot. 'I've won a fair few bob on her,' he grinned, 'and the others as well. But we can't manage four at once!'

'You've paid for them now,' said Dom, who could see his dogs would be well treated and have a good home with Aubrey. 'We've got a deal. Apart from which, I don't want them separated.'

Frederick realised it would be unkind to separate them when they had spent most of their short lives together. He raised his eyes to heaven and said to Aubrey, 'You'll have to walk them twice a day, mind.'

'I will!' said Aubrey. 'I'll get up early and walk them before school, and again when I come home. I promise. And I'll feed them too, Pa, honest I will.'

Frederick was falling in love with them all himself by now. 'Alright,' he said with resignation. 'Come on then.'

So Dom handed over their leads and what remained of their food, and as they mobbed Aubrey again, the little party moved off. Frederick opened the back doors of the van, and they all jumped straight in.

When they returned home, and the dogs spilled out of the van in all directions, the cottage did feel a bit damp, having been empty for so long, so they lit a fire in the little fireplace and it seemed more cheerful. The dogs filled the room, he knew it was madness, but the deed was done. Aubrey even encouraged them onto his bed.

'We'll have to build them some sort of kennels and a pen in the back garden,' said Frederick, rummaging for an old envelope in one of his boxes. Finding one, he began drawing up plans. 'We need your Grandmama for this,' he said. 'She was a brilliant architect in her day.'

Harriet had already arranged with the village school that there was a place for Aubrey. Mindful of the teasing that had resulted from the other kids seeing his ancient Papa at Aubrey's second school, Frederick showed him where to go on the Sunday, as he was due to start on the Monday, and kept out of sight. The boy was more confident by now, and seemed more able to take it in his stride.

'He's only nine,' Frederick told Harriet, 'and this is his fourth school.'

'Poor kid,' she said. 'He's bright enough, it's a shame his first school was such a waste of time.'

'I think he's caught up with the reading and writing now though,' said his Pa proudly. 'And he's taken to sums and woodwork very well. In fact he's going to help me with the new extension for the cottage.' He carefully didn't mention the dogs.

Harriet resolved to make sure Aubrey stayed at the village school, much improved since Frederick's day, until he could leave at 14, and in the meantime she would give him a little extra tuition when the opportunity arose. The new school requested Aubrey's birth certificate, but he knew by now that it would not be forthcoming, and simply told the new Miss that it was lost.

'At least he's speaking properly again at this school,' said Frederick to Harriet with some relief.

Harriet was busy in the house with MillyVic. They had given notice at their school, and a big collection and a fine send off were being prepared. They had been there for over 30 years, and would be much missed.

Before making too many changes, they had decided they should wait until Hugh and Mama returned, so that they could all decide together what needed to be done in the house since the Army left. 'Not so much left,' said MillieVic, 'it looks more like it's been abandoned.'

It was true, the place needed quite a lot doing to it, and Frederick said he and Aubrey could help with that too.

'There's something else you could take care of, if you would,' said Harriet.

'Yes, of course. If we can?' Frederick winked at his son.

'The place is overrun with rabbits,' she said. 'I suppose there's been no control over them since the army left, and if we start a garden for the children, they will eat everything in sight. You couldn't set some humane traps, could you? And perhaps a gun to shoot a few for the pot?'

Frederick grinned. This was a bit of a turn around since his father's day, when it had been strictly forbidden, and his gun confiscated. 'We'd love to,' said Aubrey. 'And the greyhounds can come along too. We're good at poaching, aren't we, Pa?'

Harriet's attention was caught. Poaching, she thought, Frederick has been teaching his son poaching? But more importantly, had she heard Aubrey say dogs?

'Greyhounds?' said Harriet. 'What greyhounds? Don't let Hugh see you with any greyhounds. He's going to be filling up the place with livestock – sheep and cows, for a start. He won't be wanting any dogs but trained working dogs around here.'

Chapter 36 – 1948

At last Harriet and MillieVic came bounding down the lane to the cottages, to let everyone know Hugh, Mama and Emily had arrived in England. One of the first things they had done when the decision was made to turn Brightwell into a school, was to have a telephone installed. Hugh had telephoned them that very morning to say they had docked in Southampton last night, and were staying at a hotel for a few days to recover before coming on to Brightwell. The voyage had been much quicker, and nowhere near as rough as their outward passage, and they were all in good fettle, looking forward to seeing Brightwell again.

Betsy was so excited at seeing her dear mistress again, and MillyVic reminded her Grace was no longer her mistress, but a friend. This put Betsy into even more of a dither, and she cleaned her sparkling cottage a second time, just to make sure it was ready for Mrs Sinclair.

Frederick was not quite so meticulous. He had decided it was best to hire some help with the building of the stone walls for the extension. He and Aubrey could do most of the woodwork themselves, but stone walls were different. So these had been built, and he was making a lot of sawdust as he prepared timbers for the new roof.

Now that the constant reminders of his birth certificate had ceased, Aubrey was enjoying his new school very much indeed, but he still raced home each day to walk the dogs and then help Pa with the building. With only one bedroom, he and the dogs were currently sleeping in the living room, and although he loved the greyhounds more than anything else in the world, he did not care for the sleeping arrangements one bit. He didn't have a proper bed because there wasn't space for one, and had nowhere but a cardboard box to keep his special things. His Pa knew it was unsatisfactory, and had been moving on with the extension with all due haste, until the dogs arrived and took precedence, needing kennels and a pen in the garden as soon as possible.

Harriet and MillyVic had been making preparations of their own. They had personally cleaned and swept and polished until it glowed Tristram and Grace's bedroom. They had washed the bed linen and made up the bed in readiness, with plenty of warming pans and stone hot water bottles to air the mattress first.

'It was easier when we had servants!' said Harriet as they started on Hugh's bedroom, and then on to one of the smaller rooms for Emily. 'I know Emily will be going off to college or university as soon as arrangements have been made, but she will need her own room to start with.'

Finally all was ready, and on the afternoon of the following day, the taxi was at last seen trundling up the drive. Word flew round and an entire welcoming committee quickly assembled to greet them – Betsy bobbing up and down in excitement, with her daughter beside her trying to instil some sense of decorum into the occasion. Stebbins and Lilly were carefully keeping in the background; Prudence was quiet and nervous, self-consciously plump in her retirement.

Frederick had insisted the dogs were to be left in their pen behind the cottage, much to Aubrey's disgust who was keen to show them off to anyone and everyone. Father and son followed Stebbins' example and kept to the back of the little crowd, whereas Harriet was at the forefront, telling everyone what to do, and then rushing forward to open the taxi door as it came to a standstill beside the front door.

Hugh stepped out first, closely followed by Emily, and found themselves enveloped in so many hugs by so many people, they lost count. As this was going on, Grace stepped from the taxi herself, and seeing them all congregated there, and waiting to envelop her in hugs and kisses too, she could not help herself and tears streamed down her cheeks. 'I never thought I would see this day,' she sobbed. It was the happiest day of her life, and without Tristram, the saddest too. 'If only Tristram was here,' she said sadly to Harriet. 'He would have been so proud.'

At last the pandemonium subsided, and Grace noticed Frederick at the back of the group, with a little boy beside him. She beckoned him forward and gave him a hug too. Turning to the child, and knowing full well what the answer would be, she said, 'Hello, young man? And who are you?'

Aubrey looked up at her, smiling his shy smile into her lined but kind face, and surprised her by saying, with more honesty than he knew, 'I'm not sure, Miss. I don't really know.'

Frederick stepped into the breach, and said with enormous pride and a lump in his throat, 'This is Aubrey, Mama. My son.'

'Hello, Aubrey,' said Grace, returning his smile and feeling absurdly touched by the little boy. 'I am very pleased to meet you. That means I am your Grandmama, and you are my grandson.'

'I'm not sure I can be, Miss,' said Aubrey doubtfully. 'Because Pa says I am his son. And Aunt Harriet says I am her nephew. And Uncle Hugh's nephew too. Oh, and I am Emily's cousin, as well. I'm not sure I can be all these people all at once.'

Grace laughed at the intelligence and ingenuity of her new grandson, and said, 'Yes, you can! You can be all these things and more, because we all want to get to know you, and love you, and you will become very important to us. Because that's what families do.'

And taking his hand, she turned towards the house, and led them all inside.

Chapter 37
1948 – 1954

With so many willing hands to help, Grace's expertise as an architect, and professional tradesmen too, Brightwell Manor was soon restored to its former glory, and the school opened at the start of the following term. They were besieged by proud parents and nervous young girls, all of whom were reassured on meeting the redoubtable Harriet and MillyVic, and seeing the lovely old house. The updated servants' quarters in the attics made excellent dormitories for the girls, and the wonderful reception rooms downstairs were probably the best classrooms any school had ever had, but inevitably their size and availability initially limited numbers.

In between helping in the big house and keeping down the rabbit population, Frederick and Aubrey finished the extension to their cottage and Aubrey had his own room at last. Hugh met the four greyhounds early on, and was appalled at how boisterous they were. He had seen Aubrey taking them for a walk and getting towed along in their wake.

'Four?' shouted Hugh angrily at Frederick. 'Why do you have to have four, for God's sake? You can't have greyhounds here! I'll be having working dogs, Border Collies, but more than that, animals. Cows. Sheep. Can't you control them better than that?' he demanded, but Frederick only laughed.

'Of course not!' said Frederick. 'You don't control greyhounds. You set them free and they run like the wind, and they love you for it.'

This was entirely lost on Hugh. 'Well you'll have to keep them under control when we get sheep and cattle here. And working dogs.'

'Alright,' said Frederick, tired of Hugh's attitude and willing to compromise. 'What about giving me that field near the cottages? I can put up fencing so that they are dog proof on the inside, and cow proof and sheep proof on the outside. We can exercise the dogs there.'

With Harriet demanding land on which to start a large vegetable garden to help feed the girls under her care, and space for them to do some gardening of their own, as well as a sports field for recreation and exercise, Hugh begrudged his brother the field, even though he knew there was plenty of space for all of them, and finally agreed to Frederick's suggestion.

'But if any of your dogs harm one hair on the heads of any of my animals, they will be shot!' stormed Hugh.

'Sheep don't have hair,' said Frederick with an insolent

grin, determined to have the last word, as usual. 'They have wool. Thought you would've known that.' And so saying, he walked away.

Aubrey helped his Pa carefully secure the boundaries of the newly allocated field, and a few days later a set of traps appeared, presumably secondhand from the race track, but Frederick never said. He still had his ways and means.

There was no electricity nearby, so Frederick designated his son to be the hare. He gave Aubrey a dried-out rabbit skin specially saved for the purpose, put the four dogs in the traps and stationed Aubrey far enough up the field to give him a head start. Then he released the dogs and Aubrey ran for his life. It was huge fun and wonderful exercise for all concerned except Frederick, who made bets on the dogs in his head, and shouted encouragement at his son to run faster.

Hugh's old animosity towards Frederick had reasserted itself ten-fold. He wasn't sure that having his brother living on the premises, and acting as caretaker and groundsman at the school was appropriate with so many young ladies and female teachers in the vicinity. He thought his fears were confirmed one day when he saw Frederick watching a desultory game of lacrosse. The gym teacher, Mrs Martin, had taught the girls the rules and objectives of the game, but could not seem to instil into them the excitement and enthusiasm of chasing a ball round a field and trying to score goals with a stick covered in mesh. 'You have to run faster than that, ladies!' she called, but to no avail.

Remembering the chambermaid incident, Hugh said to his brother, 'You can look but don't touch. In fact, don't even look.'

Frederick was angry at his attitude, but refused to show it. 'I was just watching the game,' he said calmly. 'It's 3 to 2 to the Blue team. I think it must be you who's having impure thoughts, Hugh. Not me.' And again he walked away.

Outraged and hurt, Frederick sought solace in his greyhounds, and as soon as Aubrey returned home from school, they went off to their field to race them. It seemed it was Frederick's week for being misunderstood, because Mrs Martin, the gym teacher, saw him shouting to Aubrey to go faster, and came across to remonstrate.

'A small boy can't possibly be expected to outrun four greyhounds, you stupid man!' she expostulated. She knew him as the caretaker and groundsman, but had no idea that he was one of the sons of the house. Frederick looked at her in amazement.

'I don't expect him to.' he said. 'You're missing the point, woman!'

And he patiently indoctrinated her into the mysteries of greyhound racing, explaining that Aubrey was the hare and the dogs were chasing the hare, competing with each other, not racing his son.

'Well, at least you got him running,' she said grudgingly. 'I can't get my girls to run, even for lacrosse.'

'It'd be more fun for them if they were being chased by greyhounds!' said Frederick, and Mrs Martin laughed at the very idea.

To Hugh's further disapproval, thereafter Mrs Martin was often to be seen chatting and laughing with Frederick. Annoyingly, she seemed to gravitate towards him and the dogs, rather than he to her, so Hugh had no legitimate cause for complaint.

Mrs Martin lived in a rented house in the village with her twin sons, who attended the same village school as Aubrey but, being younger, were in a different classroom. Her husband had been killed at the very end of the war, so she had no option but to work.

She did invite Frederick to visit one lunchtime, when she had a free period and the boys were at school, but Frederick was playing a waiting game, unwilling to put a foot wrong with Hugh watching his every move.

Frederick was more inclined to visit his Mama, and enjoyed watching the burgeoning friendship between her and Aubrey, who had taken to her extremely well. They got along famously and she was more of a mother to him than a grandmama, the only mothering he had ever really known. It was a novel experience, and although Aubrey would never admit it, he found he liked it.

Grace was so happy to be home, and adored Aubrey.

Although vaguely aware of the continuing feud between her two sons, she knew there was nothing she could do and left them to it. She was delighted to see how successful the school was becoming, even from its very first day, and welcomed Harriet and MillyVic when ever they had a moment to spare to come and regale her with their daily doings.

Word spread and there was soon a growing waiting list for places at Brightwell Manor, so Harriet asked Hugh where would be the best place to build new dormitories and classrooms for the girls. At first Hugh refused her, but Mama spoke to him at some length and he came to see it would be a good investment.

Grace missed Tristram enormously, and told Hugh he would have been so proud and pleased to see how the house had been used and the estate developed under his expert care, such that Hugh was persuaded and Harriet got her new dormitories and classrooms. Mama helped design them, with suggestions and ideas that had not occurred to Harriet, until one morning Harriet came to visit Mama and found her, as she thought, fast asleep in her bed. But she could not be roused, and Harriet quickly realised this was a sleep from which she could not be awakened.

Aubrey was devastated. It seemed anyone he dared to risk loving was almost immediately taken from him. Frederick comforted him as best he could.

'She was very old, Aubrey,' he said. 'She had a wonderful life, and she was very happy to be home. She was just worn out, and fell asleep, but I bet she is with Grandpapa now. You didn't meet him, but they were very much in love throughout their entire lives. I bet he was waiting for her, and they're back together for ever.'

Unfortunately, Grace's passing seemed to give Frederick licence to do as he had been wanting to do for sometime, and he went to visit Mrs Martin. She had continually invited him for sometime, but he realised now, it was for Mama's sake he had stayed away, not Hugh's. Once Mama had gone, he didn't very much care what Hugh thought. He knew Harriet and MillyVic relied on him for caretaking and gardening, keeping down the rabbit population and in all sorts of other ways. Consequently he was secure in his home and in his job, for which he was now being paid, and Hugh's good opinion had never mattered to him very much.

Even with Wyn gone but not forgotten, Mrs Martin made a suitable substitute, and Frederick enjoyed her hospitality on many occasions. However, she was paying rent and Frederick was not, and it was soon born in upon him that if she came to live with him in his cottage, it would save her a lot of money, and with her income and his, they could enjoy a fine life together. The problem was that there were only two bedrooms. Frederick broached the subject with Aubrey.

'You remember when we first moved in? Before we built on the extension? You were quite comfortable sleeping in the sitting room, weren't you?'

'No, Pa, I wasn't,' said Aubrey stoutly. 'The sofa was not comfortable, and I had nowhere to put my special things.'

'You did, you had a box.'

'Yes, but now I have my collections – my butterflies, and my shells from the garden, and my birds' eggs. Please don't take my room away.'

But that was what Pa did. Being younger, Mrs Martin's twin sons went to bed earlier than Aubrey, so it was inevitable they should have his bedroom. 'You're grown up now, son,' said Pa. 'You go to bed the same time as we do, so it does make sense.'

It didn't make sense to Aubrey, and he had to move all his belongings, and got rid of most of them. Grandmama had gone, and although Pa was still there, he seemed to have deserted him too. The old feeling of not really knowing who he was returned. The twins were allowed to be the hare sometimes when the greyhounds needed racing, and Aubrey felt he no longer mattered, he no longer belonged.

His feelings were further augmented when a lady called Irene came to visit. Pa was overjoyed to see her, and told Aubrey she was his daughter long before he was born. He introduced Irene to Mrs Martin and her twins with just as much enthusiasm as he had introduced Aubrey, which didn't seem quite right to Aubrey. But Irene was very kind to him, and sympathised about his having to sleep in the sitting room, and having to get rid of his collections of special things.

During her visit, Pa went out to the scullery to put the kettle on to make her a cup of tea, so that briefly Aubrey and Irene were alone together. 'Do you remember your Ma, Aubrey?' she asked.

'Not really,' he answered, not sure why she was asking, and not sure what she wanted the answer to be. 'I haven't seen her since I was seven.'

'Well, she did love you,' said Irene, knowing Aubrey would not believe her. 'She did. She might be glad to see you now you've grown up.'

'I don't know where she is,' said Aubrey. The idea had never occurred to him.

'Well, I'm not sure I should tell you this,' said Irene conspiritorially, 'but she lives in High Wycombe.' And she told him the address.

Aubrey stared at her, and wondered why she had told him that, but he remembered the address, and later, when the twins had gone to bed, and Pa and Mrs Martin had gone upstairs too, he found a piece of paper and a pencil, and wrote it down.

It wasn't much longer before 2nd April arrived and Aubrey was 15, old enough to leave school. Pa didn't really make much of it. He gave his son some extra pocket money to spend as he liked, and wished him a happy birthday, but it was obvious to Aubrey it wasn't as special an occasion as it had been when he was at the big house in Maidenhead on the banks of the Thames, and Pa had been so excited and pleased to see him.

More importantly, Pa just assumed he would now work on the estate, and did not ask him what he wanted to do now that he was leaving school, and Aubrey had no idea himself. After helping Pa with the extension, and Aunt Harriet with the building of the new dormitories and classrooms, he was handy with tools and building, but Pa didn't suggest he should apply for a job or an apprenticeship with a building company.

It continued to rankle that his bedroom had been taken from him. He hated sleeping on the sofa which was uncomfortable, and also enabled him to hear Pa and Mrs Martin upstairs in their bed. They didn't always go straight off to sleep. Aubrey knew by now what the noises meant, and it was embarrassing next morning when Pa came downstairs as if nothing had happened.

So with no school and no job of his own to occupy his time, no space of his own, and no real idea of his identity, Aubrey dug out the piece of paper with Ma's address on it, and decided, having nothing to lose, he would go and find her.

Chapter 38 – 1954

After a lengthy walk to the bus stop, a bus to the railway station, and a change of trains to High Wycombe, Aubrey was hot, tired, hungry and very thirsty.

He had bidden a sad farewell to his beloved greyhounds that morning, packed a pair of pyjamas and his tooth-brush in a large brown paper bag, and simply left. He hadn't said goodbye to Pa because he knew Pa would try to talk him out of leaving.

He had some meagre savings from his pocket money, and his birthday money, but the bus and train fares had made something of a dent in that, and he was worried about going into a cafe to spend money on food and drink, in case he did not have enough. He went to the Gentlemen's conveniences at the station and drank some water from the tap, but the basin was dirty and the whole place did not smell right.

Leaving High Wycombe station, he took the well-worn piece of paper with Ma's address on it from his pocket, but had no idea where Tockington Avenue might be. He had to ask two or three people before anyone gave him comprehensible directions, but at last he found it and, clutching the brown paper bag containing his pyjamas and toothbrush, knocked on the door.

As he stood there waiting for someone to answer, he rehearsed yet again the anxieties that had haunted him since leaving home. He had no way of knowing what sort of reception he might get. Ma didn't know he was coming, and she had left him all those years ago, so she might not be very pleased to see him again. What if he wasn't welcome? What if she sent him away? What would he do then? Where would he go? He didn't have enough money to . . .

The door opened, and Ma stood before him. 'Hello?' she said, suspicious of an unexpected caller, but then light dawned almost immediately. 'Aubrey?'

'Ma?' he said.

'Oh my God!' she exclaimed, but she was smiling. 'Come in! Come in!'

She didn't try to hug him, but she took his elbow and guided him through a door marked Residents Lounge.

'Ignore that!' she laughed, sitting down in one of the big flowery armchairs and indicating the other for him. 'We don't do B&B any more, even though we've plenty of rooms. We should really, it's a waste, but it was too much like hard work.'

Aubrey had no idea what she was talking about, and looked at her in wonder.

'How did you get here? How did you find me? You look all in. Are you hungry? Thirsty?'

Aubrey nodded in enthusiastic agreement, and admitted that he was both. Very.

'Let's get you something to eat,' she said, standing up again, and he followed her into the kitchen. 'Is soup alright?'

'Yes please!' said Aubrey, his mouth watering at the very thought. As she stirred the saucepan and buttered chunks of crusty bread, an unwelcome idea struck her.

'You're Pa's not coming, is he?'

'No. No, I'm on my own.'

'How is he?'

'Alright.'

'Where is he then?'

'He has one of the cottages at Brightwell Manor. We've been living there for a while. I had to leave the greyhounds. I shall miss them, but I couldn't bring them.'

'No,' she agreed. 'We don't allow dogs here.'

Aubrey thought that was a shame but said nothing.

She set the meal on the kitchen table and he took a seat.

'You've had quite a journey,' said Ma, as he drank the soup and munched his way through all the bread and butter. 'Would you like second helpings?'

'Yes please, that was really good.'

So she bustled back to the stove and topped up his bowl, and placed more bread on his plate. He hadn't seen that much butter in his life, with the war and the rationing.

'I wouldn't want to do that journey myself on public transport,' said Wyn, taking the seat opposite him. 'You're not going back today, are you? You can stay the night if you like.'

Aubrey was relieved at the thought of a bed for the night, but wondered what he would do after that. Then a thought struck her. 'You're not just visiting, are you?' she said with conviction. 'You've left home, haven't you?'

He nodded but vouchsafed no reply.

'You can stay here while you decide what to do,' she said. 'Alan won't mind. He's retired now. He had a business . . . lorries, deliveries, you know.' Aubrey didn't, but supposed it didn't matter. 'That's why we did the B&B. For the drivers, you see.'

Again Aubrey nodded, his mouth too full of bread and butter to answer her.

'Peggy and Sheila live next door. Molly left years ago. Went off with one of the drivers, would you believe! How she could leave Alan I do not know. He's a lovely man. And very well off too,' she added with a note of satisfaction.

Aubrey wasn't sure who all these people were, or who was related to whom, but supposed that didn't matter either. Seeing his confusion, she said, 'They're your step sisters! Lots older than you. From my previous marriage. You've got a step brother as well,' she said as a bit of an afterthought. 'Bill got married, he still lives in Reading. He was a Prisoner of War in Malaya during the war, and he's still stick thin. You don't really recover from something like that, do you?'

Aubrey supposed not, and began to feel better after all the soup and bread butter, and the knowledge that he had a bed, albeit temporarily.

'You haven't got any luggage then?' she said, eyeing the brown paper bag.

'No, I couldn't really pack anything much, or Pa would have noticed.'

'So he doesn't know you've gone?' she said in some concern.

'Well, I expect he does by now.'

Frederick did indeed know by now, and was upset. He walked the greyhounds, because that was usually Aubrey's job and he was not here to do it. His thoughts tumbled over each other as he followed them unseeingly around the field, until he realised the only place his son could have gone.

'But how did he know her address?' he demanded of Mrs Martin when he returned.

'I don't know,' said Mrs Martin. 'It wasn't me. I don't know it myself.'

After more thought, Frederick realised it must have been Irene, his daughter, although how she had found out he had no idea. Something to do with Megan, no doubt.

Next morning Frederick left in the van, now somewhat delapidated but still reliable, and headed off to High Wycombe. He too knocked on the door in some trepidation. Wyn opened it.

'Is he here?' he demanded.

'Yes,' said Wyn, 'You don't beat about the bush, do you? Come in.'

Relieved his son was safe, Frederick became angry.

'I might have known you'd be behind it.'

Wyn shrugged her innocence. 'Don't blame me,' she said. 'The first I knew about it was when he appeared on the doorstep. It's you he left. Perhaps it's your fault?'

Frederick looked stunned as the wisdom of this hit home, and followed her into the kitchen, where Aubrey was eating his mid-day meal.

'Hello, son,' said Frederick, glad to see he was alright, and overwhelmed at the love he felt when he saw him again. 'What happened?'

'Hello Pa,' said Aubrey quietly. 'I'm sorry. I didn't mean to hurt your feelings.'

'Why, though, Aubrey? What made you leave without telling us?'

'I thought you'd try to stop me.'

'Well, yes,' admitted Frederick, 'I probably would have. But we could have talked about it. If you're old enough to leave school, you're old enough to get work and make your own way in the world.'

'You just assumed I'd work at Brightwell Manor, same as you.'

Frederick stepped from one foot to the other and wished Wyn would ask him to sit down, but she didn't. 'Well, it's good money,' he offered. 'And you had a home there.'

Aubrey gave him a level look. 'Well, I did until you gave Mrs Martin's twins my bedroom and I had to sleep in the sitting room again.'

Wyn looked accusingly at Frederick. 'You didn't, did you?' she said. 'A lad of 15 needs his own bedroom!' Aubrey looked at her with the hint of smile, grateful for her support. She continued, 'And you've got a new lady by the sounds of it?'

'About time!' said Frederick in his own defence. 'No one since you left. What about you? Picking up Molly's leftovers!'

Any goodwill Wyn might have felt towards him swiftly evaporated. Aubrey sat looking at his empty plate, not knowing what to say.

'I'd offer you a cup of tea,' said Wyn, 'but you're not stopping, are you.' It wasn't a question, but it made Frederick ashamed that they had quickly lost sight of the main reason for his being there.

'Have you got any plans, Aubrey? I'd like you to come back with me and talk it through. Have you decided what you want to do?'

'Yes,' said Aubrey, which immediately brought their combined attention back to him. 'When I'm 16 I'm going to join the Army. And travel. And see the world.'

After a lengthy pause, Wyn said to Frederick, 'He can stay here til then. If he wants to. We've got seven bedrooms for him to choose from.'

Frederick could see that the sitting room sofa and a cardboard box for his things could not compete with an offer like that.

'Alright then, son,' he said, deeply saddened but wanting what was best for Aubrey. 'Is that what you'd like?'

Aubrey nodded. 'Yes,' he said. 'Until I'm sixteen.'

'Promise me one thing then,' said Pa. Aubrey looked at him. 'Promise me you'll keep in touch? Come and visit?'

And Aubrey nodded again. 'I'd like that too,' he said.